EDISON'S ALLEY

BOOK 2 OF THE ACCELERATI TRILOGY

# EDISON'S ALLEY

## BOOK 2 OF THE ACCELERATI TRILOGY

## NEAL SHUSTERMAN
## AND ERIC ELFMAN

Disney • Hyperion

LOS ANGELES    NEW YORK

First Edition, February 2015

Printed in the United States of America
10 9 8 7 6 5 4 3 2
G475-5664-5-15061

Library of Congress Cataloging-in-Publication Data
Shusterman, Neal, author.
  Edison's alley/Neal Shusterman and Eric Elfman.—First edition.
    pages cm.—(Accelerati trilogy; book 2)
  Summary: "Nick and his friends race against their foes to retrieve more pieces of
Tesla's free energy transmitter, only to see them fall into the hands of the Accelerati's
shadowy leader"—Provided by publisher.
  ISBN 978-1-4231-4806-7
[1. Invention—Fiction. 2. Tesla, Nikola, 1856–1943—Fiction. 3. Colorado Springs
(Colo.)—Fiction. 4. Science fiction.]  I. Elfman, Eric, author. II. Title.
  PZ7.S55987Ed 2015
  [Fic]—dc23          2014033469

Reinforced binding

Visit www.DisneyBooks.com

# 1 RELATIVISTIC CHEESE

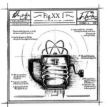

**D**r. Alan Jorgenson, undisputed commander and chief of the Accelerati, rang the doorbell of the old house, ready to meet with his superior—because in this world, even the boss has a boss. While one may presume to be the big cheese, there is always a larger, more pungent one to contend with.

And as big cheeses go, few could be more pungent than the one who gave Jorgenson his marching orders.

The housekeeper opened the door and beamed at him as he stepped in. "A right pleasure to see you, Mr. Jorgenson," she said.

"*Doctor* Jorgenson," he corrected.

"Yes, yes, 'ow silly of me."

Jorgenson looked around. The house hadn't changed in years. It never did. There was comfort in that for an agent of change like himself. Knowing that some things were forever gave him a bit of grounding.

"'E's been waiting for you, 'e 'as," the housekeeper said with a pronounced cockney accent, as if she'd been dragged from the gutters of industrial England.

To the best of Jorgenson's knowledge, the housekeeper had never been to England, much less come from there. If anything, she should've had a Germanic sensibility, as her gearworks had come from a fine watch factory in Düsseldorf. Her owner, even though he was American, preferred a British touch to his domestic life. Even the air in the house smelled of musty Victorian sensibility.

" 'E's in the parlor. Would you like a spot of tea, dear? I 'ave some nice Oolongevity, or English breakfast."

"Just water will be fine, Mrs. Higgenbotham."

"Would you prefer your water transdimensionally filtered, or just from the tap?"

"Tap will do, thank you."

"Quantum-chilled or—"

"Just *bring* it."

"As you wish, guv'nor."

The parlor, as always, was dark. The aged man in the tall red leather chair was surrounded by his perpetual cloud of cigar smoke. "Good evening, Al," he said.

Jorgenson sat down. "And to you, Al," he said back.

Such was their standard greeting.

Jorgenson waited for his eyes to adjust to the dimness, but he knew they never would, so low was the light. *What irony,* thought Jorgenson, *that this man, a luminary, would come to despise light.* Or perhaps he just couldn't bear to see luminaries who shone even brighter than he.

"I suppose I should congratulate you," the old man said, "for the fact that your team's incompetence did not bring about the end of the world."

Jorgenson grimaced as he recalled the massive asteroid that had come so close to wiping out all life on Earth only a few weeks earlier. "I take full responsibility for that debacle."

"Noble of you to accept the blame," the old man said from within his cloud of smoke, "but there were other forces at play. It was out of your control from the beginning."

For Jorgenson, the idea of anything being out of his control was like a slap in the face. Yet he had to admit that even with a mass of technology, money, and influence at his fingertips, he could not have affected the Felicity Bonk incident. "This Nick Slate boy and his friends are shrewder than we gave them credit for."

"Yes, the boy," the old man said with a sigh. "We will deal with him when the time comes. An honor I shall leave to you."

Jorgenson smiled. "Believe me, it will be my pleasure."

"But *only* when the time comes. In the meantime, there are other things to consider—"

At the creak of a floorboard, Jorgenson turned to see Mrs. Higgenbotham walk in with a glass of water that had hardened into ice the color of a glacier. "We're 'avin' trouble with the quantum-coolin' thingamajig. But you know what they say: 'When everything is right with the world, even squirrels sing.' And who wants singin' squirrels?" She patted him on the shoulder. "It'll melt eventually."

"Don't you find it curious," the old man asked, once the housekeeper had left, "that the Bonk asteroid has settled into an orbit as stable as the moon's?"

Jorgenson knew where this was going, but he played along anyway. "Some call it luck. Some say it's divine intervention—"

The old man waved his hand at the very suggestion. Smoke eddied in a lazy whirlpool. "It is neither, and you know it. Rather it is part of a plan—a very *human* plan—devised by a great mind. Unfortunately, that mind was not great enough to know what was good for it." Then the old man smiled. "Which is why *we* will be reaping the benefits of Tesla's greatest endeavor." He pointed his cigar at Jorgenson. "In the short term, it is *your* efforts that will make all the difference, however."

Then the old man blew smoke with such force that it bridged the distance between them, filling Jorgenson's nostrils and stinging his eyes. "I expect you, as the head of the Accelerati, to impress me," the old man said, with a fair measure of threat in his voice. "I will settle for nothing less."

Jorgenson gripped his chair as if it might fly out from under him. "And in the long term?" he asked. "I suspect you have a plan of your own, do you not?"

"I do," said the old man, leaning forward for the first time. "A spectacular one."

# 2 FAT MAN FLOATING

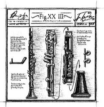

The world had not ended . . . which was very inconvenient.

Celestial Object Felicity Bonk—the unlikely name of the asteroid that had been on a collision course with Earth—rather than obliterating life as we know it, could now be seen in the night sky. It was nowhere near the size of the moon, of course, but it appeared larger than a planet.

After a brief period of celebration lasting less than a week, the world returned to its pre-Bonk patterns. The horrors of war, oppression, and reality TV, all of which might have been ended by the well-placed meteor strike, were back in force, and Nick Slate was left having to unscrew the massive screwup that had brought everything to the brink of extinction. He was taking that responsibility seriously.

Slowly but surely, Nick and his friends were gathering the strange objects that Nick had sold in his garage sale a few weeks ago and returning them to his attic. Today's recovery mission was going to be a challenge. It would require Nick and his friend Caitlin's combined powers of persuasion, iron wills, and most likely, money that they didn't have.

"How certain are you that this is the same man from your garage sale?" Caitlin asked as she and Nick approached a house overgrown with unpruned hedges and low-limbed trees.

"I could be wrong," Nick told her, "but I do remember a loud fat guy at the garage sale, and this dude certainly fits the bill."

Caitlin glared at him. "It's cruel and insensitive to call a person who is morbidly obese a 'fat guy.' I have an uncle who struggles with that, and I can tell you, it's not an easy cross to bear."

"Sorry," Nick said. To look at Caitlin, he couldn't imagine anyone in her family being anything but beautiful and slender, or at least well groomed and proportional. "I'd call him a 'large gentleman,' but there's nothing gentlemanly about him. He's a creep, at any poundage."

Caitlin nodded and sighed. "Creeps do come in all shapes and sizes."

Nick had run into him at the grocery store, where the man was bitterly arguing with the store manager over the price of a casaba melon. Nick had seen him switch a product code sticker from a less expensive piece of fruit. Although he could have ratted the man out, he let it play through, all the while awed by the guy's audacity and the fact that any human being would get into a fight over a melon. Something about the way he bickered made Nick remember how one customer had aggressively haggled over the price of an item in his now-notorious garage sale. He realized that this was the same quarrelsome dude.

"Do you remember what he bought?" Caitlin asked. Both of them were hesitant to walk up to the man's front door.

"I can't be sure," Nick said, "but I think it was a weight machine."

When one holds a garage sale, one never expects to see the junk sold to unsuspecting neighbors ever again. But when the garage-sale items are the lost inventions of the world's greatest scientist, the word "oops" doesn't begin to cover it.

Perhaps if Tesla hadn't disguised them all as normal household objects, Nick might have had a clue that the things in his attic each had a greater purpose. Now Nick understood that the inventor hadn't wanted them to be discovered by the secret society of scientists known as the Accelerati. But Nick hadn't known that at the time, and the inventions had been dispersed into the world to wreak their peculiar sort of havoc.

And yet Nick had to wonder, in spite of the clear and present danger the objects posed, if there was also a method to the madness. Perhaps everything that had happened was part of the inventor's master plan.

For instance, his brother unwittingly pulled an asteroid into a collision course with Earth using a cosmic attractor disguised as a baseball mitt. Could it be coincidence that his father had swung a celestial deflector disguised as a baseball *bat*?

Nick knew that each of the items sold in his garage sale had to be retrieved, but he also suspected that they needed to be out in the world as well—at least for a short time—because the people whose lives these objects touched were also, somehow, part of Tesla's grand mechanism. Nick found it somewhat irritating to be manipulated by a long-dead genius, but at the same time he was comforted by the thought that he might be the central cog in a machine that was crafting something truly worthwhile.

He and Caitlin had figured out that the inventions all fit together to form a larger one—the Far Range Energy Emitter, or F.R.E.E., which had been Tesla's life's work. They were the only ones who had figured that out. Exactly what the F.R.E.E. would do when it was complete was anyone's guess. All Nick knew was that he felt the need to complete it.

As they approached the casaba melon man's house, Nick began to hear a rhythmic clanking of metal on metal—a sound that anyone who has been to a gym would recognize.

"He's in there," Nick said. "He's using the weight machine."

Caitlin grabbed him before he got too close to the door, a shadow of fear crossing her face. "What do you suppose the machine does?"

Nick didn't want to speculate, because if he did, he might never go in.

"We'll know soon enough" was all he said.

Instead of going straight to the front door, they decided to do a little reconnaissance. Quietly they made their way through the dense weeds and brush on the side of the house. When they neared the window, they could feel their hair standing on end. As it would turn out, there was a reason for that.

"Boost me up so I can see," Caitlin said. Nick lowered his hands, interlacing his fingers to give her a step up, and then hoisted her higher.

He anticipated Caitlin's weight as he lifted her, but he thought he must have miscalculated, because he found her surprisingly light. It would turn out there was a reason for that, too.

"What do you see?" he asked.

"I see the machine," she said. "It's right there in the middle of the room, but . . ."

"But what?"

"No one's there."

"What do you mean no one's there? I can hear someone pumping iron."

"That's what I mean. The machine is doing it all by itself."

Suddenly the window flew open, and Caitlin was pulled out of Nick's hands and into the house by the home's large occupant.

"Caitlin!" Nick shouted.

A moment later, a hand reached out, grabbed Nick by the hair, and, with what appeared to be superhuman strength, Nick was hauled off his feet and through the window.

First came an intense feeling of disorientation. Caitlin, Nick, and the casaba man tumbled, but they didn't quite fall. Nick hit a wall and dislodged a framed photograph, but the photo didn't fall either. Instead it floated, flipping end over end until it bumped the ceiling and bounced off.

All at once Nick got it. He looked up, which was actually down, and saw the old-fashioned weight machine, its piston pumping, its cables straining. This was a weight machine in a very literal sense. It was an antigravity device that made everything around it weightless—which explained why Caitlin felt so light just beyond the edge of the antigravity field, and why their hair had been standing on end. Each clang of metal on metal created a wave of energy—invisible, but Nick could feel it pulsing through his gut, his ears, and his eyes.

"You think I don't know who you are? You think I don't know you've been spying on me?" The man's voice boomed with the same irate tone he had used when arguing with the supermarket manager. He was, indeed, very large—even more so, it seemed, with his mass unfettered by Earth's gravity. He pushed Nick, and both of them went flying in opposite directions, although Nick went much faster.

Caitlin tried to grab the man but couldn't. She just floated past him, frantically moving her arms and legs as if trying to swim in midair.

Nick hit a beam in the vaulted ceiling, and he yelped in pain. Even weightless, he still had enough inertia for it to hurt. That's when Caitlin, who had reached the far wall, flung herself into action. She pushed off from the wall, becoming a human projectile aimed right at the man in the middle of the room. He, however, was much more adept at maneuvering in free fall. With a single flick of his wrist, he shifted his entire body to avoid her, and then he flew to the far corner, where he peered down at them—or up—like a spider from the center of its web.

"You can't have it! It's mine!"

He was an intimidating figure floating in the heart of his lair, holding on to a handle that had been bolted to a crossbeam in the ceiling. Nick looked around and saw that similar handles had been strategically affixed to the walls and ceiling so the man could maneuver weightlessly through the house.

"Do you have any idea what it's like to struggle with weight all your life, and then find yourself free from it entirely? You can't possibly imagine how liberating that is. And I won't let you steal that from me!" He launched himself once more at Nick, grabbed him, and hurled him across the room again.

Nick spun, and his shoulder painfully hit the weight machine. He ricocheted off of it and, mercifully, found himself hitting a sofa that had been secured to the floor. He wanted to stay there, but the sofa acted like a trampoline and bounced him toward the ceiling.

"Please," said Caitlin, "just hear us out."

"Words have no weight here either," the man said. "Especially yours!"

Nick hit the ceiling again, but this time he was able to grab one of the handles and steady himself.

"We're not going to lie to you," Nick said. "We need the machine back."

"We're willing to pay," Caitlin said, which just made the man laugh.

"Do you think I'm an idiot? There isn't enough money in the world to pay what this thing is worth!"

"We know," Nick told him, and then he went out on a limb. "But let's talk about *you*. Ever since you turned that machine on, living without it has become harder and harder, hasn't it?"

The man pursed his lips into a thin scowl. "You don't know anything," he growled.

Nick continued. "When the machine is off, you weigh even more than you did before. Your arms are weak, your legs are weaker, and you can barely move, which is why you're so angry in the outside world. You're constantly exhausted . . . so you go out less and less."

"That has nothing to do with it!" the man shouted. He no longer looked like a spider in his web, but a cornered creature.

It wasn't too difficult for Nick to figure out what was happening to the man. When you're weightless, you don't use your muscles. When you don't use your muscles, you don't burn calories. The guy was building mass at an alarming rate.

"That machine is killing you," Nick told him. "You might not want to admit it, but you know it's true." He swung himself to a handle slightly closer. Caitlin was now behind the man, out of his line of sight. Nick only hoped she knew what she had to do.

Nick held eye contact with the man, whose face grew red, his eyes spilling tears that floated away.

"Freedom isn't freedom when you're addicted to it," Nick said.

"But I can't stop. Don't you understand? I can't turn off the machine, because if I do . . . if I do . . ."

Nick reached out and put a hand on his shoulder. "I know. If you do, then everything will come crashing down." Then he turned to Caitlin and shouted, "Now!"

And Caitlin, who had swung her way over to the machine, reached into the device and pulled out the pin so the weights slammed down, bringing the machine to a sudden halt.

The moment it did, everything—and everyone—that wasn't nailed down plunged to the floor. Gravity, clearly not pleased by their blatant defiance of the law, was punishing. Nick and the large man slammed to the ground, with only a thin layer of worn carpet to cushion their fall. Either one of them could have broken his neck or back, or any other part of his anatomy, but good fortune left them only bruised.

Grimacing, Nick pulled himself up, the sudden return of gravity making him feel weak after only a five-minute lapse.

Caitlin was disoriented but not hurt, because she had been close to the floor. She noticed that their brief battle had dislodged several things in the room, such as the sofa cushions and a photograph. The glass in the frame had shattered, and shards now lay strewn across the carpet. *What a hazard they'll be,* Caitlin thought, *if things go weightless again.*

She went over to Nick, fearing the worst when she saw the pain in his face. "Are you okay?"

"Yeah, I think so," he said.

And then she looked at the man, who now lay in a heap, his body racked with sobs. But Caitlin knew it wasn't from the pain of the fall.

As Nick picked himself up, recovering, Caitlin went to examine the man, who was not really the machine's owner, but more like its victim.

He struggled to push himself to his feet, but he could not. Caitlin recalled how astronauts who have been in space too long can barely walk when they return home, because of how quickly muscles atrophy in a weightless environment. She marveled that Nick had the foresight to realize this when they were still floating.

Each time that Nick did something wildly insensitive or generally dim, he would redeem himself by doing something brilliant and profoundly insightful. Caitlin knew that if he were *only* brilliant and insightful, she'd dislike him—just as much as if he were only insensitive and dim. It was the fact that he constantly teetered between the two states that made him so interesting.

"Why did it all have to go so wrong?" the heavy man wailed.

She knelt down to him and put a hand on his shoulder. "Maybe it needed to go wrong," she said softly, "to bring you to this moment."

He looked up at her, his eyes questioning.

Among the debris in the room was a pen. She found a scrap of paper and wrote down a name and phone number. "My uncle wrestles with obesity and a slow metabolism. He runs a clinic for people who are sick of fad diets"—she glanced at the machine—"and, uh . . . other weight-loss gimmicks."

The man took the slip of paper and stared at it.

"He'll help you get back on your feet—so to speak," she told him compassionately. "When you're ready."

He offered no resistance as they took the machine from the house, proving that maybe he was ready after all.

# 3 TESLANOID OBJECTS

Even dormant and only semi-assembled, Tesla's machine radiated energy.

Whenever Nick stood before the invention in his attic bedroom, he had no doubt that he was somehow a part of it, as were his friends, his father and brother, as well as everyone who had received one of the items.

His dad and Danny had already played their part in the inventor's master plan. Nick kept the broken bat in the attic as a memento, but it and the lost baseball glove were spent—he could sense that they were no longer connected to all the other objects. They also didn't fit into the machine. Neither did the Shut Up 'N Listen—an eerie variation on a See 'n Say toy—which had served its function by granting his friend Mitch the intermittent ability to "know the answer" even before anyone had formed the question.

The glove, the bat, and the toy were just "things" now, their purposes completed. But there was purpose left to spare for Nick and his friends and for all of the items still scattered through town.

Before the asteroid near miss, they had amassed twelve "Teslanoid Objects," as they had dubbed them. In the three weeks since, Nick had been able to recover four more. Some people had turned up at Nick's door begging him to release them from the burden, while others had to be tracked down through rumors and gossip.

Teslanoid Object No. 13. Just three days after the asteroid fell into orbit, a tired-looking woman had come by Nick's house to return a toy she had bought at the garage sale. She didn't even ask for her money back.

"Worst purchase ever," she told him.

The toy was a jack-in-the-box with such a mind-jolting finale, it rendered the unsuspecting viewer unconscious for hours, like a powerful narcotic. The woman had been using the "narc-in-a-box," as she called it, to put her fairly feral young children to sleep at night.

"But they figured it out," the woman told him, "and began using it on me so they could stay up all night eating candy and watching TV. You can't imagine what my house looks like every morning now," she moaned. "Just take it! I never want to see it again."

Teslanoid Object No. 14. When word got around school that someone's little brother had broken his arm in a windstorm, Nick thought that odd, because there hadn't been a whole lot of wind recently.

On a tip, Nick and Mitch visited a vacant lot, where they found a bunch of little kids playing with a hand bellows from the garage sale. The kids were using it to create little "dust devil" tornadoes, which they would then run into and get tossed ten feet away like rag dolls, laughing all the while. As mothers often say, "It's all well and good until someone breaks an arm."

Nick and Mitch traded very valuable video games for the bellows, ensuring that the kids wouldn't suffer any more bodily injuries, except, perhaps, carpal tunnel syndrome from overuse of a game controller.

Teslanoid Object No. 15. Mitch had overheard a couple of English teachers discussing a curious situation involving a math teacher's elderly parent. Apparently, the family had decided it was time to put Mom, now pushing ninety, into a nursing home. The woman, however, had no intention of leaving the house in which she had lived her life.

"According to Beth, who heard it from Alice," the teacher had said, "they couldn't get within five feet of her. It was like she was under some kind of protective spell."

Of course they had laughed the story away—after all, the very idea of folk magic and bad juju was ridiculous.

But the idea of unexplained science was not.

After some detective work, Nick, Mitch, and Caitlin had located the woman. It took all of them working together to broker an exchange for the electric flour sifter, which, when hand-cranked, generated a force field about five feet wide. There was no telling how large or powerful that field would be when connected to its intended power source, whatever that might be.

To seal the deal Caitlin had to promise that her father, an attorney, would give the elderly woman free legal representation in her fight to stay put.

Teslanoid Object No. 16. This one was returned to Nick unexpectedly by a man with cotton balls in his ears. Nick had completely forgotten about the item: a tarnished gunmetal-gray clarinet.

"Do you have any idea what it's like," the man asked furiously, "to listen to your daughter play her poor little heart out in a recital—only to have everyone in the audience run out screaming? Do you know what it's like," he shouted, "to have to shove cotton in your ears days after the trauma, because no matter what you do, you can't stop hearing those hideous sounds?"

Nick took the clarinet from him. "I've been to school recitals," Nick told him. "I feel your pain."

Nick took the instrument upstairs. The clarinet's bell fit perfectly over the nozzle of the hand bellows, making it clear that the creation of soul-searingly bad music was not the function of the "clarinet." It was merely a by-product.

Now, with the weight machine about to be added to the collection, seventeen objects had been recovered, and fifteen were still missing.

Hauling the bulky weight machine home would have been close to impossible under normal circumstances. But Nick had discovered that he could turn the machine on low by putting the pin in at the lightest weight. Immediately it became light enough for Caitlin and him to carry down the street and up to the attic without anyone's help.

Nick's bedroom furniture was dwarfed by the grand and mysterious contraption that was taking shape in the middle of the attic, composed of all the individual objects that fit together like pieces of a puzzle. In only a few moments, Nick figured out exactly where the weight machine fit into the device. It slipped in behind the lamp, and its frame provided a space perfectly sized for the six miniature Tesla coils disguised as hair curlers.

Caitlin crossed her arms and frowned. "How do you *do* that?"

"Do what?" Nick asked.

"How do you know exactly how it fits together? *I'm* the artist. I'm supposed to be the one with an advanced visual sense."

Nick shrugged. "I just picture it in my mind and I know."

"Careful," said Caitlin, with the slightest of grins, "or someone might accuse you of being a genius."

"Yeah," said Nick, "or an idiot savant."

Caitlin's grin got broader. "Or just an idiot."

Nick nodded. "I've been accused of that before."

He looked at the machine. He couldn't deny he felt a sense of pride each time he put another piece of the puzzle together. It made him feel one step closer to the man who had designed it. Perhaps Caitlin was right—maybe he had absorbed a smidgen of Tesla's brilliance.

"What does your dad think about all this stuff being back up here? He must wonder about it."

"He would," Nick admitted. "If he knew."

"Wait—you mean—"

"My dad has trouble with his knees—just enough to keep him from coming up here," he explained, glancing at the steep retractable attic stairs that led down to the second floor. "As long as I take my laundry to the basement, keep the room clean, and don't let food go bad, he has no reason to come up here."

"And if ever he does?"

Nick sighed. "I'll deal with it somehow." There was more to the situation with his father, but Nick didn't want to go into it.

With the weight machine in place, Nick and Caitlin went downstairs to reward themselves with champagne glasses of sparkling Dr Pepper.

After the third sip, Caitlin asked, "What's next?"

What was next for Nick had nothing to do with Tesla's devices. But he wasn't about to spring that on Caitlin. At least not yet.

"I saw an antique card catalog online that someone in town is selling. I think it's the one from the attic."

"Hmm," said Caitlin. "If they're selling it, it means they don't know what it does."

"Or," suggested Nick, "they don't like what it does and they want to get rid of it."

"Either way," Caitlin said, before taking another sip, "someone should check it out."

Nick interpreted "someone" to mean "not her." And he couldn't blame her. After all, Mitch and even Petula were a part of this, too. But it seemed like Nick and Caitlin had been doing all the heavy lifting, with or without gravity reduction. And then there was Vince, who hadn't been involved lately, for obvious reasons.

Nick said nothing for an uncomfortable moment, and Caitlin shifted as if about to get up.

"Well, I've got homework," she said.

Nick stopped her. "Caitlin," he said, "I've been thinking." He tried his best to maintain eye contact, but somehow that had been easier to do with the weightless casaba man. "Yeah, I was thinking," he repeated.

She looked at him expectantly.

"If we're not going to go hunting for more stuff this weekend . . ." he continued, "I mean, you know, stuff from my attic—I mean Tesla's stuff—not that I don't like doing that . . . I mean, I don't, but it's okay when I'm doing it with you—"

"Nick," Caitlin said gently, "you're babbling."

This interrupted his train of thought, which, he had to admit, was more like a train wreck. "What I mean to say is that I know how you like funny foreign films that end badly, and *My Big Swedish Funeral* is playing downtown."

"Are you asking me out on a date?" Caitlin asked with unbearable bluntness.

"Well . . . yeah. I guess."

"You *guess*? Or you *are*?"

Nick took a deep breath. "I am."

"Oh," said Caitlin. "Okay."

"Okay, yes? Or okay, you're acknowledging that I just asked you out on a date?"

"The second, I think."

"You *think*? Or you *are*?"

Caitlin took a deep breath, which was not a good sign. "Nick," she began, "we're in the middle of something really important. Going out on a date would . . . complicate things, don't you think?"

Nick felt his ears turning red, and he hoped his cheeks weren't turning red as well. "I think complicated is good."

Caitlin's shoulders sagged.

"Unless," Nick said, perhaps a little more belligerently than he meant to, "your heart is still set on Theo."

She looked at him as if he'd just slapped her. "It's not that, and you know it."

"Do I?"

He could see Caitlin struggling for words. *Good,* he thought, *let her struggle. If she's going to turn me down, let it be as hard for her as it was for me to ask.*

"I'm just not sure how I feel about it."

Nick got up with so much force that his chair slid backward across the kitchen floor. He wanted to storm out, but he realized that this was his house, and storming out would be weird. So he just stood there.

"Well," he said, "maybe you should get Tesla's tape recorder so it can tell you how you feel."

Caitlin rose from her chair. "That," she said, "was uncalled for."

She turned and stormed out far more effectively than Nick would have.

Nick resolved not to feel bad about what he'd said, and not to regret having asked her to the movies. Their friendship had grown since those first difficult days. It had survived the near end of the world. Was it too much to ask that their friendship take on a new dimension?

Now that Caitlin was gone, Nick returned to the attic and stood alone in front of Tesla's machine.

He was hurt by Caitlin's rejection, but, somehow, being with the machine made him feel a little bit better. He couldn't explain its grip on him. How, when he was near it, he had the urge to crawl inside it. To become a part of it. It now occupied that strange gravitational vortex in the center of his attic—the spot where he used to sit when the room was empty. Being there had made him feel like he was at the center of all things, but more importantly, at the center of himself. He couldn't get to that place now. The best he could do was be near the machine. Nick felt a growing need to tend to it.

To complete it.

Just as Caitlin had said—before shooting him down in flames—Nick intuitively knew how the objects fit in the larger machine, although he had no idea what each object's specific function in the device was, and with each part he added, the pull to completion grew. The closer he got to finishing Tesla's Far Range Energy Emitter, the more it seemed the machine *wanted* to be finished.

Nick's feeling of urgency was far preferable to the humiliation Caitlin had left him with. And so, secret and alone, he stood as close as humanly possible to the unfinished machine, trying to somehow resonate with its purpose, and longing for the day he could finally fire it up and see what it did.

Caitlin didn't even remember the walk home from Nick's house that day, she was so filled with frustration and anger. Long before she reached her front door, however, she realized she was angry at herself, not Nick.

The tape recorder that Nick had so coldly brought up had given her enough insight into herself to know that he had every right to be upset with her. Perhaps they *were* growing into more than friends. And if she was leading him on, there was a reason. Admittedly she liked him, even if she admitted it to no one but herself—but dating carried the kind of baggage that neither she nor Nick could afford right now.

In Caitlin's experience, a boyfriend was someone you thought you really liked, but once you got to know him, you spent all your time figuring out how to escape. Caitlin figured that dating would be like that until she finally got the hang of it. Only then would true love set in; only then would she find her soul mate.

She suspected that Nick might very well be soul-mate material, but turning him into a Theo would ruin that. Was there something wrong with her, that she would keep dating a boy she didn't want to spend time with, and keep spending time with a boy she was afraid to date?

"Caitlin, honey," her mother said as she walked into the house, "Theo's here."

And there he stood in the doorway, her ex/not-quite-ex-boyfriend.

Caitlin sighed. "Of course he is."

"Did you forget we were studying for science today?" he asked.

"Sorry," she said. "There was something I had to take care of."

Then she sat down, and they pulled out their science books and got to work.

*Yes,* thought Caitlin, *there definitely is something wrong with me.* And she wondered if, in the entire world, there could possibly be a more mismatched couple than her and Theo.

In fact, there was.

# ▮4▮ THE EPIC SPECTACLE OF THE HUMAN FAIL

**W**hile Petula Grabowski-Jones waited in rapt anticipation, Mitch Murló suppressed a sigh.

"Okay, here she comes," Petula said. "Watch—this is gonna be good."

This wasn't Mitch's idea of a good time, but he was willing to suspend judgment since it seemed to make Petula happy. And he wanted to keep her happy, because this was their first date that didn't involve the blissful silence of a movie theater. It meant they had to acknowledge each other's existence for an extended period of time, and actually converse. Such a thing is not easy. It had taken a while to settle on a nonmovie date that worked for both of them. She had nixed bowling as too lowbrow, and fine dining was inconceivable with Mitch, because, according to her, he had "the table manners of a lemur with brain damage."

It was thinking about himself as a lemur that made Mitch suggest the zoo. Petula had accepted, but, like everything else she did, it was for her own unique reasons.

Mitch couldn't quite say why he liked Petula. Maybe it was the charmingly irritating way she introduced herself to people ("It's PETula like SPATula, not PeTULa like PeTUNia"). Or maybe it was the way she parted her hair and braided her pigtails with quaint, yet terrifying, mathematical precision, so that even their faintly lopsided nature was by design. Or maybe it was just because *she* liked *him*. Whatever the reason, they now held hands and sat at a table at the edge of the snack bar of the Colorado Springs Zoo, watching Earth's highest mammal species—the kind not protected from Petula by the safety of cages.

"You remember how dark the reptile pavilion was, right?"

"Yeah . . ." Mitch said.

"And you see how bright the marble ground is right by the exit, right?"

"Yeah . . ." Mitch said.

"And you see that one single unexpected step, right?"

"Sure . . ." Mitch said.

Petula gestured with her hand, as if presenting him with some breathtaking vista. "Observe."

The woman who had just exited the reptile pavilion was fast approaching the nearly invisible step.

"Uh . . . shouldn't we warn her?" Mitch asked.

Petula burned him with a glare. "Is there something wrong with you?"

Blinded by the white marble, the hapless woman didn't see the step, and never had a chance. And while some other people exiting the reptile pavilion had made mildly clumsy missteps, this woman took a headlong fall; a wipeout for the ages. Her purse flew from her hands, disgorging its contents across yards of white marble, until it looked like the aftermath of a plane crash.

The woman, now prostrate as if in some odd form of worship, was rushed by half a dozen people. They helped her to her feet and gathered whatever belongings were not already being carried away by pigeons.

"That was . . . intense," Mitch said.

Petula leaned into him, in a very friendly sort of way. "Some moments are too special not to share."

"I think we should help her, though. I mean, look at her."

Even with the assistance of several bystanders, the woman seemed seriously disoriented.

Petula sighed in mild exasperation. "We can't help her, because we didn't help her."

"Huh?"

Reluctantly, Petula reached into her purse. "I didn't want to show you these, as they would spoil the surprise. But I suppose it's better if you know."

And then she presented Mitch with a series of black-and-white photographs of this exact spot. One was an image of the very scene before them, as if it had been taken two or three seconds earlier. Another was a shot of a man lying sprawled out in equal distress. And there was a third photo, of an entire family that had landed in a dog pile.

And all at once Mitch got it.

"The box camera."

Petula nodded. "I came here yesterday, set the camera for twenty-four hours, and started snapping pictures. I've been here several times before to enjoy the epic spectacle of the human fail. But I never knew when the most spectacular falls would take place. Thanks to the camera, I can tell down to the minute. The second fall will occur at three seventeen. And this third one at three thirty-two. I'm really looking forward to seeing how the family ends up like this."

Mitch was still having trouble wrapping his head around Tesla's camera that took pictures of the future. "But if we know what's going to happen, and we stop it—"

"We *can't* stop it," Petula pointed out. "The fact that we have a picture of it proves that it wasn't stopped. And the fact that we're not in the pictures helping these people proves that we won't."

"But we *could.*"

Petula balled her hands into fists. "There are no pictures of you and me catching falling people. Do I make myself clear?"

When Petula became adamant about something, Mitch knew there was nothing to do but let nature run its course without further argument.

Petula, however, did realize that it was in her best interest to control her temper. She had to remind herself that Mitch was an imbecile, but only in the way that all fourteen-year-old boys are imbeciles. She would help him outgrow it. A month ago Mitch Murló was barely on her radar. Funny how things change. She actually enjoyed her time with him, even when he made her angry. *Especially* when he made her angry. For in anger there is passion.

But then leave it to Mitch to spoil the moment.

"You know, you really should give Nick back that camera."

The mention of Nick made her feel defensive, possessive, and emotionally violated all at once. How dare he bring up the boy she'd rather go out with?

"Why would I ever do that? He still blames me for Vince's death. He hates me."

Mitch shrugged. "Maybe if you gave him back the camera he wouldn't hate you so much. Besides, Vince's death wasn't such a big deal, if you know what I mean."

Petula had to admit that the idea of Nick Slate not hating her would be a giant step toward her wish being fulfilled. And besides, she had other reasons to get back in Nick's good graces—reasons that had nothing to do with her feelings and all to do with the tiny Accelerati pin she wore secretly under the lapel of her blouse.

"I'll consider it," Petula told him, gently patting Mitch's hand. Then she pointed to a man exiting the reptile pavilion, a man destined to meet the marble in a most glorious fashion.

# 5 UNDEADITUDE

**S**ome relationships are made in heaven. Some are not. Take, for instance, the relationship between the sun and the moon. Now, *there* was a perfect union of heavenly bodies. The moon gave the earth tides, which in turn created beaches and breathtaking shorelines. Its phases helped early humans devise a calendar, and the occasional eclipse gave various civilizations cause for great theatrical events, such as human sacrifices and school closures.

But now an asteroid had come between them, and it was beginning to wreak a whole new brand of havoc. Because when a third party enters any relationship, there's bound to be some friction. Or at least some magnetic and electrical upheaval.

The first indication of change was actually rather beautiful. The aurora borealis, also known as the northern lights, which had previously been visible only near the Arctic Circle, could now be seen from any location on Earth. Sweeping flames of magnetic energy made a glorious display each night.

In every community, people would watch and marvel at the mystery of creation. And in the morning, when they received little carpet shocks while opening their bedroom doors, no one thought anything of it. At first.

■ ■ ■

Vince LaRue was no stranger to electrical shocks. Lately, his life was all about maintaining a firm electrical charge.

Death, he had found, was not all it was cracked up to be. In fact, it was a royal pain in the neck. Well, actually a pain just *beneath* Vince's neck, where the electrodes were attached.

"Vince, honey," his mother called from the annoyingly cheery part of the house, "are you still down there? You'll be late for school!"

"At this point, does it really matter?"

His friend Nick had his bedroom in an attic. Vince had chosen a basement. Both were dingy spaces, but there was a fundamental gloom about a basement that Vince had always found appealing. Especially now that he was dead.

Well, not exactly dead. Undead. Not in the vampiric sense. Not quite in the zombific sense either, but in a real-world *I'm-plugged-into-a-freaking-battery-that-keeps-me-alive* kind of sense.

He regarded himself in his bathroom mirror, which had given him mostly bad news for the past couple of weeks. After all, he had been verifiably dead for nearly four days before his friends came to reanimate him—a moment Vince never wanted to revisit. He still couldn't think of Spam or camels without feeling ill.

When he was first reanimated he just looked . . . well, dead. Pale and pasty like a fish belly. Unhealthy in a rare and special sort of way.

After a few days, though, his upper layers of skin had begun to peel. He was barely recognizable at first. He looked marvelously monsterlike. Just for fun he would go out in the early evening to parks and various other public locales to frighten the squeamish. His greatest victory had been making a young woman puke into her boyfriend's lap as they sat on a bench in Acacia Park. Of course, it could have been the boyfriend's kiss that made her barf—he wasn't all that good-looking—but Vince chose to take credit.

"The dead skin will be replaced by living skin eventually," Nick had told him.

"How would you know?" Vince asked. After all, it wasn't like there was a manual for this sort of thing.

But apparently Nick was right. His skin was clearing up, and now he looked like he'd just gotten a really bad sunburn. Although his body temperature remained a tepid seventy-two degrees, he was beginning to resemble his old self.

The biggest problem with being undead, however, was that it left a person with truly unholy body odor. And so, before donning his Grateful Dead T-shirt—which was now satisfyingly appropos—he slathered his pits with industrial-strength Right Guard, followed by a chaser of Old Spice, and then some Axe finishing spray over the rest of his body. It would, for at least a few hours, reduce his personal stench. Of course, anyone near him might wonder where on earth that smell of cat food was coming from. It wouldn't become intolerable until at least noon.

Vince had long since figured out the body-odor thing. It wasn't only that his body was purging itself of the remnants of death. Tesla's wet-cell battery had revived more than just him— it was also reanimating the dead bacteria on his body, all of which were more than happy to multiply and produce oodles of waste now that they were alive again.

What made it worse was that he couldn't shower with the electrodes on the back of his neck. The little EKG pads and tape would get wet, peel off, and he'd die again—which had already happened once. There are few things more humiliating than coming back to life on the shower floor and finding your mother standing over you, having just reattached your electrodes.

Now he had to take careful baths several times a day. For

a kid who used to enjoy stewing in his own juices, he had to admit that three baths a day was poetically just punishment.

"Vincent!" his mom called, with a standard parental loss of patience.

"Coming, Mom," he announced as he trudged up the stairs.

His mother emerged from the unnaturally merry kitchen and entered the unnaturally merry living room.

"Sit down," she said merrily. "Let me freshen up your tape."

This ritual had been added to her routine good-bye hug, and Vince was as powerless to resist it as he was the hug. Mothers do what mothers do.

Carefully, making sure the electrodes never lost contact, she removed the old tape and checked that the electrodes were secure and the EKG pads still adhered to his skin. Then she put a fresh strip of tape on his upper back, just beneath his collar line.

She hummed to herself as she did it. Vince was still amazed by how quickly she had come to accept his living-dead status. Then again, what choice did she have? It was either accept it or run away screaming. She now called Vince her "little miracle" and left it at that.

In the days after his reanimation, she kept asking him what he had experienced in his temporary afterlife. Each time he answered in a different but equally snarky way. First he told her, "They gave me wings and I played Halo." Then, "I inherited a planet, but it was blown up by the Death Star." And finally, "I was at a dinner party with our dead relatives. That's how I knew I was in hell." She didn't ask him again after that.

But the truth was, he couldn't actually remember what he had experienced on the other side. It was like that dream that lurks at the edge of your consciousness, but you just can't pull it from the depths of your memory no matter how hard you try.

As Vince walked to school, his head and shoulders in a

slouch, his mother followed one block behind in her car. She would track him until he was on school property, then leave to begin her work day at SmileMax Realty, which claimed to have the "Happiest Realtors on Earth.®" Ever since he had been resurrected, she wanted to drive him everywhere, to make sure he was safe. He had refused to allow it. This was their compromise.

As he strolled the root-buckled sidewalks of his neighborhood, he dared to consider his options. What were the long-term prospects for the undead? Would he grow into manhood, or would he be perpetually fixed at fourteen? If the latter, was that such a bad thing? And did being undead mean "living" forever?

On the positive side, his acne had cleared up, because acne, being the purging of dead bacteria, couldn't happen if the bacteria kept coming back to life.

On the downside, if he were exposed to a bad bug it would multiply much more rapidly in him than in a regular living person. He could be the carrier of any number of deadly diseases.

Which was disturbing enough to be slightly thrilling to him.

With everything taken into account, Vince concluded that he enjoyed his current state of undeaditude.

He did have to admit that he missed dreaming. But there was no sleeping for him anymore. He had only two states now: awake and dead. Since he had previously been something of an insomniac, he was used to watching old movies and playing video games all night long. Since he never nodded off now—and never even got tired—he didn't miss the end of movies.

His mother had once suggested that he disconnect at bedtime, and she could come in to reconnect him when his alarm went off, because "everybody needs eight hours of rest." But when he pointed out that he'd spend those eight hours decomposing, it quickly put an end to that idea.

On the rare occasion when a wire slipped off in a public place,

Vince had learned the trick of closing his eyes the moment he felt death coming on. That way, when he hit the floor, it would appear to any onlookers that he was merely unconscious until help arrived.

For this reason, Vince, a loner by nature, had been forced to adopt the buddy system, making sure that he was almost always under the watchful eyes of either his mother one block behind, or one of the four classmates who knew about the battery.

Mitch was the first member of their little secret society to greet Vince at school that day, at which point his mother sped away.

"Hey, Vince," Mitch said, a little too loudly, like always. "How you feeling today?"

"Dead to the world," Vince responded in as flat a tone as he could muster.

Mitch gave him a courtesy laugh, and followed him to class.

Between Mitch, Petula, Caitlin, and Nick, Vince had someone to spot him in five out of six classes. Though he hated having to be babysat, the possibility of dropping dead in the classroom was worse. Which, on this particular day, happened in English, when his backpack containing the heavy wet-cell battery slipped from his chair to the floor, disconnecting his electrodes.

Nick was two seats away when he heard the telltale thud of Vince's head hitting the desk. It brought about a titter of giggles around him, because his classmates thought he had fallen asleep.

The cover story, which came in the form of a note from Vince's mother to all of his teachers, was that Vince had been diagnosed as narcoleptic. The note said he could fall asleep at any moment, and that the teachers should not take it personally—which, invariably, they did—and, in fact, a few students were keeping a secret tally of which of Vince's teachers were the most sleep-inducing.

When Vince went down, Nick was quick to react, practically jumping over the girl between them to reconnect the electrodes. Luckily, the wires had detached from the battery and not Vince's back, because it would have been much harder for Nick to explain why he was reaching up Vince's shirt to wake him, rather than just slapping him in the face—as many of the other kids, and perhaps even some teachers, would have been happy to do.

Once the electrodes were reconnected, Vince opened his eyes and popped up in his chair as if it had never happened. "Present!" he said.

The girl next to Vince looked at Nick with an odd expression on her face.

"What did you just do?" she asked.

Nick shrugged. "Nothing. I was just going for his phone to call his mother. She wants to know whenever he has a narcoleptic episode."

But the girl wasn't convinced. "What's that in his backpack? It looks heavy."

Nick and Vince were saved by their teacher, who insisted that all attention return to her. One of these days, though, Nick knew someone would get a little too curious and realize that Vince's condition was grave—in the literal sense.

At the end of the period Vince made a beeline for the door, but Nick followed him down the hall.

"If you're expecting a thank-you," said Vince, "you're not going to get one."

"Why would I expect that?" Nick asked. "You never thanked Caitlin and me for reanimating you in the first place. And after what happened in the mortuary that day, we don't deserve thank-yous, we deserve medals." Nick shuddered. "I'm still having nightmares about porcupines and pickaxes."

He looked around, making sure none of the other students

hurrying to class were listening. "Hey, I still need your help, Vince."

Vince crossed his gangly arms, giving Nick a dead-fish kind of look. "Why would I help you? If it weren't for you, I wouldn't need this battery at all."

Vince had a point, but there was a much larger point to be made. "Whether you like it or not, we're all in this together now."

"And whose fault is that?"

Nick felt his hands ball into fists. "Will it matter whose fault it is when the Accelerati steal your battery and you're six feet under for good?"

"That'll never happen," Vince said. "I plan to be cremated."

Nick wanted to grab him and give him a good shake, but he thought that might dislodge the wires again, so he took a deep breath to calm down. Nick had to remind himself that this situation had left Vince worse off than any of them.

"Why don't you just let the Accelerati get the rest of the stuff?" Vince grumbled. "Maybe then they'll leave us alone."

Nick was about to point out that he needed every remaining item to assemble the machine in his attic, but then he realized he had never told Vince that the objects fit together. Vince didn't know, and neither did the Accelerati.

And all at once Nick understood that he couldn't tell Vince, because to finish the machine, the final object they'd need would be Vince's battery. It was a cold truth that Nick didn't want to face right now, so he pushed the thought away. All Nick said was "After what they did to you, don't you want to take them down?"

Vince hesitated. The hallway began to clear. Nick knew he'd be late to history, but this was more important.

"I'll sleep on it," Vince finally said.

"You don't sleep," Nick pointed out.

"Which means I'll have plenty of time to think it over."

# 6 OF LOBSTERS AND LUNCH LADIES

**A** power generator is an unpredictable thing. It can blow up, blow out, or electrocute people with the same happy ease with which it charges your electric toothbrush.

The larger the generator, the more power it delivers, and consequently, the more potential for devastation.

The Three Gorges Dam, capable of providing 10 percent of China's power with its thirty-two massive turbines, had been the world's largest electric power generator. But even the largest turbine is just a quantity of copper wire spinning around a magnet, and can't compare to a chunk of copper fifty miles across, spinning around the magnetic core of planet Earth. There was a new mega–power generator on the block, and its name was Bonk.

Everyone was aware of the buildup in static electricity. Most people just considered it "one of those things." Like the way Wint-O-Green Life Savers spark in your mouth when you chew them, or how sometimes dry bedsheets flash with microlightning when you shuffle your feet beneath the covers.

Petula was no stranger to the phenomenon of electric shock.

Her parents would often laughingly tell of her many near-death experiences when, as a toddler, she had repeatedly shoved forks into outlets. Eventually they became an all-plastic-utensil household. Petula remembered it enough to know that she didn't have an infant death wish—she was just trying to kill the "stinking monster" in the wall that kept shocking her for no good reason.

But now the monster was back, and it was no longer confined to the wall.

Petula knew it wasn't going to be a good day when she awoke to discover that the static she had kicked up in her sheets during the night had caused her braided pigtails to stand almost on end, like Pippi Longstocking. It took the painful touching of many doorknobs to discharge the static, and industrial amounts of hair gel to keep her braids in place.

Petula suffered through her morning classes, but ever since the day Ms. Planck, the so-called lunch lady, had invited her to join the Accelerati, the busywork of institutionalized curriculum seemed like a nonsensical waste of her time.

The problem, Petula only now realized, was that Ms. Planck had inducted her into a sleeper cell of two. They were supposed to do nothing but watch and wait.

Petula was skilled at watching, but waiting was something she could not abide. She had gathered information on Nick Slate's activities. She had reported to Ms. Planck which objects Nick had in his possession. She had taken remarkably dull pictures of the future on Ms. Planck's orders, and she kept expecting Ms. Planck to ask her to actually do something important, but no such luck.

During history class, while the teacher was droning on about Manifest Destiny, Petula decided it was time to manifest her own destiny. The instant the lunch bell rang, she made a beeline to the cafeteria.

Ms. Planck was at her usual station behind the steam table. The woman, who had worked undercover all these years, was one of the few people in the world Petula respected and one of the fewer she actually liked. But at the moment, she was holding Petula back.

There were other kids already waiting for lunch. Petula allowed them their place in line ahead of her so she could formulate her thoughts and build her resolve. When no one was looking, she reached up and felt the hidden gold pin she wore, running her thumb and forefinger over the smooth little *A* with an infinity sign as its crossbar. "Wear this close to your heart, but don't let anyone see it," Ms. Planck had told her. Well, membership had to mean more than a stupid pin. It had to be a doorway to greatness, and Petula was tired of knocking.

When Petula finally approached, Ms. Planck must have read something in her face, because she offered a conspiratorial smirk and said, "You look like you could use some food from my special surprise stash."

Seventy-five percent of surprises, Petula had concluded, were unpleasant, but she had to admit she was curious.

"Sure," she said to Ms. Planck. "What ya got?"

The lunch lady reached a pair of long silver tongs below the counter, then dropped a perfectly broiled lobster tail on Petula's tray.

"Impressive," Petula said. "Who do you usually serve this to?"

"Anyone who deserves it and isn't allergic to shellfish," Ms. Planck said.

"There are kids I know who *are* allergic to shellfish, and deserve to be given some."

"Give me their names," Ms. Planck said with a wink, "and I'll see what I can do."

"Hey," said the kid behind her in line. "How come she got the big shrimp? I want a big shrimp too!"

"Can't do it," said Ms. Planck flatly. "Serving you a bottom-feeder could be considered encouraging cannibalism. You get soy pizza. Next!"

Kids were pushing forward to get their lunch, but Petula

blocked the flow, refusing to move on. "We need to talk," she told Ms. Planck.

"Later" was all Ms. Planck said, and she then ignored her, serving up slop as if Petula wasn't there. So Petula found a table, sat down, and ate the lobster tail unnoticed by the other kids. This didn't surprise her—she was convinced she could have done a hula dance with the lobster tail on her head and, with the exception of the one kid who wanted "big shrimp," no one would have paid any attention.

*That*, Petula resolved, was one more thing that needed to change.

After school, Petula took her daily photographs for the Accelerati with the focus ring of Tesla's old box camera set twenty-four hours to the future. She snapped a photo of the newspaper kiosk, where tomorrow's headlines would appear. She took a few pictures of the digital stock ticker that wrapped around the Wells Fargo Bank building. And finally she took a shot of the front of the neighborhood bowling alley.

When she was done, she went to Ms. Planck's darkroom and developed the negatives. Together they pored over the enlargements, studying tomorrow's newspaper headlines, noting the next day's closing stock prices, and confirming that the bowling alley looked unchanged. Ms. Planck had never explained the significance of snapping this last photograph every day, and not knowing why made Petula feel even more like an outsider.

"Look," Petula said, pointing at a news headline. "The Phoenix Suns are going to beat the Lakers in tonight's playoff— that's a pretty big upset."

"Yes, it is. I'm sure the Accelerati will find the information most useful," Ms. Planck responded.

"You mean they'll place a bet?"

"Don't be ridiculous, honey. They'll buy the team."

*Thanks to me!* Petula wanted to shout. Not only was she their eyes and ears on Nick Slate and his attic, she was also feeding the Accelerati reams of priceless information about the future. But did they even know about her, or was Ms. Planck taking all the credit? It was that thought that pushed Petula over the edge.

"Enjoy those pictures," she told Ms. Planck. "Because they're the last you're going to get. As of now, I'm on strike."

Ms. Planck didn't seem bothered. She just smirked. "Really. Is it just you or the entire future-tographer's union?"

"I don't mind being used," Petula told her, "as long as I get something worthwhile in return."

Ms. Planck considered that, then said, "Maybe it's time to introduce you to the brass."

Petula's only context for that sentiment was a gangster movie she had seen once on TCM, in which being "introduced to the brass" meant a beating with brass knuckles.

"Are you threatening me?" Petula asked, and she assumed a ready position she had learned in her online theoretical jujitsu class.

"Take it easy, honey," Ms. Planck said, arching an eyebrow. "I only mean to say I think you're ready to meet some of the higher-ups in our little association."

Petula let out a small breath and smiled at the thought. This was what she had been waiting for: her moment to make an impression. With her personality and perfect elocution, she had no doubt that this was her opportunity to open the door wide.

"In that case, we have a deal," she said. "The strike has been averted."

She would enchant the visionaries of the Accelerati. And God help them if they weren't enchanted.

# 7 SHELL GAME

**D**r. Alan Jorgenson sat in his office at the University of Colorado, simmering slowly like a roast in a Crock-Pot. He had the resources of the world's most technologically advanced secret society at his fingertips. He could control the weather with the flick of a switch; he could stop time and move between the seconds; he could end the lives of his enemies as effortlessly as changing channels on a television.

So why was he letting a group of mediocre-minded middle schoolers get to him?

There was a timid knock, and in a moment the office door opened just wide enough for the person on the other side to poke his head in. "Excuse me, Dr. Jorgenson?" an impertinent doctoral student said. "I've been waiting for nearly an hour. . . ."

"And you'll wait an hour more if that's what I require," Jorgenson told him.

"Yes, sir." He unpoked his head and closed the door quietly.

Even as a distinguished full professor at a major university, Jorgenson could not escape the academic blight of doctoral students. He had to maintain his cover, at least for now, and the academic cred could one day prove useful, so he made his students research assistants and rarely had any use for them unless they had results to show him.

The young bespectacled man outside claimed to have results,

but Jorgenson's university research, no matter how important, paled next to the potential of Tesla's "lost" inventions. Retrieving at least some of those inventions would be simple: just kill Nick Slate, take the objects from his attic, and be done with it. But the Man in Charge would not allow it. Jorgenson's orders were clear. Let the boy be. At least for now.

"He will be dispensed with soon enough," the old man had told Jorgenson. "The more he spins his wheels to gather the lost items, the less we'll have to."

But "soon enough" wasn't soon enough for Jorgenson, who knew something the old man didn't: the boy was crafty. And clever. He had, more than once, outsmarted Jorgenson's superior intellect, which meant he was not to be underestimated. If he were allowed to gather too many of Tesla's inventions—and figured out how to use them—he and his friends would become formidable opponents. Such objects should not be left in the hands of children.

And to make sure that they weren't, it was best if those children were killed. Why couldn't the old man see that?

Once more came the timid knocking and the bespectacled student. "Dr. Jorgenson, I know you said to wait, but I need to teach an undergrad physics class in ten minutes. . . ."

Jorgenson sighed. "Very well." He gestured for the young man to enter.

The student held a shoe box. "I've been in charge of the TTT project. You know—the Titanium Testudine Trials."

"Ah! The tortoises."

The young man sat down across from Jorgenson, pulled from the shoe box three tortoise shells the size of coconut halves, and placed them on Jorgenson's desk. All of the shells had a pale metallic sheen about them.

Jorgenson was curious to hear the results of the study, but he feigned absolute disinterest. "Just get this over with," he said. "My time is more valuable than yours. Don't waste it!" He paused to gauge the effect of his tone on the student's psyche and was pleased to detect a tremor in the region of the young man's knees.

"W-we induced rapid growth using your biotemporal field emitter, and infused the developing cells with titanium, using three different protocols." He pointed to two of the shells. "The first two specimens didn't prove any stronger, but the third was the charm." He tapped the last shell proudly.

Jorgenson lifted one of the shells. The plastron—or underside—had been removed, leaving only the dome-shaped carapace. "And what happened to the creatures they held?"

The student lowered his head as if in respect for the dead. "They gave their lives for science."

"Indeed," Jorgenson said. "As must we all."

Then Jorgenson started sliding the three shells around on his desk, shuffling their positions again and again. "Are you watching closely? Keep your eye on the strongest one, the 'charm,' as you called it." Jorgenson spoke rapidly, his voice taking on the cadence of a carnival barker. "That's right, never take your eye off the shell, if you don't want to get shucked."

He stopped and leaned forward, smiling broadly at the younger man, who stared at the row of three shells, somewhat bewildered.

"Now, put your hand beneath the one you think is the strongest," Jorgenson said.

"My hand? Why?"

"Come, come. He who hesitates is lost."

After a moment, the student chose the shell in the middle, sliding his hand through the neural arch that had originally made room for the reptile's neck.

Jorgenson looked into the man's eyes. "Are you sure that's the one?"

"I—I think so," the student said.

"Good, good."

Without warning, Jorgenson pulled from his desk drawer a large hammer—a weapon he kept as a defense against the potential attacks of disgruntled students and irate colleagues. He held it up just long enough to register the terror in the young man's eyes, then he slammed the hammer down on the empty shell on the left. Pieces of shell flew in every direction; Jorgenson felt some flakes bounce off his chin. The student flinched and grimaced, but, to his credit, did not remove his hand from the center shell.

"Hmm. My test confirms that it wasn't the shell on the left. Now, would you like to stay with your original choice? Or would you prefer to switch?"

The student just stared at him, his eyes seeming as wide as the lenses of his glasses.

"I'm giving you the chance to change your mind, you see. The mathematical odds are much more favorable if you do—there's a fifty-fifty chance, as opposed to one in three."

"B-but—"

"I know it seems counterintuitive, but it's true."

The student was so petrified, he couldn't move even if he'd wanted to.

"Sticking with your first choice, are you? Risky." And Jorgenson reached over and removed the unchosen shell from the desk.

"Wait—you're not going to smash that one?"

Jorgenson smiled once more. "Where would be the fun in that?" Then, without warning, he brought the hammer down with full force on the shell covering the student's hand.

The young man screamed, but the hammer bounced off the shell, leaving it intact and the hand beneath it unharmed.

"Interesting result," Jorgenson murmured, and, just to be sure, he slammed the hammer down on the shell a second time, even harder. Again the hammer did no damage. "Well done!"

The doctoral student, suddenly jolted from his petrifaction, jerked his hand back and gave it a few shakes as if to make sure all of the bones and tendons were still in working order.

"So what have we learned from our little experiment?" Jorgenson asked. "What lesson do we extract?"

"You—you could have mangled me!"

"Wrong!" Jorgenson shouted. "The lesson is: *From now on, you NEVER bring me anything but your best specimen. Is that understood?*" He dropped the hammer onto the desk and picked up the pristine shell. "Now go and teach your pathetic class."

As the young man fled the office, Jorgenson examined the metalized shell more closely. His mind flooded with potential uses—indestructible tanks and personnel carriers, undentable automobiles. And that was only scratching the surface. With the 725 million dollars that had come into the Accelerati's possession, implementing those uses would be easy.

And yet, any sense of triumph was overshadowed by his recent failure. He longed for the day he could give his research assistants the task of reverse-engineering the objects that Nick Slate had in his possession. The applications and monetary rewards of those inventions, whatever they were, would be staggering in the hands of someone who knew how to exploit them.

Someone other than Nick Slate.

The old man wanted Jorgenson to wait, but he had waited long enough. Jorgenson had to take matters into his own hands.

He slipped the fortified shell into the pocket of his coat.

Then, almost as an afterthought, he placed the other intact tortoise shell back on his desk.

The boy was nothing. He was as empty, and ultimately as fragile, as this shell, which, clearly, had not protected its reptilian owner from an untimely demise.

Jorgenson brought the hammer up once more, and with all his might, he slammed it down on the third shell. It disintegrated in a satisfying burst of silver-green shards. He took a deep breath and smiled.

It was time to do the same to Nick.

# 8 "WE BOTH KNOW YOU DID THAT ON PURPOSE"

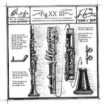

**N**ick was not looking forward to his brother's baseball game after school.

This should have been a sign that something was off—not only because he loved baseball, but also because he prided himself on being a good big brother, and these days Danny really needed him. The house fire back in Florida may not have been as momentous as an asteroid strike, but it had been just as devastating to Nick and Danny and their father. Four months was not enough time to heal from something like that. Nick's family had changed forever, and it could be years before they truly came to terms with it.

Perspective. It was a luxury Nick, his brother, and his father simply didn't have right now.

Danny's previous game had ended abruptly when a meteorite the size of a grapefruit was pulled from the sky and into his mitt. He took to the field alone a few nights after that, pulling dozens more from the sky with the Tesla-modified glove, hoping beyond hope that wishing on the falling stars would bring his mother back. The last space rock he had turned in Earth's direction was the heavy hitter.

Now Danny would be in the field again. A different field, to be sure, since the Sports McComplex they had played in was now cratered from meteor strikes. Instead they would be playing in Memorial Park on Wednesday afternoons, when the diamond was available.

The park was in an older part of town, fairly close to where Tesla's laboratory had once stood. With mixed feelings, Nick rode his bike through the neighborhood of old homes and came to a stop across the street from the site. The lab was long gone, of course; the ordinary tract house occupying the space had an iron fence and two guard dogs to keep away the lunatics who saw it as hallowed ground.

That was the problem—it was mostly lunatics. The greatest inventor of all time deserved more than the babbling fringe.

Such was the brine of Nick's thoughts as he joined his father in the bleachers while Danny took to the field.

"He'll do fine," Mr. Slate said, clearly trying to convince himself. "Baseball is in his blood. He'll do fine."

Watching Danny play baseball was a rare moment of escape for Nick's dad. Wayne Slate worked as a copy-machine repairman at NORAD—which would have been fine, if it weren't for the fact that Jorgenson, the veritable eye of the Accelerati, had gotten him the job. It was his way of keeping their whole family under his thumb.

Nick's dad didn't know about the Accelerati, of course, or about Tesla's inventions. Nick wondered, though, if his father knew that it was his very own swing of the bat—even though it missed the ball that Nick had pitched to him—that had saved the world. Surely he must have suspected, but they had never spoken of it, and Nick doubted they ever would.

After that day, Wayne Slate had slipped into a bizarre form of post-traumatic stress. He became busy. Busier than ever before. It was as if keeping the blood flowing to other parts of his body prevented it from reaching his brain, where he would have to process everything that had happened. And whenever he slowed down, he began to sink like a stone into himself.

"I'm fine," he had told Nick and Danny. "Better than fine. The world is saved—we all have a new lease on life, right? I intend to make the very best of it."

They all rose for "The Star-Spangled Banner," performed by a paunchy middle-aged guy who had once been in a boy band, and then Danny's team took the field. The woman sitting next to them on the bleacher kept looking at Nick's dad out of the corner of her eye. Finally she turned to him and said, "Your son's the one who caught that meteorite, isn't he?"

Nick could hear the discomfort in his father's voice as he deftly changed the subject. "Say, didn't I spill popcorn on you during that game? I hope the butter didn't leave any stains."

"No, not at all. Thanks for asking."

*Stains.* Nick suddenly remembered the last game. This woman said her son—one of Danny's teammates—had bought her a miraculous stain remover at a garage sale. Nick's interest in the woman was piqued. She probably didn't even know how unique the object was. *Perhaps,* thought Nick, *that'll make it easier to get it back.*

The popcorn woman slid a little closer to Nick's father on the bench. "The way you raced out there when the meteorite dragged him through the field . . . it was very moving. I'm glad to see he's okay."

"Thanks," his father said.

The woman smiled and held out her hand. "Hi, I'm Beverly—Seth Hills's mom." She pointed to the ten-year-old at third base.

Nick's father grinned. "So I suppose that makes you Beverly Hills."

She sighed. "Luckily, no. I mean, that *was* my married name, but when *that* ended, I went back to Webb, my maiden name."

Nick watched this little parental drama with a feeling resembling nausea. In just a few brief moments she had sidled up to his father and smoothly let him know that she was available. Well, his dad most certainly was not.

"So," Nick found himself blurting out, "did your husband die, like my mom did, three and a half months ago?"

"Nick!" his father said sharply. It was the first time Nick had used his mom's death as a weapon. Under the circumstances, he thought she'd be okay with that. In a way, he felt she was an ally in saving his father from Beverly, the Popcorn Lady.

"How awful," she said, backing off a bit. "I'm so sorry to hear that."

"It was a fire," Nick said. "Did I mention it happened only three and a half months ago?"

They were all rescued by a line drive to her son, the third baseman, who fielded it, getting the first out of the game.

Now that Beverly Webb had become quiet and had moved out of Nick's father's airspace, Nick realized that he had just missed a golden opportunity. If she and his father got friendly, Nick would be that much closer to retrieving the stain remover.

A storm raged in Nick now. A single word from him could ease the tension he had created. He could bring this woman into his family circle, or he could keep her out of it forever. But could he betray the memory of his mother just to get a stupid stain remover? Although, it was more than a stain remover, wasn't it? Would he hate himself if he did it? Would he kick himself if he didn't? And which was worse, hating himself or kicking himself?

Nick looked up when he heard the crack of a bat. The batter had popped a fly ball into right field—where Danny was waiting.

The ball reached its apex as the batter rounded first, and it came down toward Danny. The entire crowd fell silent with anticipation that bordered on dread, and the other fielders actually began to back away.

Everyone remembered what had happened the last time a ball was hit in Danny's direction. The sky had opened up and hurled a flaming piece of heaven at him.

This time Danny reached out his arm, held his mitt high . . .

. . . and the ball hit the ground about five feet to his left.

The fans rose to their feet in thunderous cheers—even his own teammates were cheering. The batter continued to round the bases, but no one much cared—no one even went after the ball. It was as if, by failing to catch it, Danny had just won the World Series. Danny, not knowing what to make of it, just watched the cheering crowd, and then took an exaggerated bow that brought on even more cheers.

"Go, Danny!" yelled Nick's dad, ever the proud father.

Nick also cheered his brother's magnificent error. And in that moment he got an idea.

Swinging his arm wide, he brushed his elbow against Beverly Webb's purse, knocking it off their bench and sending it down into the dim framework of the bleachers. As it tumbled, it spilled keys and loose change that clanged and tinkled on dusty struts all the way down.

"Oops," said Nick.

Beverly Webb gave Nick a gaze that was not so much cold as piercingly honest.

"We both know you did that on purpose," she said without any of the anger Nick wanted her to have.

Nick's father opened his mouth, fully prepared to defend him, but Nick didn't let him.

"Yeah, maybe I did," said Nick.

"And maybe you'll go get it," said Beverly Webb.

"No maybe about it," said his father. "Nick, apologize and get her purse."

Nick stood up. "It was a dumb thing to do. I'm sorry."

As he left the bleachers, he heard his dad say, "He's really not that kind of kid," and that bothered Nick, because it made him wonder what kind of kid he was . . . or was becoming.

The crawl space beneath the bleachers was darker than Nick thought it would be, with only a few slender beams of light piercing the gloom. The ground was littered with soda cans, gum wrappers, and popcorn. Right now the darkness was his friend, because it meant that no one peering through the slats up above could see what he was doing. He found the purse and began gathering the various things that had fallen out. Including the woman's wallet, which he now opened.

Beverly Webb thought he had knocked the purse over because he didn't like her. It was true he didn't like her—but that wasn't the reason for what he did. As long as she believed it was, though, she'd never suspect the whole truth.

Nick pulled out her driver's license and held it in a shaft of light just long enough to memorize the address. Then he slid it back into the wallet, slipped the wallet into the purse, and returned to the bench above, where he presented the purse to its owner.

"Thank you," she said. His father chose not to look at him.

"Like I said, I'm sorry."

She offered him a forgiving grin. "Apology accepted. And I get it, okay?"

Nick shrugged. "There's nothing to get," he said. Well, there *was* one thing. And now that he knew where she lived, he'd be coming for the stain remover.

# ⑨ ALL THINGS THAT FALL

According to the science of game theory, individuals tend to make decisions that favor themselves. This might seem ridiculously obvious, but science is full of things that seem ridiculously obvious yet are far more complex than they appear. Take, for instance, Newton's greatest achievement, the theory of gravity, which boils down to: "All things that fall, fall down."

And, like the theory of gravity, game theory is not as simple as it seems. First of all, "game" applies to much more than simple pastimes like Little League, or even Major League, baseball. Game theory stretches to encompass politics, economics, biology—even civilization as a whole—and it can sometimes tip the balance in life-or-death decisions.

The game Nick now played held such life-or-death consequences—for both himself and the world. He knew it, and still he played, because when you're both a game piece and a player, the only way out is through either victory or defeat. Defeat, in Nick's case, meant a world in which the Accelerati held all of Tesla's inventions and, most likely, his life in their hands. Neither of those was an acceptable outcome to Nick.

Vince LaRue was also in the game, although somewhat on the fringe. He had a very different perspective on life-or-death decisions. To him, both states were temporary, and both were a nuisance. He often wished there were a third state of being that wasn't such a royal pain, but electricity was binary in nature, leaving him only two choices: either positive or negative.

Though Vince did not show it, he was actually pleased when Nick called that night. Sure, Nick was indirectly responsible for Vince's current binary state, but he was also the driving force behind the most interesting chain of events Vince had ever experienced. After all, the world had almost ended. Perhaps it might almost end again! That was definitely worth the ride.

"Vince, I need your help." It sounded as if his friend on the other end of the phone was pedaling a bicycle uphill, which, in fact, was the case.

"With what?" Vince asked with a yawn—which was solely for dramatic effect, as the battery did not allow him to be tired.

"Breaking and entering," Nick said.

This surprised Vince, as Nick was not the burglarizing type. But people change. "I'm insulted you assume I know anything about that."

"Well, do you?"

"Of course, but I'm still insulted."

Nick quickly summarized the situation. His brother's team and their parents had gone out for consolation pizza after losing thirty-three to zero. This gave Nick a window of about two hours to retrieve a garage-sale item from one of those family's homes.

In the end, it didn't take much to convince Vince to meet him at Beverly Webb's house, though Vince made it sound like a major imposition. "The sooner we find all this junk," he said, "the sooner you'll stop bugging me, and let me get on with my so-called life." As he hung up, he felt some satisfaction that this was perhaps the only time in history that the expression "so-called life" was entirely accurate.

■ ■ ■

The sun had already dropped behind Pikes Peak as Vince rode his bike to the address Nick had given him. The shadow of the Rocky Mountains was now reaching out to blanket Colorado Springs in darkness. Vince loved how quickly night came just east of the Rockies. It fell upon the town like a coffin lid, leaving the populace bewildered until their eyes could adjust.

It was already instant night when he arrived at the boxy tract home at the top of a hill. Vince had come prepared for the job, with two pairs of latex gloves, two LED headlamps on rubber straps, and a set of lock-picking tools that he didn't actually know how to use. He had put them all into the zippered front pocket of the backpack he now always kept slung over his shoulders. The one that held his literal lifeline.

Nick was standing deep in the bushes at the edge of the property, where he wouldn't be seen by anyone—unless they knew to look for him.

"I thought you might have changed your mind," he said as Vince coasted to a stop in front of him.

"Should I have?" Vince asked, not the least out of breath from his uphill pedaling—another benefit of battery-operated existence. He walked his bike behind a bush and leaned it against Nick's before asking the question that had been nagging at him. "So how come we're breaking in, instead of negotiating for it?"

"It's complicated," Nick said, looking away. "Can we just get this over with, please?"

Vince could have pressed, but he didn't really care why this mission was different. "Did you find a point of entry?"

"Back door, front door, side garage door. They're all locked."

"Doors are never truly locked," Vince said, until he discovered the nasty double-mortise dead bolts in all three doors. "Except for these," he amended. "Did you ring the bell?"

"Why would I do that?"

Vince rolled his eyes. Was this obvious only to him? "To find out if there's a canine presence."

"Wouldn't a dog already have heard us?"

"You give them too much credit. You can poke around outside a house for an hour, but until you bang on the wall or ring the bell, most dogs won't care. But once you do, they care way too much."

The doorbell yielded nothing but silence from inside, which satisfied Vince. He led the way to the kitchen window—the one least likely to be locked.

"I used to break into neighbors' homes," Vince admitted. "Not to take anything, but to watch TV. My mom refuses to spring for the good cable stations."

The window wasn't wired with an alarm, and it was only barely latched. Together, Nick and Vince gingerly removed the screen. Then Vince used one of the picking tools as a lever to unfasten the latch.

"Easy peasy," said Vince once they were standing in the kitchen. "And I'll deny it if you ever tell anyone I said 'easy peasy.'"

He stopped short when he saw a cat-food bowl on the floor near the sink. "Uh-oh."

"What is it?"

"They have a cat. Cats don't seem to like me anymore."

This sentiment was punctuated, and confirmed, by the loudest hiss Vince had ever heard. He wouldn't have been surprised to see a mountain lion in the room with them. But it was just a common house cat sitting on top of the refrigerator.

"Boo!" Vince shouted, and the cat did an amazing feline leap, ricocheting off the hanging lampshade and out of the room. With the cat dispatched, Vince carefully pulled his backpack around so he could unzip the outer pocket. He fished out the small headlamps and handed one to Nick. "Here, put this on." Once the lamps were strapped to their heads and flicked on, Vince asked, "What is it we're looking for again?"

"A stain remover," Nick whispered, as if somehow breaking into an empty house required hushed tones.

"What does it look like?" Vince said, in a defiantly full voice.

"I don't know," Nick whispered back. "Nothing at the garage sale looked like a stain remover."

"Then how are we supposed to find it?"

"I'll know it when I see it," said Nick, his volume finally matching Vince's. "In the meantime, look for something old and . . . Tesla-like." Which was actually a helpful suggestion. "Let's fan out and check the whole house."

"Technically, I don't think two people can 'fan,'" Vince pointed out.

"Fine. You take the ground floor and I'll go upstairs."

And although Vince didn't like being told what to do, he agreed, since that would have been his plan anyway. Nick left, and Vince watched his light bob up the stairs. Vince's first stop was the laundry room just off the kitchen—which apparently was the cat's panic room, because it stood on the dryer, back arched and fur on end like a Halloween decoration.

"Boo!" said Vince again, and it fled so quickly it appeared to have vaporized.

There was nothing Tesla-like in the laundry room. Just some liquid detergent, bleach, and a few other cleaning supplies.

In the living room he found a retro Lava lamp, but he wasn't sure whether or not it was old enough to have belonged to Tesla.

Then he saw a tabloid newspaper lying open on the coffee table—the *Planetary Times*, one of those papers in which invading aliens and/or long-dead celebrities figured in every headline and photo. But the photo that caught Vince's eye was something very different.

"Nick!" he called. "Come look at this!"

But Nick, upstairs, must have been too far away to hear.

Just then a bright light began to arc across the room. Headlights! A car was pulling into the driveway.

Vince turned sharply and hurried to get Nick, but he didn't notice the coatrack. The middle hook snagged the wires extending from his backpack, they were yanked off his neck, and, once more, he became a demonstration of Newton's famous theory.

This time, Vince didn't even remember to close his eyes before he died.


Nick didn't see the headlights or hear the car doors open. The only warning he had were their voices as they stepped out of the car.

"I'm gonna hurl!" Seth said.

"I told you not to eat all that pizza," said his mother as they walked to the front door.

"I'm gonna hurl!" Seth said again.

"I'll get you some Pepto-Bismol," said his mother.

Nick bounded down the stairs. "Vince!" he whispered. "Vince—we gotta go now!"

But Vince wasn't going anywhere. He was, in fact, cadaverously positioned in the absolute worst place at the absolute worst time. He was lying like a doormat just inside the front door.

Which was now opening.


Dead bodies have been found in the strangest of places. Take the case of the Canadian tourist who, after hotel patrons complained of low water pressure, was found floating in a rooftop water tank. Or the poor soul who left this life, but whose body showed up on Google Maps for the world to see. Then there was the case of a TV series about crime-scene investigation—while shooting an episode about finding someone's mummified remains in an apartment building, the crew found someone's actual mummified remains in the apartment building where they were filming.

Beverly Webb and her son, Seth, however, were not considering the prospect of finding a dead body in their foyer when they arrived home that night. Seth was beset by the kind of nausea that can only come from eating thirteen pieces of Everything pizza, and Beverly was focused on getting him to the bathroom before he left a mess that she would have to clean.

She pushed the front door . . . only to find that it wouldn't open. Something was in the way.

"I'm gonna hurl!" Seth wailed.

Beverly pushed the door again, with all her might. It wouldn't budge. Did she really need this? What could possibly be worse than having a kid ready to puke and not being able to get in the front door?

Well, perhaps opening the front door and watching your kid puke all over the dead body in your foyer—but luckily for everyone, she didn't know about that particular dead body.

"It's happening!" yelled Seth. "It's happening now." He turned to the side, but when he saw that he was about to empty the better part of his digestive tract into the garden his mother had recently planted, he ran back to the car, opened a door, and barfed ten or eleven pieces of partially digested pizza all over the backseat, because he figured that leather was easier to clean than flower petals.

Beverly observed him with the sort of numb wonder that one might have while watching a truly bad dance performance. In the realm of all things possible, why would the universe conspire to deliver this?

She went to her son as a mother must, and patted him gently on the back. She tried not to think about the prospect of having her automotive interior cleaned and detailed, and then she remembered that she did, after all, have a stain remover that worked wonders.

"Better now?" she asked.

"No," Seth told her, but instead of an encore performance, he ran off toward the house and—wonder of wonders—this time the door opened like it had never been blocked.

Seth was not quite finished, but this time he felt he could make it to the bathroom, which was the preferred location for the tossing of tacos. Even when those tacos were pizza. But what he encountered when he got inside the house was not at all what he expected. He saw one teen dragging another out the back door.

They made eye contact.

"Whoa! Who are you?" Seth said, his spasming stomach temporarily forgotten.

The teen hesitated like a raccoon at a trash can, but then he got on with his business. He was gone in an instant, but his face lingered in Seth's mind. And before he could call out, his stomach rumbled a demand that could not be ignored.

He turned and released the last of his pizza on the kitchen floor, where the family cat had chosen precisely the wrong moment to stand its ground.

Nick had never been happier to see someone be violently ill. Seth had given him the few additional seconds he needed. Nick had dragged Vince to the side yard, but in the dark, even with the faint shimmering of the aurora up above, he couldn't find where the wires attached, and he didn't dare turn on the headlamp he was still wearing. But he did know that water conducted electricity, so rather than mess with the tape on Vince's back, he shoved the two wires right into Vince's mouth and pushed his jaw closed.

Vince's eyes, which were already open, instantly ignited with sentience.

"Don't talk, don't open your mouth," Nick said. "Just bite down on those wires until we're out of here.

Vince growled at him, but he did as he was told.

Nick could see Beverly inside, tending to her son, and from the sounds that were coming from the open kitchen window, it was clear that the kid was not yet in a state where he could tell her what he'd seen. Nick could only hope that Seth wouldn't be able to identify him.

Nick and Vince got on their bikes and pedaled away, their mission a failure on every level.

# 10 BLACK HOLES AND GRAY'S ANATOMY

The patience of scientists is a well-documented fact. Many natural phenomena move at a glacial pace, not just glaciers. For instance, in order for particle physicists to study atoms that would vaporize in a billionth of a second, they had to bide their time for over a decade as the Large Hadron Collider was built. And that was just a blink of an eye compared to the pitch drop experiment, ongoing for nearly one hundred years, to measure the flow rate of room-temperature tar. That flow rate turns out to be about nine drops per century (although the scientists monitoring the experiment somehow managed to miss the most recent drop).

The NASA scientists studying the newly orbiting copper asteroid were no exception. They were weighing the possibility of considering an examination of the factors involved in embarking on a study about sending a probe.

In the meantime, an electromagnetic charge was building up in the atmosphere without a means for it to be released. What people noticed most were the little things. Random incidents of magnetized paper clips standing on end on office desks. Cars starting for no apparent reason. Kids' braces sending out sizzling arcs of electricity. Some of these small-scale events were mere curiosities, others were nuisances, but the one thing that could be agreed upon by all is that they were becoming more and more frequent. The world's leading scientists assured the public that everything would work itself out. At least that's what they said.

Like the scientific community, Mitch Murló had great patience and a very long fuse. In fact, no one in recent memory had seen it burn down to its devastating payload. There's a reason the most destructive explosives have such long fuses. This was the day Mitch reminded everyone of that reason.

Mitch didn't know why he lost control. He had been teased about his father's prison sentence many times before. He knew firsthand that kids were cruel, especially in groups. He had always been able to take the nastiness of jerks in stride. Yes, their comments bothered him, angered him even, but they had never provoked him into a fight. Until now.

Perhaps it was his budding relationship with Petula. Maybe that gave him more confidence, or just enough anxiety to shorten his fuse. Or maybe it was the recent revelation by the Shut Up 'N Listen that his father would never be paroled. The information had left his mind in a whirlwind that was getting harder and harder to control.

"Hey, Murló," taunted Steven Gray, just before lunch, when everyone in the world is at their most irritable. "Here. I think your dad forgot these." And with that, Gray hurled a handful of pennies at Mitch. They fell on him like shrapnel.

It was old news that Mitch's dad had been convicted of robbing one cent from every bank account in the world. And although he claimed he had been framed for stealing 725 million dollars entirely in pennies, no one but his family believed his story.

The coin toss was a tired gag as far as Mitch was concerned. But this time one of the pennies lodged in his shirt pocket. His fingers were stubby, the pocket was narrow, and he just couldn't fish it out. At that moment he realized he would never fish it out. He and his family would never be free of the stolen pennies for the rest of their lives.

That's when Mitch detonated.

The fight that followed was a three-teacher battle. Meaning it took three teachers to pull Mitch off Gray. And one of those teachers wound up with a black eye.

And as they fought, in his anger, Mitch found himself turning back into a human Shut Up 'N Listen. The problem was, Steven Gray wouldn't shut up.

"Murló, when I'm done with you—" started Gray.

And Mitch finished, "—you're going to go home and play with your stuffed animals!"

Gray's eyes went wide. "Shut up! You don't know—"

"—the fifth answer on today's science test."

"That's it! I'm gonna—"

"—drop out of high school and become a rodeo clown."

Beyond that, Mitch didn't remember any other specifics, except for the satisfying feeling of his fists connecting with various parts of Gray's anatomy. And although Gray got in some of his own shots, too, he was far bloodier than Mitch when all was said and done.

Needless to say, Mitch wound up in Principal Watt's office, while Gray was sent to the school nurse. Mitch had calmed down by the time he got there, but not enough to regret what he had done.

Already waiting for an audience with the principal was Theo Blankenship, not the last person Mitch wanted to see, but definitely among the bottom ten. By now Mitch had two tissues shoved up his nostrils, which made Theo laugh.

Mitch took a deep mouth breath and held it to keep himself from losing his temper again.

Meanwhile, Mrs. Gray came to collect her boy from the

nurse's office and take him home—where he would most certainly play with his stuffed animals and wonder how Mitch had guessed his secret dream of being a rodeo clown.

After Gray and his mother left, Theo said to Mitch, "Must have been some fight. Sorry I missed it."

From Principal Watt's office they could hear the muffled sounds of a girl crying.

"Sydney Van Hook," Theo explained. "She wrote an inappropriate essay."

"So why are you here?" mumbled Mitch.

Theo looked down. "You know how Galileo School is like our biggest rival?"

"Yeah."

"Well . . . I barbecued their mascot."

"What's their mascot?" Mitch asked.

Theo shook his head. "You don't want to know."

While Mitch considered that, Theo leaned a little closer. "So, you're really good friends with Nick Slate, huh?"

Mitch had known this was coming the second he saw Theo in the waiting room. "Hey, what goes on between Nick and Caitlin is none of my business, okay? So don't ask me."

"So there *is* something going on between them."

"I didn't say that."

Theo glared at Mitch, and poked him in the chest to emphasize every word. "You tell your friend he'd better watch out . . . because jealousy is a green-eyed mobster—and if he's not careful, he'll be sleeping with the fishes."

"Uh . . . you mean you're gonna put a fish in his bed?"

"Exactly. And it'll only get worse from there."

The door to Principal Watt's office opened, and Sydney Van Hook ran out in a veil of tears. Watt beckoned Theo in with an intensity befitting the Grim Reaper.

Theo stood up, but before he went in, he turned to Mitch and said, "Whatever Nick's doing, he won't get away with it. Like they say, he's going to find himself between Iraq and a hard place." And with that, he turned and walked into Principal Watt's Office of Doom. The door closed behind him, and in a few moments Mitch could hear Theo crying.

Mitch found himself alone once more with only his thoughts and the penny in his pocket. Angrily, he tried again to fish it out, but it seemed to be stuck to some old chewing gum that had melded with the fabric.

He wished there was some way he could get back at the corporate creeps who had framed his father, but such justice was even further out of his reach than the penny.

Then, out of nowhere, a voice said, "Mind if I try?"

Mitch looked up to see Ms. Planck, the lunch lady. Without waiting for an answer, she reached into his pocket with long, tapering fingers, strong from ladling slop day in and day out. She grasped the penny and pulled it free in one try, then held it out to him.

"Penny for your thoughts?"

"Keep it," said Mitch bitterly. "I don't want it. I don't want *any* of them."

Ms. Planck sat down next to him. "I don't blame you," she said. "If it means anything to you, I don't think your father took that money."

Mitch looked at her, trying to figure out if she just wanted to make him feel better or if she meant it. She was a no-nonsense kind of woman. Mitch could tell she was sincere.

"What are you doing here?" Mitch asked. "Did you get called to the principal's office, too?"

She held up a clipboard. "Next month's lunch menu for Principal Watt to approve. He's got his fingers in every pie."

Mitch grinned. "I knew there were fingers in those pies."

Ms. Planck raised her eyebrows. "Protein! Tastes good and good *for* you."

From behind the closed door came Theo's wailing pleas for clemency. Mitch resolved that whatever punishment was levied upon him when it was his turn, he would bear it stoically.

"So I understand you're spending a lot of time with Petula Grabowski-Jones," Ms. Planck said.

"Petula has a big mouth," grumbled Mitch.

Ms. Planck shrugged. "There are worse things. She's unusual, it's true. But in a good way. And I told her the same thing about you."

"Where is this going?" Mitch wondered aloud.

She put the penny in his hand and closed his fingers around it. "Someplace worth the price of admission," she said. "I promise." Then she got up and left.

When Mitch opened his hand, he discovered something remarkable. Through sleight of hand or some other clever trick, the coin in his palm was now a nickel.

Meanwhile, Caitlin was having her own troubles. She had always been a fairly decent math student, but during today's test, she found herself stricken with such inexplicable dread that she couldn't catch her breath. She was not prone to panic attacks, and she was becoming more anxious over the fact that she was becoming anxious than by the cause of the anxiety itself. Then, when she looked around, she realized that she wasn't the only one suffering. Everyone in the room—including the teacher—was either sweating, or shaking, or moaning. One kid was chewing his pencil with such nervous intensity that he bit it in half.

In the midst of the turmoil there was, however, a calm oasis of one: Carter Black, who always sat in the back of the room and had gone unnoticed for most of his life. He was now a hot zone of focused energy and calculation. He was zipping through the test like it was nothing.

This was one of those "open book" kind of tests where calculators and other computational devices were allowed. Carter did not have a calculator. His stress-free hands were deftly flipping the beads of a small abacus—the kind of counting device used in days gone by.

Carter Black was not a math whiz by any means. In fact, he had earned the nickname "Carter Black Hole," because his brain seemed to have an event horizon beyond which mathematical concepts broke down, leading to D-minuses on all of his tests. Any other kid would have to work pretty hard to achieve such consistency.

As Caitlin's own math terror increased, Carter's focus intensified, and although at the moment even adding one plus one was a difficult stretch, she managed it, and came up with the only possible solution.

The abacus was from Nick's garage sale.

Each time Carter flicked a metallic bead, the wire that held it sparked, giving him brainpower and confidence—by stealing it from his classmates.

And so, while the rest of the room became more and more mathematically unsound, Caitlin got up out of her seat, made her way over to Carter Black, and ripped the abacus from his hands.

"Hey, that's mine!"

She slipped it into a rather heavy case that was, no doubt, woven from lead-infused fabric, and the moment she did, she felt her tension dissolve.

"Possession is nine-tenths of the law," she told Carter. Now that his math skills had sunk back to caveman levels, he was left to grapple with the concept of nine-tenths while the rest of the room breathed a communal sigh of relief, not knowing what had happened, or why it had ended.

"Pencils down," said their teacher, blotting his sweaty forehead with his sleeve. "We'll take this test tomorrow."

Caitlin gripped the abacus to her chest as if at any moment it might be ripped away by Carter Black, or the Accelerati. She had an urge to run out of the classroom, find Nick, and hand it over to him, but she knew she could make a better play. Nick hadn't given her as much as the time of day since she refused his movie invitation, and the rift between them wasn't helping anybody. But now she had an excuse to bridge the gap. The abacus could be her peace offering. Peace offerings had to be treated with care and ceremony. She would bring it to him at his house when she felt the time was right. She would watch as he placed it into the machine. And that would make them a team again, if not a couple.

As for Carter Black, he scowled at Caitlin, staring invisible daggers into the back of her head, but he didn't try to get the abacus back. Truth be told, he was relieved that his fifteen minutes of genius were over. Unnatural brilliance was uncharted territory for him. It was like rafting down a raging river, never knowing if the twists and turns would lead him to a deadly waterfall. Now he could happily go back to being the lightless singularity he had always been . . . but with the heady memory of momentary illumination.

He had read somewhere that Einstein had failed math in school. In fact, some people had considered him an idiot. Carter Black could relate—and for the first time, he dreamed of aspiring to that kind of idiocy. Thanks to the abacus, he was now motivated to do something completely foreign to him: he was motivated to try.

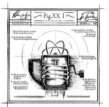

**C**halking up one more failure was the last thing Nick needed, but the chest being sold online was not an antique card catalog, as the picture had suggested. It was just an ordinary dresser. Nick and Mitch went to see it, dismissed it, and the closer they got to the door, the lower the price became, until the woman was ready to give it to them for free if they would just haul the thing away.

Nick turned back to the woman and waved his hand like Obi-Wan Kenobi. "These are not the drawers we're looking for," he said, and left.

"It's supposed to be 'you're,' not 'we're,'" Mitch pointed out as they walked away.

"Either way," Nick said with a sigh, "we're back at square one, and we don't know where to look."

In the wake of their disappointment, Mitch suggested they go for comfort food at Beef-O-Rama. Not an unusual suggestion coming from Mitch.

But as they arrived, Nick saw Petula through the front window, sitting in a booth, waiting.

"Suddenly I'm not hungry." He threw Mitch an accusatory glance and started to walk away.

Mitch stopped him. "I know you hate her," he said, "but she *has* been helping us keep Vince alive, since she's in math with him—and she feels really bad about how she didn't tell you he was gonna die in the first place. . . ."

"She didn't know *he* was going to die," Nick pointed out. "She just knew that *someone* would. How do you expect me to forgive her for not telling me someone was about to die in my house? It could have been you!"

"And it could have been *her*!" Mitch reminded him. "She put herself in danger by coming to your house—but she came anyway, because she wanted to save you. At least give her credit for that!"

Nick was still not ready to give Petula credit for anything. But maybe his anger was as misdirected as Petula had been misguided that day. She wasn't the enemy. That honor was saved for Jorgenson and the Accelerati.

"Anyway," said Mitch, "she has something to give you. . . ."

Mitch slid into the booth next to Petula. Nick took the bench across from them and watched Petula put her hands gently on Mitch's face, which was still bruised from his knock-down-drag-out fight.

"Aw, my poor pumpkin," Petula said.

"Did you really just call me 'pumpkin'?" Mitch asked.

Petula nodded cheerfully. "Because after that fight, your head looks like a crushed one."

"So?" Nick said to Petula, not caring to endure more sweet nothings between them. "You have something for me?"

Petula looked miffed. "No 'hello'? No 'how are you'? or 'good to see you'?" She tilted her head back so she could look down her nose at him. "Manners count, you know. Even in the Beef-O-Rama."

The waitress, who, like Nick, wanted to be anywhere else, took their orders absently, and ripped the menus out of their hands.

"Well," Nick said to Petula, "since it *isn't* good to see you and I *don't* really care how you are, let me just say hello."

Nick meant his comment to be as stinging as it sounded, but Petula seemed genuinely pleased by it. "That's an acceptable start. Hello to you, too. And although you can't be bothered with my personal well-being, *I* am gracious enough to care about yours. So how are you?"

"Not great," Nick said honestly. "I'm pretty disappointed by the way things are going in general, actually."

"Well, maybe this will cheer you up." With that, she lifted her backpack off the bench next to her, revealing the box camera. She handed it over the table to him.

Nick didn't know what to say. He looked over at Mitch, who was grinning.

"You convinced her?" Nick asked him.

"I only suggested it," he replied. "She's the one who decided."

"Hold on," Nick said, looking at the camera more closely, studying the bare aperture at the front. "Where's the lens?"

"I'm hanging on to that," she said. "For insurance."

"Insurance against what?" asked Nick.

Petula shook her head and sighed. "If we knew the nature of the unexpected disaster we needed insurance against, we wouldn't need insurance, would we?"

"Come on, Nick," Mitch said. "Take it. It's a step in the right direction, right?"

Nick took the camera. "Okay, fine." And although it wasn't easy, he added, "Thank you."

"You're welcome," Petula said.

The waitress brought out their malts and a basket of chili-cheese onion rings, perhaps the messiest food in the known universe—which was made worse by Mitch, who tended to talk with his hands while holding his rings, thereby flinging chili in all directions.

Mitch talked about the fight, and his visit to Principal Watt's office. Chewing thoughtfully, he said, "I got a three-day in-school suspension." Then he pondered the other half of the onion ring in his hand, as if it held the answer to one of life's unanswerable questions.

"How is it a suspension if you're in school?" Nick asked.

"Don't you know anything?" said Petula. "In-school suspension means they put you in a room with a teacher all day, but you're not allowed to learn."

Mitch shrugged. "Could be worse. I had a talk with Ms. Planck and she kind of made me feel better about the whole thing."

Nick was surprised. "The lunch lady?"

"Yeah. Sometimes I think she oughta be running the school. I mean, she *knows* things."

Nick had to agree. Like the way she had told him to dump his lunch on Heisenberg during his first day. That single act had made Nick a school legend. Ms. Planck always seemed to have the right words of wisdom when kids needed them most. She *did* know things.

*What if that's not limited only to school?* Nick wondered. *What if she has feelers throughout town?* It wasn't too farfetched to think that Ms. Planck had inside information that no one else had.

The thought stayed with him as the waitress brought the check and Nick paid his share. Mitch put enough money on the table, Nick noticed, to cover his own and Petula's tab.

"Do you think Ms. Planck might have a clue about where some of the garage-sale stuff ended up?" Nick asked as they left.

Mitch shrugged. "It couldn't hurt to ask."

"I think that's a great idea!" said Petula, and she grinned at Nick. "And imagine, it came from *you*!"

Outside the restaurant, Mitch stopped short in front of the local-interests bulletin board, which was covered with business cards, postcards, and flyers for upcoming events. "Hey, look!" he said, jabbing his finger at one of the flyers. A large photograph graced the piece of paper. "The harp!"

"What harp?" Petula said pleasantly.

Nick grimaced. Petula was like sand at the beach—she had a way of getting into everything, making the world feel uncomfortable. He took a closer look at the flyer.

According to the headline, a local harpist was putting on a benefit concert for charity. Mitch pointed at the photo of a woman sitting behind a harp.

"That's the harp from your garage sale, isn't it?" Mitch asked. "I remember seeing it there."

Just then, another diner came out of the restaurant, still wiping the grease from his lips with a napkin. He noticed them studying the flyer.

"You kids like music?" the man asked.

"Maybe we do and maybe we don't," Petula said.

The man tapped the photo of the harpist with his finger. "Well, don't waste your time. This isn't music. I don't know what it is. I saw her 'play' at a coffeehouse last week. Her harp had no strings, and yet . . ." His thoughts seemed to go far away for a moment, then he shook it off. "Anyway, whatever it was, it sure made the neighborhood dogs howl. And in key!"

As soon as he left, Petula said, "Sounds like a Teslanoid Object to me."

Nick looked at the flyer and nodded. It was the same stringless harp he had sold. The performance was two days away. "We can't take a chance that the Accelerati will get to it first. We need to find her before Saturday night."

"I'll find her," said Mitch.

"And I'll go around pulling down the flyers," offered Petula, "so the Acceleroonies don't see them."

"Accelerati," corrected Nick. He was about to tell Petula that they didn't need her help, but the fact was, they did. "Look, if we're going to let you in on this," he told her, "I have to know we can trust you."

She looked shocked by the suggestion. "Of course you can trust me," she said. "I wouldn't want to do anything to add to your bitter disappointment."

When Nick got home that afternoon, Danny was playing video games in the living room, intentionally oblivious to the real world around him.

"Lucky you didn't come with us for pizza yesterday," he said, without looking away from his game. "It made half the team sick."

"Yeah, I heard."

Through the window, Nick could see their father out back, planting a tree. Mom was the one who'd had the green thumb in the family. Perhaps this was one of his dad's ways of remembering her. Or maybe it was just another one of his ways to keep busy.

Nick went out the back door. "What kind of tree is it?" he asked.

"Blood orange, so I'm told," his dad answered. "But it won't give fruit for a couple of years."

He took a break, wiping sweat from his forehead with his T-shirt sleeve, then looked at Nick with the kind of uncomfortably intrusive gaze that only a parent can deliver.

"You doing okay?" he asked.

Nick shrugged. Actually, there were quite a few reasons why he wouldn't be, only some of which his father knew. "Yeah, fine. Why?"

"It's just that . . . you never talk about your friend," he said. "The one who . . . passed away . . . in our living room. I know the whole asteroid business made it seem less important somehow . . . but it happened."

Nick stiffened. Since that day he had never discussed Vince with his father. "Yeah, I try not to think about it," Nick told him. And then, in a sudden burst of crazy-mad inspiration, he said, "His identical twin brother is really having a hard time with it, though."

His father grimaced. "I can't imagine." Then, satisfied that had done his parental duty as bereavement counselor, he returned to the matter at hand. He pointed to the hole he was digging. "What do you suppose that is?"

Nick looked down and saw the shiny edge of something metallic and smooth. The hole, he realized, was more like a shallow trench—as though his father had started out making room for the tree, but had grown more interested in exposing the metallic rail. He had uncovered at least five feet of it— enough to reveal that it had a slight curve.

"When I hit it with the shovel, I got kind of carried away," his father said.

Nick instinctively knew whatever this was, it was Tesla-related. As such, it should not be his father's problem. "Maybe just cover it back up," Nick offered, "and put the tree somewhere else."

"Maybe so," his father said, "except . . . when you cover up strange things, they never go away completely, do they?"

*No,* Nick had to admit to himself, *they certainly don't.*

His dad sat on a stump, took off his cap, and scratched his head. "Funny thing," he said. "After that day, I couldn't stop thinking about how the bat cracked even though it never hit the ball, and how all those windows broke, and how the asteroid never did what all those genius scientists said it would do. And I can't help wondering . . . what if it was *me*? What if *I* knocked it into orbit? That's crazy, right?"

Nick could feel tears welling up in his eyes. He tried to fight them but couldn't. And when his voice finally came out, it was a whisper. "What if it's not crazy?"

His father looked right at him. "It has to be, Nick. Don't you see? Because if it's not crazy, the alternative is terrifying."

Without warning, Nick launched himself into his father's arms, and they held each other as tightly as they could. And for a while, that embrace seemed to protect them from all the terror the world could hurl their way.

Nick didn't let go until he felt his tears subside. He couldn't help but notice his father was wiping his own away, too.

"Whatever that is in the ground," Nick said, "let's just bury it and plant the tree somewhere else. It might not go away, but it doesn't have to be our problem right now."

Although Nick knew he'd have to deal with it later, whatever it was, he found another shovel and together he and his father hid the thing beneath the dirt. They planted the tree close to the house, where someday, Nick could imagine, it would spread its leaves, filling the kitchen window with a soothing green view, and give them the sweetest oranges they had ever tasted.

## 12 GOOD-BYE KITTY

**V**ince's knack for ferreting out lost Teslanoid objects had nothing to do with the fact that his unwanted childhood nickname was "The Ferret." The name originated solely from the unfortunate combination of how skinny he was, and the fact that his front baby teeth had made him look somewhat rodent-like for a time. It was the beginning of his life as an outsider.

Even as an outsider, though, he had his own antisocial circle. It was from these shadowy friends that he got leads on the lost objects—because fringe folk loved nothing more than yakking about weird stuff, and weirder people.

He was hanging out at the skate park, watching wistfully as kids did tricks he could no longer attempt without the risk of losing battery power, when a fresh lead came his way.

"Dude," said a skateboarder buddy with more scabs than flesh on his legs, "there's this lady on my street with, like, cats coming out of her ears."

"Literally, or figuratively?" Vince asked—because, considering the devices he was tracking, cats coming out of someone's ears was not entirely out of the question.

His bud just looked at him, blinking, not quite getting the question. "Dude!" he said. "She's got, like, a million of them in her house!"

Vince sighed. "Literally, or figuratively?" he asked again. "Do you actually mean a million, or just lots and lots?"

"Lots and lots," the kid said. "But here's the weird thing: they disappeared all of a sudden and now we've got, like, all these mice in the neighborhood." Then he leaned in and whispered, "She's still bringing cats to the house, though. The kitties go in, but they don't come out."

In spite of Vince's burglarizing misadventure, this definitely warranted investigation—even though curiosity might kill him instead of the cats.

The house in question was on a street that had seen better days. Even the trees were leaning away from the homes as if they wished to have nothing to do with them. As he approached the residence, he heard the cats. Faint. Distant. But it was more than that. The sound of their meows seemed fundamentally changed, although he couldn't quite say how.

Vince had discovered that when it came to Tesla's objects and their owners, front-door entries were to be avoided. Instead he went around the side and found a convenient doggy door, which was obviously not for dogs. It had been duct-taped from the outside, as if someone wanted to make sure that the critters within could no longer get out. He peeled away the duct tape, and being ferret-slim, was able to shimmy partway through.

The first thing he noticed was the mice.

They were all around him! He couldn't go backward through the tiny door, so he had no choice but to squeeze all the way inside. The mice scattered, hissing. He stood up and found himself face-to-face with a woman in the kitchen.

Big, fluffy pink slippers. Straggly hair, and a faraway look in her eyes. She was the very definition of "Crazy Cat Lady." She wielded a Swiffer floor mop as a weapon.

"Who are you? Get out of my house! Get out!"

She swung it at him, cutting a wide arc, which he was easily able to avoid.

The woman had mice clinging to her woolen sweater. But the noise these mice were making was wrong. They were mewling, like . . . like . . .

All at once Vince knew he was in the right place.

"Wow," he said, "I love your miniature cats!"

She hesitated before swinging the mop again, suspicious. "You do?"

"Of course I do! Who wouldn't? My friends told me you had miniature cats, and I just wanted to see for myself. May I?"

The woman still looked at him suspiciously, then pulled one from her blouse. It was a palm-size tabby, and very cute, if you liked that sort of thing. She held it out to him and Vince reached for it, but the tiny cat hissed at him.

"Maybe I'll just look."

"The health inspector said I can't have so many cats. But if they're small . . ."

As Vince took in the surroundings of the untidy kitchen, he could see that his friend's exaggeration wasn't all that far off. There were hundreds upon hundreds of miniature cats.

"How do you do it?" Vince asked, and the woman, thrilled to have someone more interested than appalled, was happy to talk.

"Shelters," she said. "I get 'em from shelters. You'd be surprised how many cats nobody wants. I save 'em from gettin' put to sleep and I bring 'em here. Of course, until a few weeks ago I couldn't bring 'em all—but now there ain't no limit!"

"But . . . how do you do it?" Vince asked again.

The woman gave him a smile that was missing some key teeth. "I'll show you, but you can't tell no one!"

Clearly she'd been itching to tell someone about it.

Vince followed the woman into her laundry room, where

there was plenty of dirty laundry, but none of it looked like it had any intention of getting into a washing machine. A full-size cat was sitting on the pile. The cat lady grabbed it and, holding it tight, put it in the sink and turned on the faucet.

"No, don't!" Vince said reflexively.

"Don't worry," the woman said. "I ain't gonna hurt it. I just gotta get it wet. It won't work unless it's wet."

As cats don't like water, it did its best to squirm away, but she held it tight until its fur was soggy. Then she opened the door of an exceptionally old dryer with her free hand. "In ya go!" she said cheerfully.

"No!" said Vince again.

"You're a nervous type, ain't ya?" she said.

She shut the dryer and turned it on. It rumbled and grumbled, but as Vince looked in the glass door, he could see that the drum wasn't turning. Something else was going on inside, though, because the cat was glowing.

"This is one a' them 'do not try this at home' kind of things," the crazy lady said. She shut the machine off after ten seconds, and when she opened the door, the cat was entirely dry. And the size of a hamster.

"I got the thing at a garage sale," she told him, which he already knew. "First time I used it to dry my clothes, everything shrunk to doll size. In one of the pockets I found a dollar bill the size of a cookie fortune. When I realized it wasn't just the clothes that had shrunk, I got to thinking. . . ."

The tiny cat jumped up onto her sweater and climbed to her shoulder to nestle with a host of others. "It's a dream come true," she said. "Finally, after all these years, I have enough cats."

And that line, Vince realized, was his in. He had discovered that for each of the items he had recovered, the object in question had fulfilled a need, or had slapped the person around enough to impart a valuable lesson. She might always be a crazy cat lady, but at least now she no longer had the insatiable desire to acquire more cats.

"I could use this," Vince said, "to save the puppies. . . ."

The woman was so moved, she gave it to him for free.

# 13 WALKING THE PLANCK

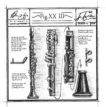

**N**ick went to school extra early the next day. He told himself it wasn't for any particular reason, but if he had used the feeling recorder it would have said, in his own voice, that his reason was very particular indeed.

There was no one he could consult about his predicament. Sure, he could talk to his friends, but they didn't have any more information than he did. Talking to his father last night had made it clear that Nick couldn't share the truth with him. He needed an outside party. Someone kindly and wise, and above all, trustworthy.

So Nick went to school early to talk to Ms. Planck, because Mitch was right—she did know things. But more than that, her advice was always like comfort food.

He found her in the cafeteria, lining up cinnamon buns and croissants on the counter. There were no other cafeteria workers present, as none would ever arrive at such an ungodly hour.

"You're an early bird today, Nick," she said when she saw him. "Got a worm to catch?"

"Couldn't sleep," he told her. "Thought I'd get a jump on the day." He dug his hands into the carton of cellophane-wrapped pastries and helped line them up.

Once the pastries were out, Ms. Planck turned to the hot items. She put sausages on an industrial-size grill, poured prescrambled egg mix into a frying pan the size of a hubcap, and started cutting up fruit. As he watched her, Nick marveled. She seemed like more than a cafeteria worker. The way she juggled all the workstations, she was more like an artist. No—a scientist! Because there truly was a science to what she did.

Outside, the morning began to brighten. The last traces of the aurora faded from the sky. There was still at least half an hour before anyone else would show up, so Nick had plenty of time to talk. He didn't know how to broach the subject . . . but just standing there watching her work and saying nothing was getting awkward, so he went for it.

"What would you say if I told you a secret society was after me, and my life might be in danger?"

She laughed. "I would say you've been watching too much TV." Then she stopped for a moment, considered, and said, "Does this have anything to do with that garage sale of yours?"

Nick snapped his eyes to hers. "How did you know about that?"

"You told me, remember? A few days before that awful business with the asteroid."

"Oh, right." He cleared his throat. "Well, the thing is, all that stuff from the garage sale . . . it was a little more important than I let on."

Ms. Planck heaved a watermelon onto the counter. "How so?"

"It belonged to someone."

Out of nowhere she produced a big, shiny cleaver. "Belonged to whom?"

"Nikola Tesla."

In one skilled move, Ms. Planck slammed the cleaver down, splitting the melon in two. "Tesla? That maniac?"

"He was a genius."

Ms. Planck hacked at the watermelon halves, quartering

them. "His experiments melted the town's generator. Colorado Springs was dark for days."

"Accidents happen," Nick said—but the thought didn't sit well with him. The man who had designed the machine in his attic was precise. He did not leave things to chance. He was not accident-prone.

Or *was* he?

"Anyway," Nick said, "I need to get back some of the objects I sold, and my friends seem to think you could help. And I guess I do, too. I mean, you know a lot about what goes on in town."

Ms. Planck continued to cut the melon until it was in serving-size pieces. "That's true. And I belong to an antiquing meet-up group. Its members are always going to garage sales. I'll bet some of your missing items might be with them." She looked at him. "You mentioned a secret society . . . Do you think someone else is after those objects?" she asked. "Do you think they might have followed you here?"

Nick glanced over his shoulder reflexively, and then felt silly about it. "No one followed me," he said. "No one knows I'm here."

"Good," she said. "Better safe than sorry." Then she took a step toward Nick, melon juice dripping from the blade of her cleaver. "Why don't you make me a list of all the items you're missing," she said with a warm smile, "and I'll see if I can help you track them down."

That sounded like a good idea, so Nick reached into his backpack for pen and paper.

In moments of extreme stress, the mind can do very strange things. Such was the case when Nick began his list for Ms. Planck.

He pulled a piece of paper out of his notebook and set it on the counter. As he fished through his backpack for a pen, the edge of the paper, which was too close to the flame under the skillet of eggs, caught fire. Nick pulled it away, but he only succeeded in moving the burning paper onto the grill, where sausages were sizzling in their own grease. The grease ignited, and flames leaped toward the stainless-steel vent hood.

And suddenly Nick was somewhere else.

In an instant he was back in Tampa. Almost four months ago. The fire! His mother! It was happening all over again. He knew he was still in the cafeteria kitchen with Ms. Planck, but that didn't erase the feeling of absolute dread inside him. The flames were all around them now, on every wall, every surface.

He grabbed Ms. Planck with adrenaline-pumped strength. "We have to get out of here!" He pulled her so hard that the cleaver fell from her hand and embedded itself in the linoleum floor. "Hurry! While there's still time!"

But Ms. Planck pulled herself free and walked back into the flames.

"No!" Nick shouted. What was she doing? He could save her! He *had* to save her! It couldn't happen again!

She went down on her knees, apparently overcome by the smoke, and Nick found himself frozen, unable to do anything but watch . . .

. . . as she pulled a small fire extinguisher from a low cabinet, aimed it at the grill, and put out the grease fire with a single blast from the nozzle.

"Well," she said, "so much for the sausages."

All at once Nick realized that the flames that had seemed so huge, so all-consuming, were in his mind; they were really confined to just a corner of the grill. The smoke was already gone—there hadn't even been enough to set off an alarm. Still, his heightened sense of terror remained.

"Now then," said Ms. Planck, "how about that list?"

Nick found he could barely breathe. He craved fresh air. He needed to clear his thoughts, because, although the fire might be out in the kitchen, it still raged in his brain.

"I gotta go." He turned and ran, almost tripping on the cleaver on his way out.

Nick ate lunch from the hallway vending machine that day. He did not want to return to the cafeteria and be reminded of the feeling he'd had that morning. Not so much the panic as the vulnerability.

He had kept his head in much worse situations. Even when Vince dropped dead in Beverly Webb's foyer, Nick had managed to stay relatively calm and knew what he had to do. But this morning had revealed a massive chink in his emotional armor—and if he was prone to irrational fear, there was a chance he could freak at the absolute wrong moment. All could be lost.

He tried not to dwell on it. School was, for once, a welcome distraction. He kept his mind on his schoolwork and his teachers' lessons. In history class, he inadvertently glanced over at Caitlin, who offered him a slim, possibly apologetic grin. It was the same grin she'd been offering him for days.

He wasn't sure what it meant. He doubted she even knew. It was awkward, and Nick didn't have the time or patience for awkward anymore. That would change when . . . well, it would change when it would change. He couldn't spend his time worrying about that now. Not when he had so much more on his mind.

Thoughts of his mom, and the fire, and the life he had lost before he moved to Colorado peeked around every unguarded corner of his brain. They threatened to overwhelm him, but by last period he had managed to smother the fire and regain, if not peace, then at least stability.

The effort had exhausted him, but his day was still not over. After school he went to Mitch's house, because they had to track down a phone number for the harpist.

Mitch's little sister opened the door, and when she saw him, she said, "You're the one who gave my brother the toy that said funny things. It's broken now."

"I know," said Nick. "Can I come in?"

She seriously considered the request, then chose to allow him entry.

This was the first time Nick had been in Mitch's house. It looked normal on the surface, but the walls seemed to breathe the absence of Mitch's father. Or maybe that was just Nick's imagination.

Mitch's room was a pigsty—and Nick sensed it was a pretty accurate reflection of Mitch's mental space as well. He hadn't known Mitch before Mr. Murló went to prison, and maybe his friend was a slob before all that, but Nick sensed that this current state of disarray was a direct result of the state of his family. It was as if Mitch's life had spun into a tornado that left its debris scattered around his room.

"I got it!" Mitch said, almost camouflaged within the mess. He waved a piece of paper at Nick. "I called the coffeehouse where the harp lady is performing—I told them I was taking harp lessons and lost her number."

"And they gave it to you?"

"Yeah, I couldn't believe it, 'cause I'm, like, the worst liar in the world."

"Did you call her?"

He handed Nick the slip of paper. "I figured I'd leave that to you."

But Nick put the phone on speaker—after all, Mitch had tracked down her number; he shouldn't be shut out of the call.

"Hello, Ms. . . . Devereaux?" Nick read the name off the flyer, certain he had mispronounced it.

"Speaking," the woman said.

"Uh . . . I had a garage sale a few weeks back?" he said, his voice unintentionally questioning. "You bought a harp?"

"Ah! You'll be wanting it back, I imagine," she said immediately. She didn't seem surprised or concerned, which both surprised and concerned Nick.

"Can we come by in the morning?" Mitch blurted out. "To talk about it?"

She instantly agreed. Nine o'clock sharp. After they hung up, Nick turned to Mitch. "Did that seem weird to you?"

"Compared to what?" Mitch asked. He had a point; any yardstick they had for measuring weirdness had been pulverized into sawdust over the past few weeks. Nick could only hope that whatever awaited him tomorrow would be less bruising than his encounter with the weightless guy.

In the meantime he looked forward to getting home so he could just hurl himself onto the living room sofa and make the world go away for a while.

Unfortunately, the world had staked a claim in Nick's living room today.

When he opened the door, his father was sitting on the couch. And sitting across from him was none other than Beverly Webb.

The situation was crystal clear to Nick. Her son, having recovered from his pizza issues, had identified him, and she and his father were waiting to ambush him with an accusation of breaking and entering.

His first instinct was to shout *It wasn't me!* His second instinct was to turn and run. But instead he simply held his tongue and waited for the ax to come down.

"Nick," his father said sternly.

"Uh . . . yeah?"

"As you can see, Beverly's here. With Seth . . ."

Nick prepared himself for the worst. But then his father said: "Seth's helping Danny with his fielding."

Nick took a deep breath and released it. "Fielding," he said. "Right."

Beverly looked at him, all warmth and understanding. "Nick, I want you to know there are no hard feelings about the other day."

"Thanks," said Nick, taking another deep breath. "So . . . where's Seth now?"

"Out back, with your brother," his father said. "Beverly and Seth will be staying for dinner. And before you say anything— it was my idea. They had a break-in recently, so I thought it best if they spent the evening with friends."

"Wow," said Nick, not sure how convincing he sounded. "Did they take anything?"

Beverly shook her head. "No—we came home and that scared them away. But Seth got a good look at one of them. Big guy. Scary."

"Probably just some pathetic lowlifes," Nick's father offered. "I'm sure they won't come back."

His father had called in an order of Chinese, since pizza was currently out of the question. Nick imagined how the dinner scene might go with Seth sitting at the table with him, then erased the scene from his mind.

"You know what? I have lots of homework," he said. "I think I'll skip dinner tonight."

His father started to protest, but Beverly stopped him. "It's okay, Wayne, really." The fact that she thought Nick was just being rude allowed him to actually *be* rude, so he brushed past her without saying good-bye and went into the kitchen to get a drink. On the way, he inconspicuously grabbed off the hallway wall the one family photo saved from the fire, and he slipped it beneath his jacket—so that Seth had no chance of seeing Nick's face.

Had Seth been more observant, he might have recognized this house as the one where he had bought the stain remover—and he might have remembered that the kid who sold it to him had just broken into his home. But it seemed that Nick had lucked out, and as long as he stayed out of Seth's line of sight, he figured he was safe.

But how long would his luck hold if Seth's mother kept poking around Nick's father?

As he stood at the refrigerator pondering these things, an idea came to him that might take care of at least one of the Beverly-related problems he currently faced.

He looked through the fridge until he found the perfect beverage: pomegranate juice. He poured himself a nice tall glass, then went back to the living room with his elbow wide.

Accidents, as Nick had pointed out that morning, do happen. He bumped into Beverly, jostling the glass, and pomegranate juice the color of blood sloshed all over his white shirt.

"Nick! Be more careful!" his father scolded.

"Sorry."

"It was my fault," said Beverly.

"No, it wasn't," said Nick, and then he caught himself. "I mean, I wish, but no—it was my fault." He looked down at his shirt. "Great. It's stained. And my favorite shirt, too."

"I'll get a napkin," said Beverly.

"Too late—it's already soaked in."

"Well, if you dab it right now . . ."

"Are you kidding me?" said Nick. "Pomegranate juice never comes out."

"Too bad," said his father. "That was a good shirt."

"It'll leave a permanent *stain*," Nick said.

"What a shame," said Beverly.

"It's ruined," Nick said, "because *nothing* can possibly get a pomegranate juice *stain* out of a white shirt." Sheesh, it felt like rubbing two sticks together to start a fire. "Absolutely *nothing*."

"Wait," Beverly finally said. "I've got a stain remover—it can get a stain out of anything." And then she held her hand out to Nick. "Take off your shirt."

Nick just stared at her. "What?"

"Give me your shirt. I'll take it home with me, and bring it back clean as new."

"Uh . . ."

"That's very kind of you," his father said. "Nick, take it off."

"Well, okay . . ." And then he had another flash of inspiration. "Here, let me just put this down." He reached over to rest the half-empty glass on an end table. Right now Nick was looking at that glass as half full.

Being intentionally clumsy, he bumped his arm against the table lamp while setting down the juice. The glass flew from his hand, dumping its crimson contents on the ivory-colored sofa.

"Oh, shoot!" said Nick.

"You're batting a thousand today," his father growled.

Nick grabbed the sofa cushion and held it out to Beverly. "Better take this, too."

Beverly sighed. "You know what? I'll just bring the stain remover here."

Then the back door banged open and Nick heard his brother enter with Seth.

"Good idea," he told Beverly. Then he bounded upstairs to the attic before Seth could see him, and pulled the spring-loaded steps closed behind him.

# 14 HOLD THAT THOUGHT

**R**etrieving the harp was going to take two people. Ideally, they'd have a vehicle for the job, but that would require Nick's father, and Nick had sworn to keep him out of it.

The best thing about a neighborhood garage sale, however, was that most of the items sold stayed in the neighborhood. As it turned out, the harp was in a house only two streets away.

Nick's dad and Danny had left early for baseball practice and would be gone all morning, so Nick knew he wouldn't face the *why-are-you-dragging-a-harp-through-the-house* conversation once he and Mitch brought it home.

Mitch arrived early. He seemed a little distracted—shell shock, Nick figured, from spending Friday evening with Petula, who could drain the life out of anyone.

Mitch yawned. "You think the harp lady'll really give it back?"

"We'll find a way to convince her," Nick told him.

"You think we'll be able to carry it?"

"It's not full-size," Nick told him. "And I remember it wasn't as heavy as it looked." But, Nick thought, Jorgenson and the Accelerati were still out there, and they might be watching. He and Mitch would have to cover the harp with something before they lugged it down the street. It wouldn't prevent the Accelerati from knowing that he had retrieved another item, but at least they wouldn't be able to see what it was.

Nick scarfed a handful of dry cereal and was headed for the door when the doorbell rang.

He hesitated. The door didn't have a peephole, or any other way to determine who was on the other side without opening it. *When,* wondered Nick, *did I become afraid of opening my own front door?*

"You expecting anyone?" Mitch asked.

Nick didn't answer. Instead, he bit back his own paranoia and swung the door wide in defiance.

Standing there was a blond girl with sun-reddened cheeks. She was as muscular as she was tall. She looked down at Nick with cool yet intense gray eyes and said, "Are you ready to go? Where's your crossbow?"

Nick tried to come up with anything resembling a sensible response. When he couldn't, he said, "Hold that thought." Then he closed the door and took a nice long moment.

"You didn't tell me you had a crossbow," Mitch said. "Can I see it?"

"I don't."

"But she said—"

"Why don't you go get a blanket to take with us so we can cover the harp. I'll deal with this."

Once Mitch had left the room, Nick took a deep breath and opened the door again.

The muscular girl looked him over. "You still don't have your crossbow." And she held up her own. It was a stainless-steel thing that looked to Nick like it would need three people to carry it.

"Uh . . . do we know each other?" Nick asked.

"Oh, right," said the girl. "Sorry. I feel like I know you, since we chatted so much online." She held out her hand. "Hi, Nick, I'm Val. It's great to finally meet you in person. Now let's kill some rabbits."

Nick was not quite up to speed, but his mental engine was primed enough to idle into the conversation. "Oh, was that today?"

"You invited me last night," Val said. "Bright and early Saturday morning, that's what you said." Then her expression got a little dark. "You didn't forget, did you?"

One thing Nick knew for sure: you don't tick off a girl who could arm-wrestle you into oblivion. Especially if she has a crossbow.

"No, I didn't forget . . . it's just that—wouldn't you know it—my crossbow's in the shop."

"No worries," Val said, reaching into an oversize gym bag. "I've got a spare." And she presented him with a crossbow that was, mercifully, slightly smaller and lighter than hers.

Clearly someone had pranked Nick by pretending to be him online and setting this whole thing up. Could it have been Caitlin? No, she'd never be that devious. But on the other hand, she had been devious enough to trick that poor jeweler, Mr. Svedberg, into telling them about the Accelerati. Before Jorgenson killed him for it, that is.

Mitch came up behind him, smiling shyly. "You can go, Nick. I got this one covered."

"But—"

"C'mon," Val prompted. "You can ride on the back of my dirt bike."

"You've got a dirt bike?" Nick couldn't believe he was allowing himself to be distracted.

"I know this great wildlife preserve," Val said, "where they let you thin out the populations."

Under normal circumstances, a girl with two crossbows and a dirt bike would be more enticing than some lady with a stringless dog-harp. But this was Tesla's dog-harp. Even as Nick thought about it, he felt the uncanny pull of the half-finished device in his attic.

"I'm sorry, but I can't go today."

She gave him a bone-crushing glare. "Oh, really? So you made me come all this way for nothing?"

Mitch pulled him aside and spoke quietly. "Nick, you should go."

"Are you kidding me? The harp—"

"I'll call Petula and we'll go get it together, right on schedule."

Nick shook his head. "Out of the question."

Mitch regarded him with an expression that was both sad and severe. "You keep telling me that we're a team, but you do just about everything yourself."

"Well, that's just because—"

"—because you think I'm a screw-up, right? Go on, say it!"

"Mitch, I don't think that."

"Then prove it. Let me do this. Let me show you I'm not a screw-up."

Nick felt cornered, but maybe Mitch was right. He did have trouble trusting anyone with Tesla's objects. It was time to show some faith in his friend.

"Go on," said Mitch. "Val's waiting."

Nick turned to Val. "Well, I guess it's okay," he said, taking the smaller crossbow from her, "as long as we're not expected to kill off all the other kids there."

"Cute," said Val. "Like I've never heard that before." She

turned and strode back to the dirt bike, her mane of hair flowing behind her. "You coming, or what?"

Nick turned to Mitch. "You promise you'll go get the harp right away?"

"Promise."

"And be careful with it—we don't know what it does."

"When am I not careful?"

"Oh, I don't know—like your entire freaking life?"

Mitch nodded, accepting the truth. "Well, then today will be the exception."

Nick turned at the rude sound of Val starting her dirt bike, which looked much more like a Harley with her on it. Well, if Caitlin thought this match-made-in-hell would rattle him, she had this coming. He resolved to go the distance just to show her, and skewer himself some critters.

So he climbed on the back of Val's bike and rode off for the hunt, trusting Mitch and Petula to do the job.

Caitlin did not know about Val. She was on her way to Nick's house with Tesla's abacus and the hope that, in addition to its mathematical properties, the device would help mend the fence between her and Nick.

Then she saw Nick cruising down the street on a dirt bike steered by a stone-faced girl with wild hair and . . . was that a weapon slung across her back?

They rode past, and Nick didn't even see Caitlin.

Needless to say, Caitlin was furious. But she didn't know who to be furious at, or what it all meant. She should have talked to Nick sooner. After all, she was the one who had stormed off after he did nothing more than dredge up the nerve to ask her out.

She continued to Nick's house in something of a rage-induced daze, intending to leave the abacus at his door. There she found Mitch in the driveway, talking desperately into his phone.

". . . and I don't know where you are, Petula, but this is the third time I'm calling," he said. "So look, I'll just come over to your house and wait. . . ."

Caitlin put the lead-lined abacus case into Mitch's hand.

"For Nick," she said. "Tell him . . ." She thought about it for a second. "You know what? Don't tell him anything. Just give it to him." Then she went back home, where she smashed a bunch of things and glued them onto canvases, creating what were perhaps her most heartfelt works of art.

It aggravated Caitlin that she cared. After all, she was pretty, she was popular, she was smart. Her life did not rise and fall on the attention of any boy. Even so, losing that attention didn't feel very good.

She had always prided herself on being a girl of action, and today that meant something more than the creation of her *mash*-terpieces, as her parents called them. There was something else that needed to be destroyed before something new could be created.

So she went into the kitchen, picked up a landline, and called Theo—because lately hearing Theo's voice on a "smart" phone just didn't seem right.

From his first few words, he sounded distracted, and she knew he was watching ESPN. He had checked out of the conversation before he'd even checked in.

After some small talk so small it was actually microscopic, she told him, "I've decided it's time we make our breakup official."

"Okay, sure," Theo said absently. "Wait—what?"

"No more studying together, no more being seen together, no more showing up at my house for food."

There was silence for a moment as Theo let it sink in. "You mean I can't even *eat* there anymore?"

"That's right. I'm sorry, Theo, but it's best this way."

"Wait," said Theo. "Is this because of what happened with Galileo's mascot?"

Caitlin had no idea what he was talking about, but still she said, "Yes, Theo, that's exactly why," and hung up.

Then she smashed the phone, and glued it to a canvas.

# 15 STRING THEORY

**U**nlike Caitlin, Petula knew about Val, because she was the one who had been impersonating Nick online. She'd been doing it for quite some time now. At first it was just for entertainment value, but more recently it had a purpose.

She had created a profile for him in a medieval weaponry chat room, and had struck up a conversation with the most intimidating girl she could find, for the purpose of blindsiding Nick exactly as she had done today.

It wasn't hard, really. Her own knowledge of Dark Age death devices had captured Val like a heretic in an iron maiden. And so, while Nick floundered at his door, negotiating with an armed teenage huntress, Petula was on the move, waiting for Ms. Planck at the harpist's house.

She had already ignored three phone calls from Mitch. She knew why he was calling, and she listened to his messages only because his increasingly frantic voice soothed her.

"This will be a feather in your cap, Petula," Ms. Planck said as she arrived. "If we retrieve this item because of you, the Accelerati won't forget it. You'll be well on your way up the secret society's ladder, and they will give you the respect that you deserve." Then she added, "And it won't look bad for me either—I need something more to show for my efforts. Do you know how close I was to getting a list of the missing objects from Nick? That would have made me the belle of the Accelerati ball!"

"The Accelerati have a ball?"

"Honestly, Petula!" Ms. Planck said, shaking her head. "That's a figure of speech." Then she suggested, "Perhaps you could sweet-talk that list out of him."

Petula knew that was as unlikely as pigs flying. Although, considering some of the experiments she'd heard about in the Accelerati's genetic research department, flying pigs were not entirely out of the question.

They arrived at the harpist's home, which was unremarkable—just one on a street of similar ranch houses. Petula reached out to ring the bell, but the door opened before she could.

The woman inside seemed to be in her thirties. She was wearing a loose-fitting flowery dress, and she had the air of contentment usually reserved for people too stupid to know that their lives were miserable.

"Hello," she said, in a rather musical tone. "You've come for the harp, haven't you? I was expecting two young men, but things change, I suppose." The smile never left her face. It was calming in a disturbing sort of way. The woman exuded a sense of inner peace and trust that made Petula not want to trust her at all.

"Come in," she said. "Stay for a moment, won't you? There's no need to rush."

Ms. Planck, however, got down to business the moment they stepped inside. "The harp is part of a collection that should not have been split up. I hope you can understand our need to retrieve it."

"Yes, of course."

"We'll buy it back," Petula said, wedging herself into the negotiation.

"And for much more than you paid for it," Ms. Planck added.

The woman just looked at the two of them, her eyes smiling as broadly as her lips, it seemed. "Oh, you don't have to pay me. Take it as my gift. I've come to realize I can't keep it. Now that it's touched my life, I'm happy to let it move on."

This made Petula even more suspicious—and probably Ms. Planck, too, because she, more than anyone, knew that there was no such thing as a free lunch.

"So then what do you want?" Petula asked. "You must want something."

Ms. Planck gently touched Petula's arm to quiet her, and said, "Can you show it to us?"

The woman led them into a den. There it sat beside a baby grand piano. It was about four feet high and was gunmetal gray with gold highlights. A beautiful object, with one very obvious problem.

"It really doesn't have strings," said Petula.

The woman chuckled lightly. "Oh, it most certainly does." Then she asked, "Would you like to hear me play?"

Petula couldn't imagine how a person could play a stringless harp, but Ms. Planck said, "Yes, we'd love to hear it, if you would be so kind."

The woman pulled up a small stool, tilted the harp so that it rested on her shoulder, and began to move her fingers in the empty space where the strings should have been.

Petula heard nothing. Nothing at all. But she could *feel* the music. It seemed to echo inside her. Not just in her bones, but in a deeper place she never knew existed—or at least had never accessed. The soundless music tapped the well of her soul.

"My God," whispered Ms. Planck. "It's strung with cosmic string!"

Petula had heard of cosmic string theory. How the universe

was made up of invisible threads stretching beyond the three dimensions that humans can experience. No wonder this woman seemed to be tuned in to something larger than herself. Because she was! She was playing the universe!

Then the howling began. Just as the man at the Beef-O-Rama had told them, this delicate melody, out of the range of human hearing, was calling to dogs like an ultrasonic whistle. And they sang with it, harmonizing. Like the man said, it wasn't music, but whatever it was, Petula wanted it to last.

But Ms. Planck said, "Thank you. It's lovely, but we really need to go."

The woman looked up—not at Ms. Planck, but at Petula, who had crossed the room and was now standing just a few feet away from the harp. The soundless music had drawn her. She felt betrayed by her own legs, and would have to find a way to punish them later.

"You want to play it, don't you?" the woman said kindly. "I think you should."

"No!" said Ms. Planck, and she pulled Petula back, whispering into her ear. "Cosmic strings are capricious and unpredictable. You don't want to touch them."

"But . . . but just a single strum couldn't hurt."

"Of course it could! Look at her." They both turned to the smiling woman, whose eyes seemed to be seeing through them to another place entirely. "Clearly she's lost her mind!"

Then Ms. Planck addressed the woman. "We really do need to go. Petula, grab the light end, and be careful not to touch the strings. I'll take the base."

The woman stepped back and let them lift the harp. They moved it to the doorway, where Ms. Planck put down her end. "Wait here," she told Petula, then went back to the woman.

"I can't just take the harp without leaving you something."

The woman heaved a sigh that seemed both blissful and melancholy. "Yes, I know," she said.

"It's not what you want, but it's necessary."

"Yes, I know," she said again.

Petula was much more interested in the harp than the transaction. Even silent, the invisible strings seemed to resonate. So Petula reached out a single finger, moved it toward the seemingly empty space, and as soon as she felt the tiniest bit of resistance, she plucked the unseen string.

The effect was immediate. It was intense, and too much to process all at once. If that's what a single string did, Petula couldn't imagine what playing all of them would do—especially if you knew how to play.

Ms. Planck must have felt the vibration, because she snapped her eyes back to Petula. "I told you not to!"

"I didn't mean to! My hand slipped!"

"It spoke to you!" the woman said, overjoyed by the prospect. "What did it tell you? What did it say?"

Petula just shook her head.

"Enough!" said Ms. Planck. "Thank you for your assistance, but we're done here." Then she pulled something out of her pocket. It wasn't money, but a small silver ball about the size of a cherry. She dropped the silver marble at the woman's feet and took several steps back. Suddenly things began to change. The colors in the den started to fade. Piano strings broke with harsh twangs.

Ms. Planck returned to the harp and lifted the heavy end. "Time to go," she said.

Petula couldn't help looking back. What she saw would have made a lesser person scream. The woman's skin was puckering. Her clothes began to tatter. Still she smiled. Still she held Petula's gaze.

"What *was* that?" Petula asked Ms. Planck. "What did you do?"

"It's called a temporal accelerator. You might call it a time bomb."

Now Petula understood. Everything within a field of about ten feet around the woman was aging at incredible speed—including the woman herself. In the blink of an eye, she looked fifty. Sixty. Eighty. Her hair grayed, her skin wrinkled, and her body withered before Petula's eyes.

"Don't worry, dear," she croaked from within the time field, in the voice of a very old woman. "I am complete . . . and all is as it should be. . . ."

Then her smile became the fleshless grin of a skeleton. Her bones crashed to the ground and disintegrated. The piano collapsed, and when the field faded, all that remained of the den was a rusty piano soundboard on a dusty, crumbling floor. The entire room had been consumed by time.

"We do the things we must do," Ms. Planck said. "Don't think too long on it, Petula."

And so, Petula resolved she wouldn't, not if she wanted to be a full-fledged member of the Accelerati. Even though she had just seen a woman disintegrate before her eyes, she couldn't let emotions or regrets get in the way. They had come here for the harp; they got the harp, end of story.

Except that the dead woman was right. The harp *had* spoken to her. Not in words, but in the silky vibration of feelings. Of intuition. Only now was Petula able to put that feeling into five simple words:

*"You must complete the circuit."*

# 16 HARP FAILURE

**M**itch was waiting at Nick's front door, dreading the moment he'd return from his wildlife adventure. Things hadn't gone the way Mitch had planned. In fact, they hadn't gone at all.

Once Petula finally called him back an hour later, they'd walked over together to retrieve the harp, but it wasn't there. Neither was the harpist.

"It's not like it's your fault," Petula had told him when they left empty-handed.

"Then why does it feel like it is?"

"Force of habit," Petula told him, "because you usually *are* to blame. Come on, let's go to my house."

Then she dragged him over for old movies and enforced snuggling, until she had to use the bathroom and he could escape. It wasn't that he didn't enjoy his time with Petula, but she was like a cinnamon fireball candy—one was fine, but a whole mouthful could be painful.

Finally, a little after four, Mitch watched as Val dropped Nick at the curb and sped off to her tree house, or wherever a girl like her lived.

Nick seemed in pretty good spirits. But those good spirits wouldn't last for long.

"So how was it?" Mitch asked, walking up to him, trying not to telegraph his own anxiety.

"Pretty good, actually," Nick told him. "I bagged a gopher that I'm pretty sure was already dead, and the tire of a parked Mercedes. That's when Val decided to call it a day. Is the harp in the attic?"

"Oh, hey, look what Caitlin brought." Mitch handed Nick the abacus. "She wanted me to give it to you."

Nick perked up. "Caitlin?"

"Yeah, she said . . ." Mitch hesitated. "Um, she said not to say anything."

Nick frowned. "Fine. Where's the harp?"

"Well, here's the thing . . ." said Mitch, and he left it hanging.

"You didn't get it," Nick said.

"We went, but when the harp lady didn't come to the door, Petula and I looked in a window. It was like a whole room had caught on fire or something—all that was left was ash. I think maybe she spontaneously combusted."

Nick shook his head. "No," he said. "The Accelerati got to her first."

"We don't know that," offered Mitch.

"*I* know that," insisted Nick.

"How would they find out about her?"

"The same way we did. They must have seen the flyer somewhere."

"Well," Mitch suggested, "maybe they spontaneously combusted, too."

"Just go home, Mitch," Nick told him.

"I'm sorry," Mitch said. He was waiting for Nick to tell him that it wasn't his fault, like Petula had.

But Nick didn't. "Go home, Mitch. I'll see you in school on Monday, okay?"

The disappointment in his voice was too dense for Mitch to cut through, so he left without another word.

Nick watched his friend go, resisting the kinder part of himself that wanted to tell Mitch it was okay, because it wasn't.

But if it was anyone's fault, it was Nick's, for not doing it himself. Saying *that* to Mitch would have been more hurtful than not saying anything at all. And really, there was no way to know if Nick could have gotten there first anyway.

If the Accelerati had the harp, Tesla's machine could never be finished. Nick had to somehow get it back. This was their biggest setback yet.

Nick went up to the attic to consult with the machine. It was odd, but he did feel that the machine could communicate with him. *"Complete me,"* it said. *"You're running out of time."*

It had waited for years, in pieces, here in the attic. Why, then, was its need so urgent now? Deep down Nick knew the answer. It had something to do with the asteroid. And the carpet shocks. And the worldwide aurora.

The moment he had turned on the stage lamp, attracting people to his garage sale, he had set something in motion, and it was speeding toward an unseen end. He only hoped he could get there before the Accelerati did.

The secret society had the clear advantage. They had money and manpower on their side. What did Nick have?

In moments of weakness, he thought it might be best to hand everything over to them, and get out of this deep water before he drowned in it. But then he would think of Jorgenson—that smug, self-important jackass. Whatever he would use Tesla's inventions for, it wouldn't be good.

And there was more driving this rivalry. Maybe it was petty and childish, but Nick just couldn't let Jorgenson find out about

Tesla's great machine. It was not what Tesla would have wanted. Nick knew that as certainly as he knew that it was *his* purpose to complete it.

Just when he had finished installing the abacus—sensing instinctively where it went—a voice behind him made him jump.

"Can I be scared yet?"

Nick turned to see his brother at the top of the attic stairs. Nick hadn't even known he was home. The expression on Danny's face was more an accusation than a question.

"Huh?"

"You told me a few weeks ago not to be scared by all the weird stuff, because you'd be scared for both of us."

"There's nothing to be scared of anymore, Danny," Nick said. "The asteroid didn't hit us. Everything's okay." Nick was aware that he wasn't being very convincing.

Danny eyed the collection of odd objects. "Sometimes I come up to the attic when you're not here," he said, "and just look at it."

Nick couldn't read his brother's face. "You shouldn't do that."

"And you shouldn't be getting all this stuff back. There's something wrong with all of it, and you bringing it here just makes it worse."

Nick couldn't deny that. "Maybe it has to get worse before it gets better," he said.

"Or maybe it just gets worse," said Danny, the expression on his face harder than Nick had ever seen it. And then he said, "He was nuts, you know."

"Who?"

"Who do you think? Tesla."

Hearing Danny say the name was surprising enough to make Nick gasp.

"I might not be as smart as you," Danny said, "but I'm not

stupid. I hear he nearly blew up the whole city, like a hundred years ago or something."

Nick couldn't look at his brother. Instead he considered the collection of objects in front of him. "You need to have experiments that don't work before you get to the ones that do."

"I don't trust a crazy dead scientist," Danny said. Then he took a deep breath and let it out. "But I trust you."

Nick felt a huge sense of relief. If Danny trusted him, maybe he was worthy of that trust.

"If you want me to help, I will," Danny said. "What do you want me to do?"

"Just look out for Dad," Nick told him. "Where is he?"

"Off with Spiderly Webb," Danny said, using what had become their secret nickname for Beverly. "They went to see Seth in his school's production of *Scooby-Doo: The Musical.* I told him I'd rather shove needles in my eyes. Dad gave me his death stare but let me stay home."

At the sound of a rattle from outside, they looked out the small attic window to see Vince coming up the driveway, hauling the old dryer on a handcart. One more object claimed! The day hadn't been a total loss.

"Come on," Nick said, "let's help him bring it up."

Danny put up his hand for a brotherly fist bump, and Nick obliged. As their fists touched, there was a loud electric snap, and something flashed—not just between their hands, but also in Nick's mind.

"Ouch!" said Danny, shaking out his hand. "I swear, you can't touch anything anymore without getting a shock."

"It's just static," Nick told him. "Like the aurora. It's from the asteroid. . . ." Something had occurred to Nick, setting his mind on fire. His attention flew back to the center of the room.

"I wish it would stop," Danny said.

"Maybe we can *make* it stop," said Nick, never taking his eyes from the machine. "Maybe we're *supposed* to. . . ."

Caitlin got a text from Nick later that afternoon. All it said was: *Memorial Park. 5:00.*

It was the first communication she'd had from him since she had chosen friendship over saliva exchange and then seen him ride off with that crazy-haired girl on a dirt bike.

Why couldn't boys understand that sometimes "I like you as a friend" means "I like you *more* than a boyfriend" or "I like you too much to ever break up with you"—because that's all the boy-crazy girls in school ever seemed to do: find the boy, break up with the boy, hate the boy, find the next boy, rinse and repeat, over and over.

She had been through the cycle once with Theo, and she wanted off that merry-go-round before the next revolution.

But on the other hand, maybe the way to stop the merry-go-round was to get on with someone you trusted and shut the thing down.

She found it a major triumph that she could understand all this about herself without the insightful playback of the tape recorder. It made her realize that she didn't need it anymore. For the short time she'd had it, it had given her exactly what she needed when she needed it.

*Maybe it needed to go wrong to bring you to this moment.*

And maybe things needed to go wrong between her and Nick to bring her to *this* moment.

She held on to that thought as she left for Memorial Park, ready to say yes to anything Nick asked. She had to trust that the merry-go-round was no match for the two of them.

• • •

Shadows were already getting long by the time she arrived. The park was not in her favorite part of town, and she had no idea why Nick wanted to meet there, but she knew it had to be important. Nick was not a frivolous texter.

People had already started to arrive with blankets and lawn chairs. The same thing was happening in other parks, open fields, and yards. The silent fireworks of the aurora borealis were more spectacular every night. Flowing colors chased each other across the sky with such brilliance you could barely see the stars anymore.

Finding Nick in the growing crowd was like playing a game of Twenty Text Messages.

*I'm by the big tree.*

> *i c lots of big trees.*

*By the parking lot.*

> *North lot or south?*

*The one by the fountain.*

> *The broken one?*

*Yeah.*

When she found him, they gave each other a standard "hey" "hey" greeting that seemed off but not awkward. She was expecting awkward. She didn't know how to read "off."

"I want to show you something," Nick told her, and he led her across a field where no sky watchers had set up camp yet. Memorial Park was very big and very flat. Up ahead was Pikes Peak Avenue, which bordered the northern edge of the park.

"Where are we going?"

"See that street?" He stopped and pointed. "Foote Avenue?"

"Yes . . ."

"Tesla's Lab was once up that way. And this field around us—this is probably the field he electrified. He shoved three lightbulbs into the ground, turned on the Tesla coil back at his lab, and the bulbs actually lit up!"

"Is that why we're here? To talk about Tesla?"

Nick didn't pick up on her disappointment and kept going. "He was using the town's generator to power the coil—but what if he figured out that he didn't have to? What if he discovered how to pull power right out of the air?"

Caitlin shook her head. It wasn't so much that she didn't understand, it was more that she didn't want to.

When she didn't say anything, Nick reached toward her. "What if you could harness *this*?" And he touched her shoulder, delivering a small shock.

"Ow! Stop it."

"Imagine that, multiplied billions of times! Imagine the aurora pulled from the sky, and into a machine right on Earth!"

And although today's meeting wasn't at all what she had expected, she had to admit that she was intrigued. "You mean the F.R.E.E.?"

"That's what it's for, Caitlin! There's all this energy being generated by the asteroid, but it's being wasted! Tesla figured out a way to harness that free energy. He figured out how to use it!"

Once Nick said it, she knew it was true—but instead of feeling amazed, she felt troubled. Clearly Nick had become addicted to the idea of completing the machine—if "addicted" was the right word—and she feared that knowing the machine's purpose would only intensify his addiction.

She could understand his need to give himself over to something larger than himself; he had just lost his mother. He didn't speak of the tragedy much anymore, but she knew it colored everything he did. Obviously the machine provided distraction and relief. But the Accelerati were a ruthless, soulless bunch. The machine could not save him any more than it had saved Tesla from Edison.

"It's too big a responsibility, Nick," she told him. "It's too much for you to handle."

"That's why I need you, Caitlin." There was desperation in his eyes. Desperation, sincerity, and determination. "What happened last week—me asking you out and stuff—it doesn't matter," he said. "There's a bigger picture, and we've got to work together. We can't let stupid things come between us."

Caitlin shrugged, but a shrug wasn't what she was feeling. The "stupid things," as Nick called them, *did* matter to her.

"Maybe I do want to go to the movies with you after all."

Nick shook his head. "We don't have time for that." Then he sighed. "There's something else you need to see." He led her to a small sign standing alone and mostly forgotten at the edge of the park. It read:

HISTORIC MARKER

DEDICATED TO

NIKOLA TESLA

1856–1943

The wooden posts were almost rotted through, and the small bronze plaque riveted to the weatherworn plywood sign was tarnished, evidencing years of neglect.

It was, to say the least, underwhelming.

"That's it?" said Caitlin. "That's all he got?"

"That," said Nick bitterly, "and the alternative school they named after him."

Now Caitlin was beginning to understand Nick's feelings. It was a sad little marker for such a great man—but what she saw as a disappointment, Nick took as an insult. He was indignant. And angry. She saw that Nick was on the edge of a place she didn't want him to go.

"Tesla had a vision, and we're a part of it," he said. "You and me, we're the only ones who know about the Far Range Energy Emitter. It's up to us to make it a reality. To prove to the world he was right—and complete his life's work."

Although part of her could see Nick's point, another part of her was worried about his increasingly strange behavior. What had begun as a quest had turned into an obsession. A potentially dangerous one. So she reached out to him, and bearing the shock that came with it, put a hand on his shoulder, gently trying to bring him back from the edge.

"Tesla hid it because he thought the world wasn't ready for it," Caitlin reminded him. "Maybe it's still not."

Nick looked at Caitlin with a steely intensity that made her shiver.

"I don't care if the world's not ready," he said. "*I'm* ready."

And up above, the aurora began to shimmer.

# ⓱ FREEZE!

The following evening, emboldened by their acquisition of the harp, the Accelerati made their move.

It was a rainy Sunday night and Nick was alone in the house. His father had taken Danny out for dinner with the Webbs, or the Hillses, or whatever the plural is for a single mom and her offspring, but Nick had to avoid being seen by Seth, so he refused to go. Considering his bristly relationship with Spiderly Webb, his father didn't insist.

"Remind her about the stain remover," Nick told his dad as he left.

Then, about half an hour later, he microwaved himself up a frozen burrito.

"You want one?" he asked Jorgenson.

"No, thank you," Jorgenson said. "Maybe after I clean out your attic, but not right now."

So Nick made only one, and he sat down at the kitchen table and began to eat, pondering his growing sense of purpose and his need to defeat the Accelerati before they defeated him.

"Something to drink, maybe?" he asked Jorgenson. "We've got juice and milk, though I think the milk might be expired."

"Very kind of you," Jorgenson said. "If I feel dehydrated I'll let you know."

In a dim corner of his mind, where the electrical impulses of his brain were currently not able to reach, Nick felt a mild sense of unease. There was something wrong, but he couldn't quite figure out what it was.

There was a clatter of heavy footsteps on the stairs as two other men in pastel-colored suits struggled to get the weight machine down from the attic.

"Turn it on," Nick told them. "It'll be easier. Just make sure it's on the lowest setting."

And when they couldn't figure out how to turn on the weight machine, he did it for them.

"Thank you," one of the men said.

"Don't mention it."

There were four or five people in Nick's house, all members of the Accelerati, going up and down the stairs, in and out of his attic. He wondered if he should be concerned, and then he realized how silly that was. There was nothing unusual about this, nothing unusual at all, and he laughed at himself for thinking there might be.

And yet . . .

As he watched a woman leave his house with the antique toaster that had nearly killed him twice, his stomach began to react in a way that his mind could not.

He looked down at his half-eaten burrito and somehow knew that the feeling in his stomach had nothing to do with his dinner. And since the inner voice in his mind had been shut down, his gut took over, like the battle bridge hidden deep within a ship.

And the voice from the battle bridge commanded him to call Caitlin.

When Nick's number appeared on her screen, Caitlin hesitated. Last night she had seen a strange side of him—a side that maybe hadn't even been there before. It was as if he were possessed. Not by any sort of spirit, but by an idea so powerful it was all-consuming. She knew that what Nick was doing was important, but she also knew he was in over his head—they all were. But she answered the phone, because although the path Nick was headed down was getting thinner and more fraught with peril, she knew she would journey with him, no matter where the journey ultimately led.

"Hello?"

"Caitlin, there's something I need to ask you, and it's important," Nick said.

She found herself holding her breath, knowing his question would take her by surprise, which it did.

"Should I be worried that the Accelerati are here?"

"What? Where are you?"

"At my house. Should I be worried they're here?"

Caitlin stood up. "Wait, start over. What are you talking about? They're there? Why are they there?"

"Oh, they're just taking stuff out of my attic," he said casually.

"Is this some kind of *joke*?"

"You know what?" Nick said. "I'm probably just being silly. I shouldn't have called."

Suddenly Caitlin figured it out. "Don't hang up," she said. "Answer me this—is Jorgenson there?"

"Yeah, him and a few others."

Caitlin ran her fingers through her hair so rapidly she almost tugged some of it out. "Nick. Listen to me carefully. Remember I told you that Jorgenson has this thing on his key chain that messes with your head and makes you think everything is normal when it isn't?"

"Oh yeah," said Nick. "I remember that now." He hesitated on the other end of the line. "What about it?"

"Nick—he's using it on you!"

"You think so? Should I ask him?"

"No! Don't ask him anything! What you have to do is get his keys away from him and turn it off!"

There was a moment of silence on the phone. "Don't you think that would be rude?"

"Nick, do you trust me?"

"Yeah, usually. Mostly. Yeah, I do."

"And do you trust Jorgenson?"

Another moment of silence. "Not . . . particularly."

Caitlin hoped he'd be able to make the logical leap, even though his logic center was scrambled. "So if you trust me and not Jorgenson, doesn't it make sense that you should do *exactly what I say*?"

"Yes, that makes sense."

"Then do it. Do it now. Sneak up on him, take his keys, and *turn it off*!"

"Okay, Caitlin, if that's what you think, I'll do it."

Caitlin hung up her phone, ran downstairs and out the door, then jumped on her bike and pedaled as fast as she could to Nick's house.

Caitlin's request seemed strange. It seemed fundamentally wrong. But his battle bridge told him he needed to trust her.

He went up to Jorgenson, who waited in the foyer as another one of his friends went upstairs for more items from the attic. Nick was about to tap Jorgenson on the shoulder and ask for his keys; then he remembered that Caitlin had told him not to alert Jorgenson of his plan. So he smiled and politely asked him again if he wanted a burrito.

Jorgenson shook his head, and the moment he turned to look the other way, Nick reached into the pocket of his pretty vanilla coat, pulled out a key chain, and saw the object Caitlin had told him about: a little glowing fob.

He pressed the fob's button with his thumb, its light went out, and Nick's mind returned in full force.

Jorgenson cursed himself for letting his guard down. So far he had retrieved only half of the objects from the attic. But even without the benefit of the neural disrupter, there were five Accelerati present and only one Nick Slate.

The old man who had given Jorgenson his marching orders did not want Nick Slate harmed, but Jorgenson was already going against those orders with this raid. If the boy was hurt, or even killed, the old man would eventually forgive Jorgenson, because the end always justifies the means.

Nick held the key chain in his hand. "Give that back!" Jorgenson commanded, hoping the authority in his voice would stop the boy long enough for them to subdue him. But it didn't.

Nick pushed Jorgenson—just hard enough to put him off balance—then raced partway up the stairs. He grabbed a heavy antique fan from one of Jorgenson's associates and pointed it in Jorgenson's direction.

"Freeze!" Nick said.

"I don't think so," Jorgenson answered with a smile, and he gestured for his associate to take it back.

And so Nick, who wasn't bluffing, turned it on.

Nick was taking a gamble. He hadn't personally seen the fan in action—he'd only heard about if from Vince. And he didn't know what setting it had been turned to. But since he needed every ounce of help he could get, he turned it to ten, its coldest temperature.

The effect was immediate. Frost formed on the walls, and the humid air condensed into snow. The Accelerati woman directly in front of him froze solid in about two-point-five seconds. Nick turned off the fan and touched the woman's shoulder with his finger. She tipped over and fell down the stairs, a solid chunk of ice that nearly bowled Jorgenson off his feet.

Nick walked down a few steps, careful not to slip on the frost, and with one finger on the controls, he aimed the fan at Jorgenson. "Make one move, and I'll polar-ize you."

And Jorgenson moved—in one swift motion, he pulled from his pocket a remote control.

Nick knew what it was. It was the same type of device that had killed Vince with a push of a button—and now it was aimed at him.

Nick didn't hesitate; he turned the fan on again. Jorgenson dodged, but the blast of icy air caught his arm. The remote, covered in frost, fell out of his hand. Jorgenson looked down, grimacing in pain—his arm, from elbow to fingertips, was frozen solid.

Nick hurled himself down the stairs, taking advantage of Jorgenson's disorientation, and grabbed the remote from the floor.

Jorgenson jerked his shoulder, and his arm flung back. His hand hit the door frame and his frozen pinkie snapped off like the delicate finger of a china doll.

Nick pointed the deadly remote at him and said, "Run."

And he did.

As Jorgenson took off, he bumped into one of his associates who was coming through the door. The associate quickly sized up the situation and did an about-face. Two more Accelerati came down from the attic carrying objects.

Nick pointed the remote at them. "Put those down, grab the frozen lady, and go," he ordered. *"Now!"*

And, seeing the remote in his hands, they did as they were told.

Nick followed them out into the rain. Jorgenson was getting into an SUV that held the objects taken from the attic.

"When I said run, I *meant* run!" Nick shouted, and he aimed the fan at the car.

The SUV, drenched from the downpour, instantly froze solid, and its idling engine, unable to handle the sudden change in temperature, blew apart, sending the hood flipping into the air.

"Run!" Jorgenson yelled to his minions. "Just run!"

Nick followed them down the driveway. There had been few moments in his life more rewarding than watching Dr. Alan Jorgenson sprint down the street, trailed by three of his henchmen struggling to carry a fourth, frozen one.

Nick stood at the curb with the remote and the fan, not yet ready to relax, not yet convinced that Jorgenson didn't have another trick up his sleeve, until he heard a voice to his right.

"Nick, turn that thing off before you freeze the whole neighborhood," Caitlin said, coasting up to him on her bike. "You got rid of them."

As she reached over and turned off the fan, Nick found himself falling to his knees, his adrenaline spent just as quickly as it had surged.

"Hey!" Caitlin jumped off her bike and helped him back to his feet. "Are you okay?"

"Yeah," he said with a half smile. "Thanks to you."

She smiled back, and Nick hoped she might give him a spontaneous hug. He suspected her battle bridge wanted to. But unfortunately her head was in control and didn't allow it.

"They could come back. . . ." Caitlin pointed out.

"Not for a while," Nick told her. "They have some wounds to lick."

At that moment Vince arrived on his bike as well. He looked at the frozen, blown-out SUV and said, "Uh . . . did I miss something?"

"Kind of," Nick said, but he didn't want to talk about it.

"Right," said Vince, giving one more glance to the ruined vehicle. Then he apparently dismissed it as Not His Problem. "Anyway, I just wanted to show you this." In spite of the rain, he was wearing a pair of sunglasses. "Check it out," he said. "The wires run up my shirt, into the eyeglass frames, and connect to little patches behind my ears. Much more convenient than tape on my back—or electrodes in my mouth."

"Electrodes in your *mouth?*" Caitlin repeated.

"I . . . uh, had to reanimate him on the fly," Nick told Caitlin, but he didn't go into details.

"I was ticked off about it at first," Vince said, "but then I realized what you risked to pull me out of there. If it was me, I probably would have just taken off and left you to rot. Literally. So I guess I owe you one." Then he caught sight of the object in Nick's hand, and he took a step back. "Hey, if that's what I think it is, would you mind aiming it somewhere else?"

Nick looked down to see he was still holding the killer remote. He also had Jorgenson's neural disrupter fob in his pocket. The disrupter might come in handy, but the remote didn't belong anywhere in this world. So he dropped the remote to the ground and crushed it beneath his shoe.

Then he went to the SUV, which was beginning to defrost, and opened the back, revealing the items from the attic.

"Whoa," said Vince. "I really did miss the whole show, didn't I?"

"Tell us everything," said Caitlin. "Every juicy detail."

"Let's get this stuff back upstairs first," Nick said. "And when we're done, let's roll this wreck down the street—I don't want my dad wondering about it."

As they carried the first objects into the house, Caitlin noticed something just inside Nick's front door. "Ew, what's that?"

Nick looked where she was pointing and grimaced. "Nothing for you to worry about."

He got a napkin, reached down, and picked up Jorgenson's thawing pinkie. Then he took it to the bathroom and heartily flushed it.

# 18 EDISON'S ALLEY

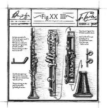

**A**tomic Lanes, in downtown Colorado Springs, was a bowling alley that had resisted modernization like a stubborn child resists spinach. It operated in its own peculiar sort of time field. Everything within its boundaries, from the parking lot to the back alley, was a relic from an era gone by, and perhaps best forgotten.

While newer complexes boasted color-coordinated neon balls and 3-D replays, Atomic Lanes featured beer-bellied guys with names like Rufus and Duke wearing age-worn bowling shoes that were too large and too tight at the same time. It was a place where men kissed their bowling balls more often than their wives, and no doubt their wives played things like cribbage and mah-jongg and other arcane table games that allowed them to show off big hair and bigger nails.

This was the bowling alley that Petula was required to take a picture of once a day. Of course, that was before the Accelerati had run off with the lens from her camera—which was why she had been willing to give the useless box part to Nick.

This was also the bowling alley to which Ms. Planck brought her the following Monday after school.

"Why are we going bowling?" Petula asked in a voice as flat as the Great Plains.

"If you want to meet the Accelerati, this is how it's done."

Petula couldn't imagine a secret society of cutting-edge

scientists hurling balls at pins for recreation. But then, hadn't she read that Tesla had been an avid billiards player? And hadn't Richard Feynman, the father of quantum physics, played the bongos? Petula supposed great minds needed simple pleasures to vent the by-products of genius.

The place was dimly lit and reeked of spilled beer and the malignant ghosts of cigarettes. Orange plastic chairs were worn maroon in the seat, and all the balls were black, with chips around the finger holes. That wasn't a problem, because most people who bowled here brought their own.

Case in point: the man in the lane to their left. He bowled alone, with his designer ball, no doubt brushing up on his game for some tournament that would require even more hair gel than he wore now. In the lane to their right was a family with three children too young to successfully lift a bowling ball, much less throw one. With the bumpers up, however, every ball they dropped managed to meander its way down the alley, bouncing off the rubber sides like a lethargic pinball, until it hit the pins hard enough to make them wobble and occasionally tip over.

And Ms. Planck said, "Show me what ya got."

Petula restrained a glare, and grabbed a ball. Then, with all the strength she could muster, she heaved it down the waxed aisle toward the pins, which always looked like grinning skeleton teeth to her.

Petula was breaking no teeth today. Without the benefit of kiddie-bumpers, her ball dropped into the gutter with a belligerent thud, and rolled off into oblivion. She knew this would happen, and she was furious. Petula detested any activity that she wasn't already extremely good at. Her second attempt got a little closer to the pins but still dropped into the gutter.

"There, are you happy?"

Ms. Planck grinned. Petula took it as sadistic.

"Relax. Your problem is that you don't have the right ball," Ms. Planck said. She reached into her ball bag and pulled out a polished orb of royal blue that seemed to swim with galaxies all the way down to its core.

"Arresting, isn't it?" said Ms. Planck. "But, like so many things, looks aren't its best feature." Then she turned it around and showed Petula a small dial camouflaged against the resin surface. She made a few adjustments to the dial and then, with perfect form, threw her ball down the alley. Kinetic energy was exchanged from ball to pins, and they flew with the familiar thunder of what should have been a strike. But it wasn't. The two outermost pins remained standing, making the lane look like the mouth of a six-year-old who's been making the tooth fairy work overtime.

"Tough break," said Petula, feeling a twinge of joy at Ms. Planck's misfortune.

But Ms. Planck didn't seem to mind. "Ordinarily, a seven-ten split is a bad thing. But not today." Then she threw an intentional field goal right up the middle.

The pins reset and Petula went for her ball, but Ms. Planck stopped her. "For now you're a spectator." She tweaked the dial on her ball again and rolled. This time three pins were left: the seven and the ten pins again, with the five pin right between them.

"They call this split 'the three wise men,'" Miss Planck said. Like the last time, she missed all of them with her second shot.

"Should I be keeping score?" Petula asked.

"Not necessary when you know what the score will be." In the next frame Ms. Planck's first ball left a pattern that was extremely improbable, if not entirely impossible. The entire back row still stood. And so did the head pin. Then she handed Petula the ball to finish out the frame. Petula threw a gutter ball, of course, which is exactly what was required.

"Now," said Ms. Planck, "for the crowning glory." This

time she didn't dial anything on the ball. She just went to the line, and she hurled a perfect strike. And the moment the pins cleared, things began to happen.

As dim as the light around them was, it dimmed even further, and the far end of the lane began to drop, until it became a ramp leading down to a hidden place beneath the bowling alley.

"To gain admittance to the Accelerati Lodge, one must bowl a precise combination of pin patterns, on this lane," Ms. Planck explained. "The chance of bowling the patterns naturally is about one in one hundred billion, which is why it is necessary to have a key-ball that can be programmed to hit certain pins and not others."

Petula noted that one hundred billion was also the number of stars in the galaxy. This, she knew, was not coincidence. Everything the Accelerati did was by design. She loved that about them.

To their left, the lone hair-gel man was still practicing his game, and to their right, the young family was still doing whatever it was that almost, but not quite, looked like bowling. None of them seemed to notice that the lane between them had become a passage to some secret hideout.

"Aren't you worried someone will see?" Petula asked.

"The moment I hit that strike," Ms. Planck explained, "light began to bend around our lane, rendering it invisible. We simply entered everyone's blind spot."

Next to them a boy no older than four stared right at Petula. "Mommy," he said, "those people over there just disappeared."

"That's nice, honey," said the mother absently. "Now finish your milk."

"You see?" said Ms. Planck. "People don't miss what they never really noticed in the first place."

As they headed down the ramp to the Accelerati Lodge, Petula had to ask the obvious question.

"Why don't you just have a door with a lock?"

Ms. Planck bristled. "If you have to ask that question, then you're not one of us yet."

When it came to the Accelerati, form was far more important than function. They were all about style, elegance, and panache. Their evil designs were truly about design.

For instance, if they determined that there was a need to end your life, they wouldn't just end it. They would first have you end the life of someone else who needed ending, who in turn had just ended the life of someone else for them, and so on, like a procession of fishes in which the smaller one is always swallowed by the larger one behind it.

Thus, the Accelerati member who designed the bowling-pin combination lock had been applauded and received the organization's highest honors before he was killed—by someone else who needed to be killed.

Their lodge predated the bowling alley by several years. When a local businessman decided to build the recreation spot directly above their underground lair, the Accelerati saw it as an opportunity. For who would ever imagine that humanity's greatest minds were hiding underneath a bowling alley? And although it was called Atomic Lanes, the Accelerati's secret experiments made it only slightly radioactive.

Petula knew none of this. All she knew was that she was required to take a picture every day, showing what the bowling alley would look like one day in the future. Since the Accelerati had no enemies powerful enough to attack them, the photos weren't to warn them of outside threats—but rather to let them know if, over the next twenty-four hours, they would accidentally blow themselves up.

"Welcome to the Great Hall," Ms. Planck said, throwing

open a pair of ornately sculpted bronze doors. The room before them, however, seemed no larger than a closet.

"That's some Great Hall," Petula said, with her familiar flatness.

"Have you ever heard of Zeno's paradoxes?"

Petula did not answer, because admitting that she did not know something was not part of her chosen lifestyle.

"One of them is the concept on which the Great Hall is based."

Petula stepped forward, only to find that with each step the other end of the room seemed twice as far away as before; it expanded until she found herself standing in a cathedral-like library. Huge windows seemed to be looking out on seventeenth-century Venice, with gondolas gliding gracefully by outside.

"Ah," said Ms. Planck, "Italian Renaissance Day. Each day of the month a different holographic theme is projected. We're in negotiations to sell the technology to Apple."

On the walls were artworks by great artists, familiar in style if not in composition.

"Most of the pieces in this room were presumed lost in fires and other natural, and not-so-natural, disasters."

Petula didn't want to think about how they came to be in the Accelerati's possession.

Just beyond the Great Hall they reached a rotunda where a larger-than-life-size statue of Thomas Edison held up a light-bulb, his expression grim.

"Our founder," Ms. Planck noted as they passed it. "Obviously."

Several hallways led to other wings of what seemed to be a sprawling underground complex. It didn't actually appear to be underground, but instead woven into the infrastructure of Venice. At least for today.

Ms. Planck led Petula through a door that read RESEARCH

AND DEVELOPMENT. "Don't dawdle, Petula, he doesn't like to be kept waiting."

No one had ever accused Petula of dawdling. But there was so much to see, both within the walls and outside the windows of the Accelerati Lodge, that it was hard not to be distracted.

"He, who?" Petula asked.

"Dr. Alan Jorgenson, the Grand Acceleratus."

"You're not serious—he's not actually called that, is he?"

"Don't mock him, Petula," Ms. Planck told her quietly. "He's not a man who suffers mockery lightly."

The R&D wing, which overlooked the pigeon-filled holographic expanse of St. Mark's Square, was bustling with activity. In the middle of it all stood a tall man in a silk suit that almost seemed to glow with vanilla-toned pearlescence.

"Evangeline!" he said, taking Ms. Planck's hand and kissing it. "So good to see you!"

Until that moment, Petula had never considered that Ms. Planck had a first name other than "Ms."

Then the Grand Acceleratus looked down at Petula. His smile was difficult to read. She couldn't tell if he was pleased to meet her, or if he was considering whether she would taste better chewed or swallowed whole.

"And you must be the new fledgling I've been hearing so much about."

Petula held out her hand for him to shake. "Petula Grabowski-Jones," she announced, then added, "future Grand Acceleratus."

It was a calculated move that paid off just as she'd hoped. Jorgenson did not hold out his hand—because it was bandaged—but his smile changed from predatory to genuine. "We appreciate ambition here," he said. "I suspect you'll do well."

"What happened to your hand?" Petula asked.

The Grand Acceleratus sighed. "An accident while out in the

field. One of my associates was frozen, along with my arm. I lost my pinkie in the process."

Although Petula found the very idea funny, she kept herself from laughing.

"Poor Helga," Ms. Planck said. "How is she doing?"

"Recovering nicely, thanks to our pressure-defroster," Dr. Jorgenson told her. "And on the bright side, it proves the viability of human hibernation. Once we have the device that caused it, we can sell the technology to NASA for a fortune." Then he gestured to a large window that looked in on one of the research rooms. "You're just in time—I think you'll enjoy this."

In the center of the room was none other than the cosmic string harp that Petula had helped snag for them. Workers placed watermelons on three low platforms around the harp, and then left the room.

Once they were gone and the room was sealed, a pair of mechanical hands descended from the ceiling and began to play the harp. Petula expected to feel the same soul-searing vibration she had experienced in the harpist's house, but she felt nothing.

"That can't be right," Petula wondered out loud, and Jorgenson, guessing what she meant, rapped on the window that was between them and the harp.

"High-density leaded glass," he told her. "We're perfectly safe out here."

The mechanical hands played the invisible strings with increasing intensity. All at once the three melons exploded, splattering the room and window with fleshy shrapnel.

"Remarkable!" said Ms. Planck. "Absolutely remarkable!"

"Wait till you see this next test," Jorgenson said.

Petula found herself raising her hand, as she never actually did in school. Questions, she believed, should never await permission. But in the presence of the Grand Acceleratus, she couldn't help herself.

"Uh, excuse me," she said, "but I don't think that's what the harp is for."

Jorgenson put his unbandaged hand on her shoulder. "Creators never understand the potential of their creations," he said. "It's left to us to complete their vision."

The workers went back into the room, this time with a single melon, and set it down. Then they carried in what looked like a huge metallic tortoise shell about the size of an overturned bathtub. They placed it over the melon, and exited.

The mechanical hands played with the same intensity for over a minute. When they stopped, the workers went in and removed the shell, revealing that the melon had not been damaged at all.

"Splendid!" said Jorgenson. "Not only is the tortoise shell material resistant to impact and radiation, it also deflects cosmic string dissonance. Whenever we create a weapon, we strive to also create the perfect defense against it—for ourselves."

Then he took a long look at Petula, as if pondering a major purchase. "What are your views on vengeance, Ms. Grabowski-Jones?"

Petula considered how she might best answer. "Well," she said, "some people believe vengeance is a dish best served cold. But I believe it shouldn't be served at all—it's better as an all-you-can-eat buffet."

Jorgenson grinned once more and nodded his satisfaction. Then he presented her with a small glass vial. It had a tiny computer chip inside.

"I would like you to use this to make Nick Slate's life miserable."

Petula took the vial and sighed. "According to him, that's what I do best."

# 19 A CLUB, A POLE, OR A STICK

With the pieces back in place, Nick finally allowed himself to relax a little. But when he ventured close enough to touch the incomplete machine, he could still feel the presence of all of the other wayward objects out there.

Not enough to know *where* they were, only *that* they were.

This is how he knew that the harp was still intact and hadn't been consumed in some sort of localized disaster in the harpist's home. He could sense it resonating with all of the objects in the machine, as well as the ones still to be recovered.

He looked up at the window in his ceiling, the glass pinnacle of the attic pyramid, and wondered whether it was there to bring light in, or to channel energy out. Perhaps both.

Of course, all of this was just intuition. The farther Nick got from his attic, the less he trusted these feelings. He often wondered if he was just deluding himself—until he stood in the presence of Tesla's great creation again, and found that absolute, undeniable sense of interconnectedness. It was so comforting, so overwhelming that, were he a weaker kid, he might never leave his attic.

But he wasn't weak. And now that he had faced the Accelerati head-on and fought them off, he felt more confident than ever.

"Confidence can be dangerous," Caitlin had told him. "You might have scared them away, but they'll be back—and when they come back, they'll hit hard."

"Then we'll hit back harder," Nick had responded. But he knew they needed a plan.

And so, on Monday evening, Nick gathered his friends under the guise of a school project. Caitlin, Vince, Mitch, and Petula climbed the steep steps into the attic for a meeting of the minds.

Nick's dad allowed them their space, and if he had any suspicions about their activities, he kept them to himself. Just to be on the safe side, though, Vince wore a hoodie so Mr. Slate couldn't really see his face—and if he did, and trapped Vince in a conversation, Nick told Vince to pretend he was his own twin brother.

"The gravity's getting stronger," Nick said to the others in his attic. To prove it, he took off his shoes and set them on the floor next to him. "My bed and desk are nailed down, but everything else migrates to the center."

The shoes did not appear to move.

"Fail," said Vince.

"It's like the hour hand of a clock," Nick told him. "Look again in five minutes." Then he noticed that Vince's body odor was ranker than usual.

Petula, of course, was the one who had to comment. "Ew, did something die in here?"

"That would be me," said Vince. "Thanks to you."

Vince didn't seem bitter, just resigned, which was the way he had lived his pre-undead life. Today he wore a shirt proclaiming YOLO on the front, with the second *o* crossed out and replaced with a hand-scrawled *t*. Nick noticed he was looking a little green under the neckline. Vince noticed him noticing.

"I think I'm growing moss," Vince casually announced. "I really should do a science project on myself."

"If the Accelerati nab you," Caitlin said, "I'm sure they'll do it *for* you."

"Which is why," Nick said, getting back to business, "we have to make sure they don't. We can't just wait until they take the next swing. We need a strategy."

"Why don't we hide everything?" suggested Mitch. "It doesn't all have to be here in your attic—we can put the stuff in different places."

Nick threw Caitlin a look that she threw back at him.

"We can't," Nick told them.

"Why not?" challenged Petula. "Seems like the logical thing to do."

Nick had considered that idea himself, but every time he thought about taking the machine apart, he felt like something was being torn from his insides. That feeling had to mean something, It couldn't be ignored.

"Because we just can't," Nick said, a little more forcefully.

He stood up, walked over to the machine, and touched it. The static shock it gave him was a taste of something far greater. Something he couldn't yet explain.

"Nick," said Mitch, "you're acting really weird. I mean, weirder than usual."

Nick turned to him. If they were to be a part of this, they needed to know everything. He pointed at the objects. "Take a closer look," he said. "I mean, really look."

Mitch was the first to catch on. "It's a single machine," he said.

Nick nodded. "Exactly."

Petula let out a soft whistle. Vince drew his knees up to his chest.

"Caitlin and I figured it out just before the asteroid was bonked into orbit."

"You could have told us," said Vince.

"It was the end of the world," Nick reminded him. "And you had just died. At the time, it didn't seem all that important."

"So what does it do?"

"Tesla dreamed of bringing free wireless energy to the world. This is how he was going to do it," Nick explained. "This machine needs to be here. It needs to be completed. And we're the ones who have to complete it."

There was a moment of silence so loud it seemed to echo.

Then Mitch said, "Nick, your shoes."

They all looked; in the five minutes they had been talking, Nick's shoes had migrated about two feet closer to the machine. Now they all could see the gravity of the situation.

"How can you be sure we're the ones who have to complete it?" asked Vince. "I mean, it's just a feeling, right?"

Nick nodded. "That's true, but it's a pretty strong one."

"I don't know about any of you," said Vince, "but I'm not much of a believer in feelings. My mother is all about feelings. They lead to nothing but motivational greeting cards and designated 'happy places' all over our house. I'd rather have cold hard facts in my cold dead hands."

Caitlin turned to Nick. "What do you think we should do?"

"All the garage-sale stuff stays here," said Nick, in spite of Vince's reservations. "And we continue to build the machine. The Accelerati might have the harp, but they haven't gotten their hands on anything else yet, as far as we know."

"How are we supposed to protect all this stuff from them if we keep it here?" asked Mitch. "And, for that matter, how do we protect ourselves?"

"I don't know!" Nick said, exasperated. "That why I brought you all here—I thought maybe together we could figure it out." He looked toward the machine again. "If this thing could just tell us what to do . . ."

His voice trailed off. The machine couldn't talk, but that didn't mean it wasn't communicating with him on some deeper level, where words couldn't reach. "You know," he said slowly, "I think the answer is right in front of us."

They all followed his gaze. Caitlin was the first to understand. "You want to use Tesla's devices as weapons against the Accelerati?"

"I don't *want* to . . . but I think we *have* to."

"Then we're no better than them!" Caitlin said.

"Yes we are," Mitch said, "because we're gonna weaponize them for the sake of good!"

"There's a difference between using the inventions as weapons," Nick explained, "and using them to defend ourselves."

"Is there?" Caitlin asked. "That sounds like the argument for every war in history."

"They already killed Vince," Nick told her. "And Jorgenson tried to kill me the other day. Sorry to tell you this, Caitlin, but we're already at war."

Caitlin stood up, crossing her arms. "I have no intention of killing anyone. Do you?"

Nick turned his gaze away. "I think I already have."

Caitlin gasped and the others looked equally shocked. Nick's shoulders sagged with the weight of his confession. He hadn't told his friends about this part of his encounter with the Accelerati. "I froze one of them with the fan. I—I might have killed her."

"No, you didn't," Petula blurted, and when everyone turned to look at her, she giggled nervously and said, "I mean, they're the Accelerati, right? I'm sure they figured out a way to defrost her."

And since that was what Nick wanted to believe, he didn't question it. "Thanks," he said. "I hope you're right."

"So you have a plan?" Vince asked. "Or are you going to keep that from us, too?"

"We'll each take one object to protect us," Nick said. "The rest stay here, in the attic. And if Jorgenson comes after us with his braniac flunkies and his fake smile and his stupid vanilla suit, we'll smack him down so hard he'll have to crawl away."

Mitch looked up suddenly. "Vanilla suit? What about a vanilla suit?"

"It's what he wears," Caitlin told him. "The Accelerati all wear these weird pastel suits."

"They're made of Madagascan spider silk," Nick added.

". . . and in a certain light," mumbled Mitch, "they seem to shimmer . . ."

Then Mitch Murló took a deep dive into himself.


Humans have the uncanny ability to distance themselves from anything real. Sometimes, for their own protection, they create stories that pass for history because creating meaning is so much easier than searching for it. The stories become symbols on a page, and in the end the page is replaced by electronic strings of ones and zeros floating in a cloud that is not really a cloud at all. The truth is filtered through so many levels of unreality that we can't remember what transpired over the course of time, or even what we had for breakfast this morning.

Our relationship with money is much the same, and few people knew this better than the Murló family. Thousands of years ago, money was something tangible—a string of shells or beads at first, then precious metals in the form of coins that everyone agreed were worth a certain amount. The coins gave way to worthless paper, but everyone chose to agree that the bills were worth something, too.

Then paper was replaced with the same endless string of ones and zeros that had swallowed all of human history. The world's wealth no longer existed in material form. It was a concept in the cloud that didn't actually exist . . .

. . . which is why a computer programmer with great skill

and the right amount of inspiration could figure out a way to steal unreal pennies from theoretical bank accounts and amass three-quarters of a billion dollars in less than five seconds, by clicking a single button on his laptop.

Now Mr. Murló was in prison, perhaps for the rest of his life, and the Accelerati had a secret bank account of untold millions that existed only because computers agreed that it existed.

Throughout his father's first year of incarceration, Mitch had tried to wrap his head around how something as imaginary as digital money could ruin so many lives—while improving the lives of the monsters who had used his father and then discarded him.

And so, when Mitch finally connected the dots and realized that those monsters were the very same people they were fighting now, his mind whirled in a feedback loop of fury. It was as if he had left the attic and gone to a faraway place, a place where time and space curved around on itself, allowing Mitch to repeatedly kick his own butt for not realizing it sooner.

While Mitch traveled in his own head, the others made plans in the attic. It was decided that Nick would keep the fan and Jorgenson's neural disrupter for his defense. Vince would take the narc-in-the-box that rendered people unconscious, since, by his own admission, it suited his personality. Petula was assigned the torturous clarinet, because the others could easily imagine her playing an instrument of torture. Mitch would get the dust-devil bellows, because most of the video games they had traded for it were his. And Caitlin—the conscientious objector of the group—agreed to hold on to the force-field sifter, since it was truly the most defensive of all the objects.

Mitch hadn't heard any of this. When he returned from his unhappy place, there was only one thought on his mind.

"Where's the remote?" he said with an uncharacteristic growl.

They all turned to him, a bit thrown by the snarl.

"Huh?" said Nick.

"The remote that freaking Mr. Vanilla Suit tried to kill you with. You said you broke it. Well, I want the pieces. Where are they?"

The others looked at one another, not sure what to make of this.

"I . . . threw it into the fireplace, Mitch," Nick said. "I burned it up."

Mitch stood, his fingers balling into fists so tight he could feel his nails cutting into his palms. *"WHY WOULD YOU DO THAT?"*

"Because," said Caitlin, her voice calm, as if she were trying to talk someone off a ledge, "it was too dangerous."

"It wasn't dangerous *enough*!" Mitch yelled. "It could only kill one of them at a time. I want to kill them *all*! I want them all dead! Every last one of them! I want them dead *now*." Tears burst from his eyes. He couldn't control them; he didn't even try.

Nick stood up. "Mitch, what's wrong?"

"Nothing!" he screamed. "Who said anything was wrong?"

"Mitch, that thing was made by the Accelerati, and we—"

Then Mitch blurted, *"—can never destroy the Accelerati with their own technology."* He covered his mouth with his hands. It had come out like a belch. He hadn't meant to say it, but then, he never meant to finish the sentences that he did whenever he was angry—the ones that were undeniably true—thanks to the strange power he had absorbed from the Shut Up 'N Listen. Just like the answers that had flown from his mouth when Nick needed to know how to save the world. Or the things Mitch had shouted in the heat of his fight with Steven Gray. It was only when his emotions were running high that these unintended phrases came out.

Sometimes they were helpful, sometimes they were just annoying, but they were always true, and right now he did not want the answer to be true.

"Shut up!" he yelled, but not to anyone else in the attic. He was yelling it to himself. And he bounded down the attic ladder, with no clue as to where he wanted to go, except out.

Nick followed him, not only because he cared about his friend, but also because he saw an opportunity. What they needed more than anything else right now were answers, even if they weren't the answers Mitch wanted to hear.

Nick caught up with him in the foyer and grabbed him.

"We can beat the Accelerati—" Nick prompted.

"—*with a club, a pole, or a stick,*" Mitch finished.

*Okay,* Nick thought, *less than helpful. I've got to be more specific.* "The Accelerati's next attack will be—"

"—entirely underfoot," Mitch blurted.

Interesting, thought Nick. But what did it mean?

"Please," said Mitch, "don't make me do this!"

"Don't you see, Mitch? You could be the key to everything—if I can come up with the right words. Whatever made you so angry, hold on to it, just until we get the answer."

But Mitch's anger was shooting out in many directions; right then it hurled itself at Nick. He burned Nick a gaze and tried to pull out of his grip, telling him, "No, I won't do it!"

"The Accelerati want to kill us, but we can save our lives by—"

And out of Mitch's mouth came the words "—*shaking hands with Dr. Jorgenson.*"

Once more he covered his mouth. Nick stared at him, like somehow Mitch had betrayed him, and he let go of his friend's arm. "What?" Nick asked. "What did you say?"

"It wasn't my fault!" yelled Mitch. "You made me say it!"

Mitch turned and stormed out before he could say anything else, and this time Nick didn't follow him.

Vince lingered in the attic after the others had left. He glared at the collection of objects before him, all aligning for a single purpose.

What Nick felt as compulsion, Vince was beginning to feel as repulsion.

When Nick returned to the attic, he seemed surprised that Vince was still there.

"Pretty cool how you figured out that it all fits together," Vince said. "But even if you get every single item back, including the harp, you're still going to be one item short. You know that, don't you?" He shifted his backpack on his shoulders. The backpack holding the battery.

Vince couldn't read Nick's expression. He might have been wary, or scared, or sad. Or maybe a little of all three. "We'll cross that bridge when we come to it, Vince."

"Yeah," said Vince. "I guess we will." And he left without another word.

# 20 LAPTOPS AND TABLETS AND PHONES, OH MY

**W**orldwide, lightning usually causes about eighty deaths and three hundred injuries per year. But the steadily increasing number of electrical storms in the past few weeks had laid waste to all previous statistics. Folks on all continents were getting fried like flies in a bug zapper. But of course, unless it happened to you or someone you knew, it registered as little more than distant thunder. Something to be filed away under "Stuff Happens."

So far, the only major entity affected by the electromagnetic weirdness was the airline industry, which experienced random navigation and telemetry issues. More than one airplane had landed at the wrong airport. In one instance, vacationers in plaid shorts and mouse ears en route to Orlando found themselves landing, with no explanation, in Honduras, where the resident rodents were more likely to give rabies than rides.

Meanwhile, the Slate household was dealing with its own electromagnetic woes: a sudden and inexplicable *lack* of power.

"Nick, get up! We're late!"

It was his dad's voice. Nick opened his eyes and reflexively looked at his alarm clock. The screen was dark.

"Power failure!" his father shouted up the ladder to him.

"How late are we?" he called down.

"No clue!"

Nick grabbed his phone, but it was dead, even though he'd left it charging. The power must have been out all night.

He quickly pulled on some pants and a shirt, hurrying downstairs with his shoes untied.

Danny ate Cheerios in the unlit kitchen. "I don't like eating in the dark. I can't see if there are bugs in my cereal."

"It's not dark," Nick pointed out. "Just dim."

"I don't like eating in the dim either."

As it turned out, no one's phone was working, so they were forced to consult Great-Aunt Greta's grandfather clock, which was always off by ten minutes—fast or slow—and thus was only slightly better than nothing.

"We needed to be in school either three or twenty-three minutes ago," Danny griped. "Can any of Tesla's stuff help with that?"

Nick shrugged. "Not any of the things we have."

"Figures."

Nick's father was running up and down the stairs and cursing as he kept remembering things he had to bring to work.

Apparently their bad luck was nowhere near an end, because when they went out to the car, it didn't start.

Mr. Slate pounded the steering wheel in frustration. "I can't even call to let them know I'll be late," he complained.

"Maybe the whole grid is down," Nick suggested, "and NORAD is out, too."

"NORAD doesn't lose power," their dad said flatly. "Even when the world was ending it didn't."

Nick could see, through the dreary, morning haze, that the lights were on in the house across the street. So their father went to use their neighbor's phone while Nick and Danny rode their bikes to their respective schools, which were in opposite directions.

Nick was usually observant, but he was so preoccupied with

thoughts of the Accelerati that he didn't notice how cars stalled when he pedaled next to them. He wasn't aware of the neighborhood lights flickering off as he approached and flickering back on after he had passed, or that traffic lights were winking out, causing near collisions.

Instead, his mind was filled with the very unpleasant prospect of having to shake Jorgenson's hand.

Mitch's prophetic blurts were never wrong. So did this mean that, to save their lives, they would have to enter a truce with the Accelerati—or worse, join them?

Nick locked up his bike, and as he walked into school, the hallway light flickered out. Then, when he went to hand his tardy slip to the Attendance Czar, all the lights turned off in the main office.

"Don't panic," he heard one of the secretaries say. And then: "That's funny, the flashlight on my phone isn't working."

That's when Nick knew. He quickly left the office. When he was farther down the hall, the lights in the office came back on, but the fluorescents above his head went out.

Deep in his head Nick could hear Dr. Alan Jorgenson's mocking laughter.

For the entire day it felt like there was a storm cloud over his head. Wherever he went, anything nearby lost power. The calculators in his math class, the SMART Board in English, all laptops and tablets and phones were entirely drained of juice.

"I don't know what they did to me," he told Caitlin during lunch, in a dim half of the cafeteria, sounding more desperate than he meant to. Here he could see exactly how far the nullifying field extended. It had a twenty-foot radius all around him.

"Don't panic," Caitlin said. "It's not like it's going to kill you."

"No," Nick admitted. "But once people figure out I'm the one causing their hardware to crash, *they* might kill me."

"The Accelerati are trying to keep you off balance, that's all."

"Well, it's working."

Caitlin took a deep breath. "You have to figure out what's doing it. There must be some sort of device or . . . ray or . . . something."

Nick looked down at his clothes. He'd already checked his pockets. He'd even gone so far as to brush his hair, on the off chance the mechanism was disguised as a fleck of dandruff.

"For all I know," Nick said, "they could have replaced my deodorant with energy-suck spray."

Caitlin smirked. "Well, it's good to know you use deodorant." Which made Nick blush only slightly.

Then she reached over and gently took Nick's hand. She didn't even hide the gesture—it was in full view of everyone. The fact that no one was looking didn't matter; it was daring in that anyone could have seen it.

"Well," she said, "whatever it is, it doesn't wipe out all electricity."

And although Nick blushed a little bit more, he didn't mind at all.


Rumors about Nick's involvement in the strange energy drain began to circulate, and before lunch was over, he was summoned by the principal. Suspicions were further verified when he entered the main office and the lights went out again.

When he opened the door to Principal Watt's office, the man looked up, smiled at Nick, and then his head promptly flopped down into the plate of Chinese food he was eating.

Having seen Vince die on multiple occasions, Nick quickly put two and two together and realized that the man must have a pacemaker. So he promptly left the way he came in.

Principal Watt soon regained consciousness, only slightly suffocated by the egg foo yung in his nostrils, but no worse for the wear.

Nick decided it was time for him to make an early exit from school.

# 21 BAGELS AND LOCHS

**F**ortunately, Vince stayed home from school that day, so he did not have to face a lethal failure of his electrical life-support system. He was still reeling from the revelation that Nick would eventually need the battery back, and the fact that Nick had known this for weeks and hadn't told him.

To date, Vince had collected several items for Nick, never knowing that each one was bringing Vince closer to his own doom. And now there was one item in particular he had to find out about, in spite of himself; one that occupied all of his thoughts—but he couldn't share that with his mother.

"You can't stay home from school without a reason," his mom said that morning.

"How about death?" he said flatly as he ate his raw vegan breakfast consisting of freshly juiced vegetables and seed cheese, a diet that delighted his mother. He had found, to his absolute horror, that his undead intestinal tract digested animal protein far too slowly. Although he still had intense cravings for hamburgers and pepperoni pizza, he had to admit it could have been worse. If he had been embalmed, he would have been left with an insatiable desire for iron-rich foods, such as liver and human brains. Knowing his mother, she would've made him eat spinach instead.

"You can't use the 'D-word' as an excuse for everything," his mother said. She crossed her arms defiantly. "If you're not feeling well enough for school, you should see a doctor."

Vince exhaled a long, heavy sigh. "There is no doctor for this, Mom. There's only one cure, and I'm plugged into it."

"We don't even know what *it* is," she pointed out.

"Which is why," Vince whispered to her, "we don't want anyone else to know, do we?"

Though she was frustrated, she couldn't disagree. So she picked up her purse and went off to work in a huff.

"I have houses to show, but I'll be back by five," she said on her way out the door. "Please don't leave me any messes."

Vince knew there was one house his mother could never show, however, for the simple reason that it was no longer there. And that particular missing house was the real reason Vince stayed home.

After downing what could have been a life-threatening dose of carrot/beet/kale juice, he left to visit the curiously vacant lot upon which had once stood an unremarkable residence. Unbeknownst to Nick, Vince had seen a picture of what could very well be the missing house. *That's* what had caught his attention in the tabloid newspaper during his and Nick's botched break-in—just before he was rendered inconveniently dead.

The house in question was an ordinary two-story tract home, perhaps with the same floor plan as Vince's, since it was in the same development. Its absence was hard to miss in the middle of a street of identical homes. There had been police tape around the property for a while, but the police had never arrived to investigate. The only investigation was conducted by a group of men and women in vaguely luminescent pastel-colored suits.

In the few weeks since the house had vanished into thin air, nothing much about the property had changed. Vince walked up the front path, which ended abruptly at a pit that went down about ten feet. The remains of electrical conduits, pipes, and a sewer line poked out of the ground, sheared off cleanly. Even the foundation was gone, as if the house was a tooth that had been extracted, roots and all.

In the backyard, things got even more interesting. Behind where the house used to stand was a detached garage. It was still there, but only partially.

Vince knew that Nick was on the premises when the house disappeared. He'd been standing right at the front door. The woman inside had possessed one of Tesla's devices, although Nick hadn't known which one.

Vince made his way around the crater to the garage. The front half of the structure had been sheared clean away, and inside he could see half of an old refrigerator, half of a lawn mower, and half of a bunch of other things you'd find in a garage. Lucky for Nick, thought Vince, that the Teslanoid Object had been positioned toward the back of the house so its field extended only to the front door. Had it been any closer, half of Nick might have been taken instead of half the garage.

Vince knocked on the doors of a few surrounding homes.

At the first few houses, no one answered. Either the owners weren't home, or they didn't want to deal with the creepy dude on their front step.

Finally one door opened for him. The woman at the threshold looked somewhat like a dried apple, with big hair the color of faded cotton candy.

"Wha'cha sellin'?" she asked, and before Vince could answer, she added, "Whatever it is, I don't need it anyway, but I've got a couple bagels in the toaster, so you might as well come in." She led him to her kitchen. "The only visitors I get," she noted, "are people who want my money."

"Is that so?" Vince asked politely.

"Including my relatives," she added as she served him the bagel with a dollop of whipped cream cheese. Vince wondered fleetingly how well he would digest it before he decided his undead intestines would just have to deal.

"Okay, give me your pitch," the old woman said, "and it better be good."

"Sorry to disappoint you, but I'm not selling anything and I don't want your money. I just want to pick your brain."

"Not much left to pick, sorry to say," she told him with a laugh. "That field's gone to seed."

Vince suspected she had more up there than she gave herself credit for. "I'd love to know about the person who owned the house," he said. "The one that disappeared."

The old woman took a bite of her bagel and chewed it slowly. "That would be Sheila McNee," she said finally. "Used to play bridge with her until she got too high-and-mighty for the rest of us."

"So you're not in touch?" Vince asked.

The old woman shook her head. "I haven't heard hide nor hair from her since . . . the incident. These strange G-men in funny suits came by asking questions. Told us her house went up in a freak quantum event." Then she leaned a little closer. "But there was nothing freak about it. It was the globe."

Vince's ears perked up. Immediately he remembered a globe at the garage sale. Metallic, with the landmasses engraved into it. He might have considered buying it himself, had the battery not been calling out to him, for what turned out to be obvious reasons.

"The globe . . ." he repeated, prompting her to continue.

"I never told them about it, if that's what you're asking. But something tells me you're the one who needs to know." She took another thoughtful bite. "She said it took her places."

"Where?" Vince asked.

"Anywhere," the old woman said, "everywhere. I thought she was nuts. Right until the day she vanished along with that dust trap of a house."

"Do you know where she might have gone?" Vince asked.

"Well," said the old woman, "she was always threatening to go back to Scotland, where she grew up. Said we Americans had grown 'a wee bit tiresome.'"

Vince took the last bite of his bagel, thanked her, and left. There was no doubt in his mind that what the woman had told him was true. And if he did have any doubts, all he had to do was take out his own copy of the *Planetary Times* and turn to page 17. Next to the article about the new alien Mafia was a grainy, blurry photograph of a suburban house, much like the other houses on this block, that had been spotted by scuba-diving monster hunters at the very bottom of Loch Ness.

Vince returned home with an uncharacteristic bounce in his step. Just because *he* knew where the globe was didn't mean Nick had to know. And as long as it remained lost at the bottom of a lake a continent away, Nick could never complete Tesla's machine.

Which meant he'd never come to Vince for the battery.

# 22 NO IDIOT

While Vince spent the rest of his day luxuriating in the secret knowledge that he was safe, Nick was trying to avoid busy intersections and hospitals and any other place where a sudden loss of electricity might be a serious problem. He was forced to take a weaving path back home.

Had he thought about the power station, he would have avoided it as well. But, as fate would have it, he rode his bicycle within ten feet of its largest transformer, which was obscured by an ivy trellis. When Nick got too close, all of the nearby homes and businesses went dark. And, with the sudden overload of stolen energy, Nick's left shoe burst into flames.

He leaped from his bicycle, rolled in the grass, ripped off his shoe, and flung it into the street—where it stalled every car that attempted to pass.

Now that the shoe was far enough away from the transformer, the area lights blinked back on. Nick approached the smoking remains of his poor Converse. Gingerly he picked it up, and he found the most damaged spot on the left side of the sole.

He bent the sneaker back, cracking the rubber open, and pulled out a small, shiny microchip that had been underfoot all day.

■ ■ ■

Getting the chip onto Nick's person had been Petula's crowning achievement of the week.

She knew she couldn't hide it anywhere in his clothes, because boys do occasionally change their clothes. She couldn't embed it under his skin, because he would have noticed the excruciating pain. Then, when they were in the attic, Nick took off his sneakers, finally giving Petula her opportunity. Shoving it into one of the soles while everyone else was watching Mitch turn into the Incredible Hulk had been a stroke of genius.

She had no idea what the chip would do when she activated it later, using a remote code.

"It won't damage him," the Grand Acceleratus had assured her. "It will just remind him that we are ever-present, and ever-watching."

After she had successfully planted the device, she reported to Ms. Planck, as instructed.

"If you continue to impress Dr. Jorgenson," Ms. Planck told Petula as they unloaded buckets of foodstuff from her minivan and wheeled them to the cafeteria, "you'll rise in the ranks in no time." Then she smiled at her. "I'm proud of you, Petula. You'll make a difference in this world."

The foodstuff, Ms. Planck explained, was pressed plankton, which took on the flavor of whatever you mixed it with.

"Isn't there an old sci-fi movie where everyone's eating pressed plankton—but it turns out to be made out of people?" Petula asked.

"Don't worry," the lunch lady said with a laugh, "people are currently much more expensive than plankton."

Petula wondered to herself if "currently" implied there would be a time when they weren't. She decided it was best not to entertain that line of thought. She concluded that if they ever did start serving people, Ms. Planck might be the first to go, since her name was halfway to plankton already.

Petula watched as the green foodstuff magically became beef ragout and chicken à la king. "It's twice as nutritious," Ms. Planck told her. "A better world through proprietary technology," she intoned. "In other words, technology that *we* own."

This was one of the Accelerati's many, many mottos.

"What do you suppose the Grand Acceleratus will want me to do next?" Petula asked, anxious for an answer, but fearing it as well.

"Whatever it is," Ms. Planck said, with a penetrating look, "you'll do it." Then she smiled and handed her a healthy portion of plankton à la king.

Theo was no idiot. He was as clever as he needed to be, when it served him to be so—and when it came to the grand buffet of revenge, Petula was not the only one in line. Theo was ready to dish himself up a heaping serving of "chow mean."

His relationship with Caitlin, which was never all that great to begin with, had finally ended, formally and officially. He was relieved, really—the world almost ending had given him pause for thought. Why cling to one girl just because she was beautiful and popular? Who needed a trophy girlfriend when he had a shelf full of actual trophies? The problem was the undeniable sense of humiliation. To be dumped for Nick Slate was unbearable. It was, as they say, adding insulin to injury. It simply could not stand.

Being a thorn in Slate's side was not enough—he had to be the entire rosebush. He had to surround Slate in so many thorny brambles that the slightest move would slash him to bits.

Theo knew there was some secret business going on with Nick. The way he always spoke in hushed whispers to his friends. The way odd things had started happening as soon as he moved into the neighborhood. If Theo could get to the bottom of it, and find some key bit of information, he knew it would be worthy of blackmail. Then he'd have Nick exactly where he wanted him.

So Theo kept his eyes and ears open, and he finally struck gold when Nick's friend Vince walked away from his locker without remembering to lock it. Once the hallway had cleared, Theo scavenged through the locker, looking for something incriminating. He hadn't really expected to find anything, because Vince was on the periphery of Nick's circle of friends. Then he saw the official-looking document that was taped inside the locker the way other people put up posters. Theo didn't know what to make of it at first, but when he pulled it out and read it, the truth became alarmingly clear.

It was Vince's death certificate.

Not a fake either, but the real deal, with an embossed government stamp and everything. Theo knew this could only mean one thing:

Zombie apocalypse.

While Nick's left shoe was bursting into flames, Theo was hiding behind a tree at Nick's house, waiting to pounce. Unfortunately, Theo had grown bored and was playing a game on his phone. When it suddenly flickered out, lifeless, as it had so many times at school that day, Theo became preoccupied with it, and Nick caught him by surprise instead of the other way around.

"Theo, what are you doing here?"

Startled, Theo fumbled his phone. It bounced off of Nick's oddly bare foot.

"Ouch," Nick said.

Nick only had one shoe on. The other was a melted mess in his hand.

"Aha!" Theo said. He wasn't sure what his *Aha!* was about, but anyone holding a melted shoe had to be up to something blackmail-able.

"If you're here to talk baseball with my dad, he's not home. Come back later. Like after the next ice age." Nick limped into his house. He tried to close the door behind him, but Theo wedged his foot in.

"You think I don't have a clue," Theo said. "But I know everything."

That satisfyingly stopped Nick in his tracks. He turned back to Theo. "What, exactly, do you know?"

And Theo pulled out his exhibit A. "One death certificate, sealed and signed by the county recorder, for—drum roll—Vincent LaRue."

Nick stepped closer, gazed at the death certificate with what seemed an acceptable level of worry, then said, "So what?"

"Isn't it obvious?" Theo said. "You're behind a zombie apocalypse!"

Nick looked at him with horror. At least Theo thought it was horror, until Nick impatiently pointed out, "You can't have a zombie apocalypse with only one zombie."

"Aha!" Theo shouted, finally having a reason to shout it. "So you admit it! Vince is a zombie!"

"Not exactly," Nick said. "Zombies rot continually. Vince only rotted once, and he's getting over it." He held up the melted shoe. "Look, I've got other stuff to deal with right now, okay?"

But Theo had Nick where he wanted him. "Of course, I could keep this whole zombie thing to myself . . . under one condition. . . ." Theo paused for dramatic effect, and then, to his own surprise, kept on pausing.

"Well," asked Nick, "what do you want?"

*What* do *I want?* Theo wondered. *What do I* really *want?*

Telling Nick to stay away from Caitlin wasn't enough. Telling him to disappear off the face of the earth was getting close, but on the other hand, what a waste of a good blackmailing that would be. The skilled extortionist could keep his prey on the end of a string like a yo-yo, yanking at will. Nick could be that yo-yo.

"Just do what I tell you," he managed, "when I tell you to do it." Theo figured that would allow him enough time to figure out what he wanted from Nick, and to learn proper blackmail skills.

Nick shook his head. "I really don't have time for this."

Then he reached into his pocket, pulled out his keys, and pushed a button on a little oval fob; it glowed soft blue. It was the only electronic device in the house that seemed to be working at the moment.

"Could I see that death certificate?" Nick asked.

For an instant Theo hesitated, thinking he shouldn't hand it over. But then the thought changed to *Why not?* There was nothing unusual about giving his one piece of crucial evidence to Nick. Nothing unusual at all. In fact, come to think of it, there was nothing odd about Vince having his own death certificate hanging in his school locker. At the moment it seemed like the most natural, normal thing in the world.

"Sure thing," said Theo, putting it in Nick's hand.

Nick's eyes scanned the document, then he folded up the paper and stuffed it in his back pocket. "Can I ask you a favor?" Nick asked.

*Why would I do a favor for you?* was Theo's first thought, but he heard himself say instead, "Sure, okay." He wondered why he said that, but then wondered why he was wondering, and wondered why he was wondering why he was wondering, and before long he was dizzy from the spiraling mental feedback and had to sit down.

"I need you to give a message to Caitlin," Nick said. "Here, let me write it on your forehead."

Nick came toward him with a ballpoint pen, but Theo shook his head and said, "No."

Nick stopped, surprised. "No?"

"You should use a Sharpie instead," Theo said. "Easier to read, and it won't come off."

"Why didn't I think of that?" said Nick, grabbing one from a kitchen counter.

"Because there are two types of people in the world," Theo put forth. "The ones like me . . . and the ones like you."

"I couldn't have said it better myself."

Nick wrote his message, which required more forehead space than Theo had, so it curved around his left eyebrow and down to his cheek. Through all of it, Theo had the nagging sensation that allowing your sworn enemy to write on your face with a permanent marker wasn't the best choice, but it was crushed by a much more powerful feeling that assured him everything was perfectly all right, and he was overthinking it.

When Nick was done, he gave Theo the key chain with the glowing fob. "Give this to Caitlin, too. Just make sure you keep it in your pocket until you get to her house." Then Nick reached over toward a laundry basket. "Oh—and can you wear this pair of underwear on your head, too?"

Theo had to admit it seemed like a reasonable request.

Caitlin was glad she was the one who had answered the door. Had it been her mother or father, she would have had a whole lot of explaining to do, because, though Theo could be monumentally obtuse, he'd never before arrived at her house wearing a Fruit of the Loom beret.

"Hi, Caitlin," he said brightly. "There's a message for you on my forehead."

Even before reading it, she knew this was Nick's doing. Theo handed her the key chain with the Accelerati's mind-numbing fob, which explained it all. She considered turning it off, but then decided the only way for poor Theo to retain his dignity was to not know he had lost it. She removed the wayward underwear, which, mercifully, appeared to be clean, and brought Theo in.

The message on his forehead, written in clear block letters, was simple. It said:

FOUND THE POWER DRAIN.

CALL YOU TONIGHT. THEO'S AN IDIOT.

"Is everything okay?" Theo asked, a little vaguely. "Because . . . I feel like things might not be totally okay, and I don't know why."

Caitlin sighed. "Everything will be fine in a minute," she said. Then she got her art supplies, sat him down, and began scrubbing Theo's forehead with paint thinner.

# 23 POWERLESS

When the power went out in the University of Colorado's Physics Building, darkening Dr. Alan Jorgenson's office, he looked up from a plate of flavorless takeout sushi on his desk. He knew that Nick Slate was now close.

Jorgenson pulled up his venetian blinds, letting in the remaining light of early dusk, and sat down. He took one more piece of bland albacore draped over blander rice, then leaned back in his chair to chew and wait. Should the boy be on the offensive, Jorgenson was well equipped to defend himself with any number of Accelerati devices at his immediate disposal. A quantum eviscerator that would transport the boy's intestines to a spot precisely halfway between the earth and the moon. A tungsten particle beam that would blast him to the Canadian border. And if all else failed, there was the old-fashioned revolver in his pocket.

His secretary came to his office door a moment later.

"I'd buzz you," she said, with the slightest cringe, "but . . . the power outage . . ."

"Yes, yes," Jorgenson said dismissively. "Send the boy in."

His secretary was astonished. "How did you know?"

"For the same reason I am *in* this office and you are outside of it, answering my calls," he told her.

She turned and left, and a moment later Nick entered.

He looked beaten. That was Jorgenson's first impression, and his first impressions were usually correct. He had an air of absolute defeat about him that made Jorgenson want to gloat, but he suppressed the urge. He'd have plenty of time for that later. Instead he continued to eat his sushi, which suddenly tasted a whole lot better. It tasted almost as fine as victory.

"What did you do to me?" the boy demanded with delicious desperation. "Why does the power keep dying all around me?"

"I haven't the faintest idea what you're talking about," lied Jorgenson. "Perhaps it's the effect of one of the inventions that you and your little playground friends have so blatantly abused."

"You did it!" Nick shouted. "I know it was you! It had to be you! Make it stop!"

Jorgenson forced a false sigh, and got down to business. "Very well. I promise that your life will return to normal, and you will continue your lackluster existence without any further interference from me . . . on the condition that you surrender all of Tesla's devices."

He watched as Nick bit his lip, considered the proposal, and then, instead of speaking, put out his hand for Jorgenson to shake.

Instinctively, Jorgenson raised his own hand, but then he hesitated. He had lost the pinkie of his right hand and it was still painful. The memory made him hate Nick Slate even more.

"You'll forgive me if I don't shake your hand," he said, displaying his bandages. "You and your father shall give us unrestricted permission to retrieve the objects in your attic, and shall cease and desist in all efforts at recovering the others. Finding those objects will be our task now, as it should have been from the beginning."

He turned and reached behind him for an expandable file

folder that was growing far too fat for anyone's good. He called it his "nuisance folder." Mostly it held things relating to Nick Slate. After briefly leafing through it, he pulled out a simple yet comprehensive agreement.

"I took the liberty of preparing this document a few weeks ago, back when I believed you'd be sensible and would agree to it without causing unnecessary strife."

When he turned back, Nick had the slightest smile on his face. Clearly the boy was relieved to have this over with.

"Here is the document," Jorgenson continued, laying it on his desk. "As you are a minor, your surviving parent must sign it also. I expect it to be delivered by hand back to this office within the hour. You shall remain . . . 'powerless'. . . until it is done."

"Of course," Nick said, and he held out his hand. "Shake my hand, Dr. Jorgenson, and I promise to do what needs to be done with that piece of paper."

Jorgenson kept his hand at his side. No doubt the boy wanted to give his injured hand a sadistic squeeze. "Just the signatures will be fine."

"I'd feel a lot better," the boy said, "with a handshake. . . ."

Now Jorgenson was getting irritated. The twilight was fading, and the room was growing dark. The sooner Nick left, the sooner the lights would return. "A handshake implies respect," Jorgenson said, keeping his hands by his side. "Need I say more?"

Nick held out his hand a moment longer, then his eyes narrowed. "Fine." He picked up the paper. "Like I said, I'll take this and do what needs to be done with it." Then he left, closing the door behind him.

Jorgenson sat back down and popped the last piece of raw fish into his mouth as the diminishing sunlight sliced through the blinds. The boy was bitter. Not a surprise—abject defeat will do that to a person.

What *was* surprising, however, was the fact that the lights in the room did not return after the boy left. Was he lingering? Jorgenson walked into his outer office, where the lights were also off, and stopped at his secretary's desk.

"Where's the boy?" he barked.

"He left five minutes ago," said the woman.

"No . . . that isn't possible. . . ." He stormed past her and into the hall.

Farther down the hallway, Jorgenson could see that the ceiling lights were still on. But as he walked closer, the fluorescents flickered out above him, matching his strides. He came to a sudden, slightly nauseated stop and he patted himself down, searching for the tiny chip. The little cretin must have found it before he arrived, and pretended not to know! Somehow he had placed it on Jorgenson—but how? The boy hadn't even touched him.

And then Jorgenson remembered turning his back on Nick to pull the document from the file . . . and the smile—no, it was a grin—on Nick's face . . . and the single piece of sushi sitting on the table between them.

That's when Jorgenson understood the chip wasn't on him. It was *in* him.

Jorgenson's wail would have registered a ten on the fury scale, had such a measuring device worked within a twenty-foot radius.

There was nothing more satisfying than outsmarting a genius. Nick had embedded the tiny chip between the limp slab of fish and rice while Jorgenson's back was turned. It was small enough, Nick hoped, to be swallowed whole. He was already on his bike, pedaling away across the lawn of the physics building when he heard Jorgenson yell from somewhere inside—indicating that the man had effectively swallowed his pride.

Now the chip was Jorgenson's problem, and Nick hoped that his digestion was nice and slow. He had heard that the large intestine could, on occasion, trap things for years. It would serve Jorgenson right!

But Nick's mission had only been a partial success. Mitch's little prophesy-belch had said that their lives could be saved by shaking Jorgenson's hand—but Nick knew how those little truth-burps worked: they implied no more than what they said. Nick didn't necessarily have to surrender to the Accelerati—all he had to do was shake the man's hand.

Unfortunately, that was going to be much more difficult than Nick had expected.

A few minutes later, when Nick felt he had put enough distance between himself and the Grand Acceleratus, he took a moment to stop at a street corner and throw the surrender document in a trash can, thereby fulfilling his promise to Jorgenson, by doing *exactly* what needed to be done with it.

# 24 RUH-ROH

**W**hen Nick arrived home, Beverly Webb was there with his father.

His life was filled with interlopers. Like last time, Beverly had come over under the pretense of bringing her son to play ball with Danny. Clearly, though, her interest was in their father.

Was it wrong for Nick to want him to stay in mourning? It had been less than four months since the fire. Sure, the woman's presence here didn't constitute a "date," but her intentions were obvious.

"I brought that stain remover, Nicky," she said.

"It's Nick," he said. "Thanks." No one called him Nicky but his mother.

He took the thing from her. It looked like an old-fashioned washboard. *Of course,* thought Nick. He remembered it and its buyer, thanks to the memory-enhancing Oolongevity tea he had drunk a few weeks ago. But the washboard had been purchased by some guy in a Hawaiian shirt.

"Be careful with it," Beverly said. "It was a birthday present from Seth—it has sentimental value."

"Uh . . . okay." Nick should have left right then—taken the thing up to the attic and made himself scarce, but he lingered a moment too long. "How does it work?" he asked.

"I don't know how it does what it does," she said, "but rub

anything against it, and it removes the stain without damaging the fabric."

That's when Seth came bounding out of the downstairs bathroom, passing Nick on the way to the stairs. Nick whipped the washboard up to hide his face, and for an instant he thought Seth hadn't seen him. But before he reached the stairs, Seth spun on his heels.

"It's you!" he said, pointing an accusing finger. "Mom, it's him!"

"Him who?" Beverly asked.

Nick had to think fast. "Him who's about to make you and Danny hot fudge sundaes!"

There wasn't an ounce of ice cream in the house, but it distracted Seth just long enough for him to say, "Sundaes?"

"Yeah!" said Nick, which gave him the time he needed to herd Seth into the kitchen and out the back door, pushing it closed behind them so no one else could hear.

"You were in our house!" Seth said. "You and your friend! I saw you both! You're burglars!"

Nick could have denied it—after all, it would be Seth's word against his—but he suddenly realized he had an ace to play.

"Fine," Nick said. "You know my secret, and I know yours."

That gave Seth pause. "Huh?"

"You forgot to get your own mother a birthday gift. She said you got the stain remover for her at a garage sale—but you never went to that garage sale. If you did, you would have remembered this house. Your father bought it, not you!"

Now Seth looked like a kid who'd been caught copying answers from his classmate. "You don't even know my father!"

"Goofy glasses? Drives a green Saturn? Likes Hawaiian shirts?"

Seth gasped. "How do you know that?"

"Oh, I know lots of things. Not just me, but my burglar friend, too. All my friends. We *all* know what you did!"

"But . . . but . . ."

"Here's what I think happened: your dad brought you back to your mom's, and at the last second you realized you didn't have a gift for her, so you grabbed the only thing you could find in his car. You didn't even know what it was, and your dad probably doesn't even know that you're the one who stole it from him."

"And I would have gotten away with it, too," moaned Seth, "if it wasn't for you rotten kids."

"So," said Nick, putting his arm around Seth's shoulder, "here's what we're going to do. We're going to keep quiet. About everything. No one needs to know about how you totally forgot your mother's birthday and stole your father's stain remover, and no one needs to know about me and my friend visiting your house the other night."

"Yeah, yeah, sure," said Seth, nodding so furiously Nick thought he might give himself a concussion. "One thing, though—why were you there?"

"Why do you think?" said Nick, holding up the washboard. "To get this back."

"Is that all?"

Nick shrugged. "That's it."

"But if you wanted to keep it, why did you sell it in the first place?" asked Seth. "That was dumb."

"Tell me about it," Nick said simply. "So are we good?"

"Yeah," said Seth. "We're good."

Then Danny came barging out the back door. "Dad says you're making us sundaes!"

"Tell you what—what if I take you both to DQ?"

"That seals the deal," Seth said, putting his hand up for

Danny to high-five. Danny obliged, because any deal that involved ice cream was fine with him.

They all ended up going out for ice cream, as if they were a family, which made Nick miserable. At least they took two cars, so Beverly and Seth could leave from there—but Nick noticed how, before she shook his dad's hand good-bye, she glanced at Nick—as if she would have given him a hug if Nick weren't there.

Once Nick got back, he grabbed the washboard and took it upstairs to the attic. Before fitting it into the machine, he couldn't resist rubbing his pomegranate-juice-stained shirt against it. It did remove the stain, just as advertised. But it did even more: the fabric wasn't just cleaner, it looked newer. Nick examined the washboard more closely. When he tilted it toward the light, it seemed to have an artificial depth, like one of those three-dimensional postcards. On a whim, he rubbed the torn knee of a pair of jeans back and forth across the washboard's surface. After five strokes, the tear was repaired.

So the thing didn't just purge stains, it undid *all* damage. It made things new. He tried to figure out how he might use it against the Accelerati, then he caught himself. He was thinking like them, and that wasn't good. Maybe he should stop messing with it and just let it take its place in Tesla's grand device.

He quickly found exactly where it went. Caitlin was right— he was getting better and better at completing the puzzle. He could intuitively see the way it all fit together—sensing not just the parts, but the whole.

He noticed something about the washboard, though, that gave him pause. Two posts extended from it; one was engraved with a dash, the other with a plus sign. Positive and negative. He knew what was supposed to be connected to those two posts.

Vince's battery.

For Tesla's machine to live, Vince would have to die.

Nick had told Vince they'd cross that bridge when they came to it, but with each object he added, the bridge came closer and closer.

Downstairs, his father was on the phone, and he could tell it was with Beverly. Hadn't they had enough of each other for today? When his father guffawed in response to something, it set Nick on edge. Did she think she could be a part of *their* whole?

He idly wondered if he could remove her like a stain, and then he laughed off the idea. But the darkness of the thought lingered.

Meanwhile, in Kiruna, Sweden, there were undocumented reports of a man's head exploding for no apparent reason.

All the police were able to piece together, besides skull fragments, was that he had been chewing on Life Savers at the time. This detail may not seem important, unless you consider the effects of triboluminescence, which is the phenomenon that makes Wint-O-Green Life Savers spark when you chew them . . . and the fact that Kiruna sits atop the world's largest deposit of iron ore.

## 25 DEEP HOODOO

For some, the failure of the University of Colorado's sewage treatment plant marked the beginning of the Colorado Springs Dark Time, as history would eventually come to call it.

In truth, however, the darkness was being distilled long before then, beneath an unremarkable downtown bowling alley. Ironically, the team of cutting-edge scientists cultivating that darkness saw themselves as luminaries—great bringers of light. Of course, the light they offered always came with hefty price tags. If the Accelerati had their way, they would control every source of energy in the world except sunlight—and if they could somehow claim ownership of the sun, they would do that, too.

As for the university's waste-processing woes, all the trouble-shooters knew was that an unexplained, traveling power outage had begun in the physics building, been tracked for a day and a half around campus, and finally settled permanently at the sewage treatment plant, where the power remained out despite the attempts of a dozen different electricians to get it back on.

The Army Corps of Engineers was called in, but by then the sewage plant had been out of commission for several days and the university was virtually uninhabitable. Classes were canceled, dormitories evacuated, and people in neighborhoods downwind were advised to stay indoors with their windows closed. There was, of course, a contingent of the population who believed that all of the things occurring in town, from the vanishing house to the near-satanic stench, were in some way supernatural. These were the same type of folk who saw the aurora and other electrical phenomena caused by the orbiting asteroid as mystical signs.

*Typical,* thought Alan Jorgenson, *that the masses would treat simple science as so much hoodoo.* He blamed the sewer stoppage entirely on Nick Slate, of course, in spite of the fact that he was the one who had put the power-draining chip in play in the first place.

Jorgenson's superior was heartily amused by the whole thing and just about laughed in his face during Jorgenson's next visit.

"The boy has something you don't, Al," the old man said, waving his nostril-offending cigar in the air. "He has innate cleverness, and the ability to think on his feet in a most inspired way."

It was difficult for Jorgenson to hide his indignation—especially from a man as observant as the Grand Acceleratus's wizened boss.

"You may be a genius," the old man said, "but intelligence is only one-third of the formula for true greatness. Perspiration and inspiration are the other two-thirds."

"Well, sir," Jorgenson said though gritted teeth, "you certainly are making me sweat, so I have two parts to his one."

The old man chuckled. "Well said—although I suspect the boy is making you sweat far more than I am." Then he rang a little bell, calling for the housekeeper. "I look forward to meeting this scrappy boy wonder." Jorgenson was sure he said that only to get further under his skin.

"That may prove impossible," Jorgenson told him.

The old man snuffed the stub of his stogie in an overfilled ashtray.

"Need I remind you that he still hasn't given us the list of missing items? And until he does—"

"I feel confident we can find the remaining items without Nick Slate."

The old man sighed. "I know your feelings on the matter, Al—but if the boy's life becomes forfeit to serve the greater good, you had better assure me that the greater good will be served."

"It will, sir. I have no doubt."

"Well, I have *my* doubts," the old man said. Then Mrs. Higginbotham arrived with a single tray holding his dinner, which put an end to their conversation.

But that was fine. In fact it was more than fine—because finally Dr. Alan Jorgenson had what he needed from the old man: grudging permission to erase Nick Slate from the equation. Permanently.

# 26 AGENT OF PANE

It is an accepted anthropological fact that people live in bubbles. Even in a modern, interconnected world, people's lives consist of the familiar, the mundane, the routine. The same circle of people, the same meals, the same TV shows, the same Web sites. To most people the "outside world" becomes a place seen only through layers of shaded glass, until it can barely be seen at all.

Although Caitlin Westfield prided herself on her worldliness, and on being above the mundane, she was a bubble dweller as well. Her life was all about the trials of middle school, her artistic endeavors, and more recently, irritating matters of the heart.

After the asteroid didn't end life as we know it, most people reacted by retreating deeper into their comfort zones than ever before. The objects Tesla had left behind, and Nick's obsession with them, made it very hard for Caitlin to do the same.

While Nick put together his puzzle, Caitlin was beginning to piece together her own. And she couldn't help but notice the various effects of the earth's new satellite.

In truth, no one could miss them, from the fabulous aurora to the nuisance of doorknob shocks. The news treated these things as minor curiosities. Even when airplanes began to have compass issues, the only reports that seemed to get aired were the ones where pilots landed at the wrong airport, which turned something potentially serious into a laughing matter.

It was while Caitlin was helping her mother with the laundry that her vague sense of concern began to congeal into true foreboding.

When she reached into the dryer and yanked out some bedsheets that had just finished their cycle, she was hit by a shock that knocked her backward into her mother and slammed the two of them against the laundry room wall.

"My God, are you all right?" her mother asked.

Caitlin wasn't quite sure. The shock had hurt more than any of the others she had received over the past few weeks. It was jarring, and for a moment she thought she might black out. In that befuddled moment she was forced to face what she had been refusing to consider.

*This could be bad.*

Danny had dragged the asteroid from the heavens, and then Mr. Slate had knocked it into orbit, turning it into a massive electrical generator, which created beautiful lights in the night sky and annoying static—but what if that static was more than just a nuisance? If the asteroid was a generator, could it be overloading?

"Caitlin, honey, talk to me! Are you all right?"

Caitlin took a deep breath, and got her bearings. "I'm fine, Mom. Just a shock is all." She carefully grabbed the sheets again. Even in the light of the laundry room, the sparks within the sheets could be seen as tiny little flashes, discharging with faint, arrhythmic snaps. "See?" Caitlin said, trying to downplay it. "Just static."

Her mother seemed both upset and a little bit frightened, but her own emotional charge passed. "Well," she said, "maybe we'll air-dry from now on."

Petula was also becoming more and more aware of the strange occurrences brought on by the asteroid in orbit. Most interesting to her was the increasing number of times kamikaze birds would fly into the glass of her living room window. It was as if the disturbance in the earth's magnetic field had caused the neighborhood bird population to lose all sense of direction.

Petula could relate—and she wondered whether she was the bird, or the pane. Surely there was the potential to be either. She could be the victim or the agent of forces unseen.

From the moment Petula became a junior pledge of the Accelerati, she knew that she was playing in a new league, with far higher stakes.

They had killed Vince. True, he was now connected to a device that made death little more than an inconvenience—but they probably hadn't known the battery existed when they placed the deadly remote in Nick's house.

They had killed an innocent harpist. True, for some reason, the woman didn't seem to mind the fact that she was being killed, but that didn't lessen Ms. Planck's act of murder.

Could Petula condone and forgive such acts? And if called on to kill with her own hand, could she do it? Petula knew, with absolute certainty, the answer to that question.

Maybe.

Petula despised the Great Maybe. She had always valued certainty, but she was coming to understand that "maybe" was a comforting answer to life's most difficult questions. It allowed one to avoid consulting one's own moral compass for as long as possible—and with the Earth now so weirdly magnetized, who knew in which direction her moral compass would point? Best to let it spin unchecked for a while.

The problem was not her indecisiveness, though. Her concern was how coldly decisive the Accelerati were. She suspected—no, she *knew*—that things would not end well for Nick if Dr. Jorgenson, the Grand Acceleratus, had his way.

"As long as he's useful to us, he'll be fine," Ms. Planck had assured her—as if that was comforting. For all Petula knew, Ms. Planck would end his life herself once he ceased being "useful," whatever that meant.

"The Grand Acceleratus already tried to kill him," Petula reminded Ms. Planck. "Nick told me so."

"Only because Nick was holding a weapon on him—a weapon that froze his arm, and left him without a right pinkie. Dr. Jorgenson can't be blamed for trying to defend himself, can he?"

It all sounded so reasonable. Petula was sure that if Nick were killed, the Accelerati would have a reasonable explanation for that, too.

There was so much for her to weigh. Being part of the Accelerati had already made her special; it could also make her great—not just in her own mind, but in the world outside of it. *Is this the price of being great?* Petula wondered. Being willing to sacrifice anything and anyone in the pursuit of greatness?

When put that way, the answer became clear:

Maybe.

On Saturday, Petula was called before the Grand Acceleratus again. Ms. Planck bowled their way in, and once more they crossed through the Great Hall overlooking a glorious vista. Today it wasn't Venice; it was a rain forest canopy.

"Try not to irritate him," Ms. Planck warned. "He's had a rough week."

As Petula and Ms. Planck strode through headquarters, the few Accelerati present noticed the heavy, gunmetal clarinet in her hands and whispered to one another, clearly knowing what it was, if not what it did. She fought the urge to show them.

She had brought the clarinet at Ms. Planck's insistence.

"Jorgenson asked for it, and he's a man who gets what he wants," Ms. Planck had told her.

She led Petula past the scowling statue of Edison and the research department, down a flight of stairs to an impressive wooden door with a brass knocker that seemed entirely out of place. But what was she thinking? *Everything* down there was entirely out of place.

Jorgenson opened the door.

"Miss Grabowski-Jones," he said. "A pleasure to see you again."

She reflexively held out her hand to shake, but he displayed his bandaged right hand.

"Sorry," she said. "I forgot." She and Ms. Planck stepped inside.

"Welcome to my private residence."

The well-appointed living room was decorated with minimalistic modern furniture, and it had large windows on three sides. Through the magic of high-definition holographics, the room appeared to be suspended ten stories above New York's Times Square.

Ms. Planck smirked. "Not following the rain forest theme? I would have thought you'd go for something more pastoral."

"That shows how little you know me, Evangeline," Jorgenson said, and then he quickly returned his attention to Petula. "Some like the tranquillity of nature outside their window; I prefer to exist at the very crossroads of humanity." He took out his phone and tapped the screen several times. With each tap the scene beyond the windows changed to another hub of civilization. The Champs-Élysées in Paris. Tiananmen Square in Beijing. The Brandenburg Gate in Berlin.

"I can be in all these places with the touch of my finger."

Petula would have been impressed by the display if Jorgenson hadn't been so impressed with himself. Yes, he was the Grand Acceleratus, but his self-importance rubbed her natural contrariness the wrong way, and she found herself saying, "Yeah, but they're just pictures."

Ms. Planck put a firm hand on her shoulder to remind her to watch herself. Jorgenson didn't seem offended, though. He took her comment in stride.

"Reality is subjective," he told her. "It can be whatever we choose it to be."

"Yeah, but they're still just pictures," Petula said again. And she reached out and brazenly tapped the CLEAR button on his phone interface. They were left in a room with a lot of windows looking at nothing but huge black plasma screens a foot beyond the glass. "It's not reality if I can turn it off," she said.

Ms. Planck squeezed her shoulder until it hurt and said, "Dr. Jorgenson, I'm sorry, she didn't mean—"

Jorgenson put up his pinkieless hand for silence, then waved to dismiss her. Ms. Planck threw Petula a disciplinary glare before she left the residence, closing the door behind her.

Once Ms. Planck was gone, Jorgenson smiled at Petula—that same moray-eel kind of smile she had seen before. "You pride yourself on being an irritation in the lining of the world," he said, his voice soft. "But we irritations eventually become the pearls. I see the pearl you could be, Petula."

It was the kindest thing that anyone had ever said to her. Was it crazy for her to think that the man might be sincere?

"I'm sorry if I insulted you," she said. "But I think pictures shouldn't just show us what we want to see—they should show the truth."

Jorgenson nodded. "Like the pictures your camera takes."

"Which are always true."

Jorgenson finally got to the business at hand. "But I see you've brought me a gift."

Petula had almost forgotten the clarinet she held by her side. "Well, it's not really a gift, since you asked me to bring it, and especially since I can't leave it with you."

His countenance took a turn toward stormy. "And why can't you?"

For the first time in this encounter, Petula became uncomfortable. "Nick gave it to me—and he'll know I don't have it anymore. He's . . . connected to this stuff somehow."

Jorgenson waved his hand again. "Nonsense. Why would he know? He doesn't know you gave us the camera lens, after all."

"Only because he has the camera it came from," Petula insisted.

"Come, come," said Jorgenson. "He's not any more connected to these objects than your mother is connected to your clothes dryer."

"Actually," said Petula, "my father does the laundry, and he always seems to know when the load is done, even before it buzzes." Jorgenson said nothing, so she pressed on. "You want Nick to trust me, don't you? I can't do anything that will make him suspicious."

Jorgenson sighed and put out his hand. "At least let me see the instrument."

Reluctantly, she gave it to him.

He examined the clarinet's many buttons and valves. "I used to play, you know."

"Marching band?"

Jorgenson's cold eyes flicked to hers. "Hardly. The Harvard Symphony Orchestra."

More self-importance. If it were anyone other than the Grand Acceleratus, she would not have tolerated it.

He positioned his good hand and his wounded one on the instrument, put the mouthpiece to his lips, and blew.

What came out of the other end was not music. It was the most horrific and distressing series of sounds Petula had ever heard. Pain could not adequately describe the experience. It made her want to rip her ears off and stomp them like cockroaches. She had played the clarinet only once herself, out of curiosity—but there must have been a sonic buffer zone for the player, because what had sounded to her like nothing more than bad music had left her parents screaming and scrambling to call 911. Now she understood why.

Jorgenson played for the better part of ten seconds, and each second seemed to stretch toward an infinity of anguish. When he was done, Petula found herself on the floor, her ringing ears still not ready to trust that it was finally over.

Jorgenson took the clarinet from his lips and looked curiously at Petula, who was struggling to recover. "Remarkable," he said. "Those were supposed to be the opening strains of *Rhapsody in Blue*, but apparently that's not what came out."

"Not even close," she said, glaring up at him. "I think Gershwin should rise out of his grave just to smack you."

Jorgenson regarded the clarinet for another moment. "Yes, this will weaponize nicely," he said, satisfied. Then he held it out toward Petula. "In the meantime, I leave it in your capable hands."

Petula stood up and took it, wondering what the catch was. In her experience, gestures of goodwill were just camouflaged favors that would one day need to be repaid. It couldn't be that he genuinely trusted her. *Nobody* genuinely trusted her—not even the members of her own family. Not even her Chihuahua, Hemorrhoid, who would always sniff the food she set out for him and look up at her as if weighing the possibility that she might be poisoning him again.

No—she knew Jorgenson's gesture came with a price. And she suspected what that price might be.

"Tell me, Dr. Jorgenson . . . what happens to Nick when you have all the things he sold in his garage sale?"

"Then we'll be done with him." He quickly added, "And you will advance heartily up the ladder here."

"Done with him how?"

He didn't answer the question. Instead he said, "Miss Grabowski-Jones, there comes a time in each of our lives when we must decide whose side we are on. Whether we are we going to serve the great cause of humanity, or wallow with the swine. You don't appear to be the wallowing type."

"I'm not," Petula said, indignant at the suggestion, but also torn, because she knew that swine are eventually slaughtered to put bacon on the Accelerati's plates.

Jorgenson, sensing her pensiveness, changed the subject. "By the way, you'll be pleased to know what we have in store for the time lens you gave us," he said. "We plan to build a telescope that we will train on the windows of world leaders. Imagine if we knew, twenty-four hours in advance, what the most powerful people in the world will be doing tomorrow!"

"It would make *us* the most powerful people in the world," she said.

"Precisely. But in the meantime, I've found another use for it." He reached up and pulled down what Petula, until now, had thought was just a weird ceiling lamp. It descended as Jorgenson tugged on it, revealing it to be the lower end of a periscope.

"Really?" Petula couldn't help but smirk. "What, are we in a submarine?"

Jorgenson grinned and tapped his phone once more, turning the vista beyond the large windows into a seascape full of circling sharks.

"Reality is what we make it," he said, gesturing to the periscope.

"Still just pictures," she said, but she moved closer to take a gander.

The periscope must have been able to pass through some undetectable spatial void in the bowling alley, because its head—which contained the time-leaping lens—was mounted on the building's roof.

Most periscopes turn, giving a 360-degree view, but this one was fixed and focused on a single magnified spot, some miles away, zeroing in on tomorrow.

Petula gasped, recognizing it right away. "It's Nick's house."

"It behooves us to know what he'll be up to, before he's up to it," Jorgenson said.

And so Petula gazed once more into Nick Slate's future, just as she had when she developed the picture that had predicted Vince's untimely death . . .

. . . and just like then, what she saw changed absolutely everything.

This time, however, she knew exactly what she had to do.

# 27 COWARDLY NEW WORLD

On the day Nick Slate retrieved the twentieth object, and added the "stain remover" to Tesla's Far Range Energy Emitter, two hundred and thirty-one verifiable instances of ball lightning were reported to the National Weather Service.

Bizarre pictures were being posted by people on every social media platform, which was not unusual—except *these* bizarre pictures featured throbbing blobs of atmospheric energy.

Ball lightning is extremely rare. So rare that for many years science refused to accept that it existed. It's no surprise that Nikola Tesla was the only scientist ever able to produce it in his laboratory.

When ball lightning does appear naturally, it can take many forms. It can be a pulsating, sparking orb of light in the night sky. It can seem to be a blinding halo atop a flagpole or lightning rod. It can look like an ethereal jellyfish with deadly high-voltage tentacles. Or it can shoot across the sky like a fireball. Small wonder, then, that its appearance has often been interpreted by some as divine. And who's to say it's not?

Perhaps, as some thought in the wake of Armageddon's near miss, a heavenly host had descended to observe these unprecedented happenings on planet Earth, and Gabriel the archangel was, at that very moment, breathing deep so he could at long last blow into his horn, heralding the arrival of Judgment Day.

Or maybe it was just a whole lot of weird lightning.

Mitch Murló could not have cared less about the massive static charge that was building in Earth's atmosphere. He did know that judgment was coming, though. It was coming for the Accelerati, and he was the one passing judgment.

Mitch had been spending his time plotting. This was a curious thing, because Mitch never plotted. He usually just went with the flow of life. He was comfortable being a follower, especially when it came to Nick, who always seemed to know exactly what he was doing, even when he didn't. As furious as Mitch had been the day he stormed away from the summit meeting in the attic, deep down he knew that Nick's choice to use Mitch's anger to get some answers was the right one.

The day that Nick was facing power-failure issues, Mitch, like Vince, stayed home sick, and he really was. He hadn't slept, and he had a splitting headache from hating too hard—when your mind is overwhelmed with the kind of caustic, concentrated contempt he felt for the Accelerati, your head begins to throb. His mom, who had to go to work, left him with Tylenol, canned chicken soup, a game controller, and a kiss on the forehead. Once she was gone, Mitch called his father.

Getting through to a prison inmate was always an ordeal, and it was especially difficult when the call was not prearranged. In the end all he could do was leave a message, and then play the latest version of *Grand Theft Psycho* to pass the time, running down pedestrians indiscriminately. No matter how many people he killed and maimed with his monster truck, though, he felt no better.

Finally, at noon, a call came in with the familiar recorded voice announcing that "a prisoner at Colorado State Penitentiary is calling collect."

"Dad, I found them," he said once his father was connected.

As calls from inmates were monitored and timed, he had to get to the point right away.

"Found who? Mitch, are you okay? You don't sound right."

"I found the creeps who did this to you. They're a secret society called the Accelerati, they wear suits made from spiderwebs, and I'm going to take them down."

There was complete silence on the line, and Mitch was afraid the call had dropped. Then he heard his father's deep strangled gasp, like he'd been holding his breath in shock while Mitch was talking.

"Mitch, don't. Don't even try," his father said. "Just forget about them."

"I can't. I won't."

"Mitch, listen to me." His father's voice was stern, sharp. "Stay away from them. They're dangerous."

"I know. I don't care."

"There are things you don't understand! You don't know what these people are capable of," his father warned.

"And they don't know what *I'm* capable of," Mitch told him.

The truth was, Mitch himself didn't know what he was capable of. He was now officially a loose cannon, and he liked that idea just fine.

While Mitch planned vengeance, Caitlin became a news junkie. She found it amazing how much pointless drivel filled the airwaves and Internet when it came to current events. So much so that important things vanished in the loud camouflage of celebrity sightings and car chases.

What Caitlin was able to tease out from the world soup offered glimpses of something very grim.

Entire flocks of geese were freezing to death, flying into the Arctic Circle instead of toward warmer climates. A record number of ships were getting marooned—not sinking, just lost at sea, unable to get their bearings and find land before running out of fuel. Power plants were going off-line with no official explanation. Not enough of them to cause a panic, but enough to raise a red flag for anyone who wasn't focused on the latest high-speed chase.

Caitlin was too distracted in English that morning to write a coherent essay on *Brave New World*. *Cowardly New World* was more like it, considering how everyone seemed to be hiding from a truth that was becoming clearer and clearer to Caitlin: it was only a matter of time before the billions of little shocks ignited the atmosphere or electrocuted every living thing on the planet.

She caught up with Nick between first and second period. His eyes were bloodshot, his manner skittish. He was filled with nervous energy. *Just like the world,* thought Caitlin. *Sparking with no way to release the charge.*

She had come to realize that he was right—it was his task to assemble the machine. But he had to hold himself together in the process.

"We can cross the washboard off the list," Nick told her. "I got it back and added it to the rest."

"That leaves twelve things to find," Caitlin said.

"We just have to keep at it," Nick said. "We'll get them eventually, I know it."

Nick treated each find like a victory in a game, but *eventually* wasn't good enough anymore. He had directed Caitlin's attention to the big picture, but now there was an even bigger picture that he didn't see. He was already obsessed with the machine—how much worse would he be if he knew they were running out of time?

"Maybe we can't do this on our own," Caitlin dared to suggest. "Maybe we need to turn this over to—"

"To who?" Nick stared at her as if she had just slapped him.

"The Accelerati? The government? No! This landed in my hands for a reason. I was meant to do this, Caitlin. *We* were meant to do this."

His manner was getting increasingly intense whenever he spoke of his place in the workings of the mysterious machine. Nick saw himself as not just the steward of Tesla's dream, but as an inheritor of it.

"I'm just saying we need help."

The late bell rang, and Caitlin had the urge to race to class. How strange that mundane things like school schedules still held sway over her life when such larger things were brewing. She resisted the desire to leave, and pressed Nick one more time.

"This is too much for us to do alone. Just promise you'll think about it."

"All right," Nick said. "I promise."

Nick resented the fact that Caitlin didn't trust him to do this himself. But maybe she was right. He wasn't all-knowing and all-powerful. When he stood close to the machine, he felt like he knew things—but he wasn't sure what those things were. It wasn't that the machine spoke to him. It was more like listening to music. Even if you've never heard the tune before, you can sense the next note. You can predict where it needs to go next. This instinctive sense inspired confidence. Maybe too much confidence. Perhaps he did need to take Caitlin's advice.

And so, during lunch, he lingered at the back of the line and approached the food counter after all the other kids had been served. He was a bit embarrassed to approach Ms. Planck after freaking out in the cafeteria for no reason the other morning, but he had unfinished business with her.

"Ms. Planck?" he said, getting her attention. Then he slipped a folded piece of paper beneath the glass sneeze-protector.

"Remember our conversation last week? Well, these are things I'm still trying to find. Anything you can do to help would mean the world to me."

Ms. Planck took the paper and carefully slipped it into her apron with a warm smile. "Of course, Nick. It'll be my pleasure." Then she gave him a double helping of lasagna.

Vince didn't have Nick's uncanny ability to figure out where things went in Tesla's invention—but it was pretty obvious to him that the globe would fit comfortably in the drum of the dryer. That would make it the centerpiece of the machine. Inconveniently, it was now at the bottom of an extremely deep, extremely murky Scottish lake. One that might or might not have a monster in it. As unfortunate as that was for Nick, it was very fortunate for Vince, who had no desire to give up his life so the contraption could be completed.

He had no idea that Nick had just unknowingly handed the Accelerati a list of every missing item. But even if Vince *had* known, it wouldn't have changed a thing. He doubted the Accelerati were readers of the *Planetary Times*. And even if they were, he doubted they would have caught the small photo on page 17 of the previous week's issue. As long as Vince kept silent, no one would know where the globe was and no one would ever complete that machine.

Wayne Slate's interest in the electrical anomaly besieging the planet was mostly limited to its effect on the photocopy machines at NORAD. He repaired the older, analog variety, much more common than one might expect at such a high-tech, cutting-edge installation. These vintage copiers transferred toner through an electrostatic charge. Thanks to the atmospheric interference, all the pages were coming out completely black.

What began to concern Wayne more than his additional workload, however, were the huge unmarked personnel carriers ferrying people into the massive stronghold under Cheyenne Mountain.

Of course, this was the government—they always knew things no one else did. But the commotion seemed eerily similar to when, only a few weeks earlier, important people had scurried beneath the mountain to hide from the end of the world.

Danny had grown up in Florida, where unexpected thunderstorms were a way of life; thus he found nothing unusual in the increased electrical activity. He actually enjoyed pranking his friends by shuffling his feet on the carpet, then sneaking up behind them and touching their earlobes, delivering a shock that would make them jump.

He knew his brother was probably involved in something he shouldn't have been, but he idolized Nick; therefore, while he sensed that Nick was in over his head, he chose to believe that Nick could handle it.

Sure, maybe there were creepy inventions doing creepy things in their creepy attic. But hadn't Nick just taken him and his new friend Seth out for ice cream? He wouldn't do that if he were in any sort of *real* trouble, would he?

So Danny continued to shock his friends and watch the non–northern lights, convinced that everything was fine and that in his next game he would finally catch a ball for real.

Through all of this, some fifteen thousand miles away, Celestial Object Felicity Bonk was growing excited—in the electrical sense. And she couldn't wait to share some of that excitement with the planet below.

# 28 A DOG THAT DIDN'T GET HIT BY A TRUCK

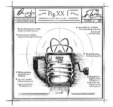

To say that the world was caught unawares would be untrue. There was more than enough evidence that Felicity Bonk was ready to go bonkers. But the aurora was so beautiful, so heavenly, that most people had a hard time believing anything could be seriously wrong.

The grounding of all aircraft due to severe navigational issues drove the reality home. A world without flight was unthinkable—almost as terrifying as a world without television—which seemed a possibility, too, because broadcasts were fading, and satellite dishes were searching for signals lost in the magnetic haze.

People had panicked when Felicity Bonk was on a life-ending collision course with Earth, but most didn't have the energy to panic again. They just waited for whatever miserable thing was coming next.

Petula Grabowski-Jones was that miserable thing.

On Sunday morning—when the first announcements were being made about the world's grounded aircraft—Petula announced herself at Nick's house with a door pounding that could wake the dead.

The moment Nick opened the door, she grabbed him and shook him, until he knocked her arms away.

"What was that all about?" he asked.

"It was coming eventually. I just wanted to get it over with."

Danny, eating breakfast, peered out from the kitchen. "Is that the weird girl with the braids? I thought you hated her," he shouted.

"Everything's relative," said Nick, which Petula seemed to take as a compliment.

Nick knew Petula would barge in and make herself at home if given the chance, so he stood in the doorway, barring entry. "What's up?" he asked.

"The harp," she said. "I know where it is."

That statement piqued Nick's interest enough to allow her in the front door, at least as far as the foyer. "So the Accelerati don't have it after all?"

"No, they do," said Petula, "but I found out where they're keeping it."

And although this was great news, Nick had to wonder, "How did you find out?"

"Never mind how," Petula said. "That's not important."

"If none of the rest of us have been able to find it, how did you?"

Petula released something between a grunt and a sigh. "Okay, fine. I was at the mall and this lady in a pastel-blue pants suit got hit by a semi."

"She got hit by a semi? At the mall?"

"In front of the mall!"

"Which mall?"

"It doesn't matter! What matters is what came flying off her shattered body." And Petula held out a pin—a tiny gold *A* with an infinity crossbar—the pin that every Accelerati wore. "When I realized she was one of *them*, I followed her."

"How could you follow her if she was killed by a truck?"

"Not her! I mean her dog! She had a dog that didn't get hit by the truck. I followed the dog."

"What kind of dog?" asked Danny, who had joined them in the foyer.

"The kind of dog that knows how to return home after their master gets run over by a truck, okay?" Petula said with increasing frustration.

"Go on," said Nick. "What happened next?"

"It led me right to the Accelerati's lair."

Nick took a long look at Petula. There was something about her that seemed both sincere and devious at the same time. He didn't know what to make of it.

"Why should I believe any of this?" he asked.

Petula reached over to shake him, but stopped, apparently realizing she had already gotten that over with. With her hands limp by her sides, she said, "Look, I know I've never given you a reason to trust me. But this time you have to. I do know where the Accelerati are hiding the harp, and we can get it back. If you don't believe anything else, believe that."

And in that moment, Nick found the scale tipping in Petula's favor. He pulled out his phone. "I'm calling the others."

He was dialing as his father emerged from the kitchen. "Did you say someone got hit by a truck?"

It was the first time that the five of them had been together since their summit meeting in Nick's attic. Now they stood in the garage, where it all began, and Nick looked at each of them in turn. Vince, Mitch, Petula, and, of course, Caitlin. Now he just had to sell them on the mission and convince them they could succeed. It would be hard, because he wasn't entirely convinced himself, but now that he knew the harp was within his reach, the risk didn't seem to matter.

"We can't just walk into the Accelerati's headquarters and take the harp," Caitlin said.

"That's exactly what we're going to do," Nick said. "They won't be expecting it—we'll have the element of surprise on our side."

"Bring it on," Mitch said, more emboldened than Nick had ever seen him.

"There's only five of us and a gazillion of them," Caitlin pointed out.

"I don't think there's all that many," said Petula. "Especially not on a weekend."

"What," said Caitlin, "are they all home watching sports?"

"Maybe," said Petula. "I mean, they must have normal lives when they're not being Accelerati."

Each of them had their defensive item with them. Vince brought the narc-in-the-box, Mitch the windstorm bellows, and Petula had gone home to get the clarinet. Nick took the frost fan down from the attic, and Caitlin brought the force-field sifter, which would theoretically make them impervious to attack. They had jury-rigged the devices with carabiner clips so they could hang from their belts, freeing up their hands. Nick couldn't help but think they looked like a pathetic pack of superhero wannabes.

Through all of this Vince had been silent. This was nothing unusual—he was a kid of few words. So the words that came out of his mouth now caught them all by surprise.

"Give me one reason why I would walk into the Accelerati's hideout and bring them my battery," Vince said. "I might as well just unplug myself now."

No one said anything for a moment. This was the first time Vince had drawn a line in the sand. Today was supposed to be a day for solidarity, but Nick found himself wanting to rip Vince's dark glasses off of his face so he could look Vince in the eyes. Then he remembered that the glasses were connected to the battery, so he couldn't do it.

"Whose side are you on, Vince?"

"I've never been on any side," he told Nick. "I just bought something in your stupid garage sale and got sucked into something I never wanted to be a part of."

Caitlin stepped forward. "None of us wanted to be a part of this, Vince, but here we are."

"Here *you* are."

"Should I smack him?" Petula asked.

"I don't think it will make a difference," Mitch said. "But smack him anyway."

Nick put up his hand to stop Petula.

"Vince," Nick reasoned, "this is a chance for you to do something that matters."

Vince shook his head. "None of this matters," he said. "I know for a fact that you'll never finish that machine!"

Nick remained calm. "Because finishing it means you'd have to die? Maybe for good?"

There. The truth was out in the open. He waited to see how Vince would react. Vince just shook his head, and Nick had the strange feeling that Vince knew something he didn't.

"You'll never even get that far," Vince said. "Trust me—even without my battery, you're screwed."

It was hard to read Vince's emotions through those dark glasses. Impossible to see where his eyes were focused. The standoff continued for a few more seconds, then Vince handed Nick the narc-in-the-box.

"I'm not going," he said. "I may be dead, but I'm not suicidal." And he left. Just like that.

"We don't need him," Mitch said.

Oddly, it was Petula who was the most perturbed by Vince's vanishing act. "But . . . but he *has* to be there!" she said.

Nick hooked the narc-in-the-box onto his belt. "Forget him. We'll do this without him."

## 29 EARWAX-DEEP

**F**ive minutes later, a pickup truck pulled into the driveway. Petula put aside her worries about Vince's unexpected departure and took everyone over to meet the driver: her cousin Harley. She engaged in a very short negotiation with him, as he would do anyone's evil, or non-evil, bidding for a price.

Once the bargain was struck, Harley drove them in the back of his pickup, beneath unsettlingly troubled skies, to a run-down bowling alley in a questionable part of town.

"Atomic Lanes?" said Caitlin. "You've got to be kidding me!"

"This is where the dog went," Petula told them as she hopped out. "Let's go inside."

Harley, who had no interest in their mission except that it had earned him twenty-five bucks plus lunch, was content to wait in the parking lot, blasting death metal—an appropriate sound track for their assault on the Accelerati.

As it was Sunday, the alley was hopping with die-hard bowlers, families, and birthday parties.

"Get shoes, pick a ball, and pretend like you're here to bowl," Petula told them.

"You're joking, right?" said Caitlin.

"We don't want to draw attention to ourselves," Petula whispered.

"Uh—we've got a fan, a bellows, a flour sifter, a clarinet, and a jack-in-the-box clipped to our belts," Nick pointed out. "How could we *not* draw attention to ourselves?"

Petula ignored him, went to the counter, and requested lane five, even though it was already taken. "We'll wait—it's my lucky lane," she said, batting her eyelashes at the disinterested clerk.

"Lane five is a secret entrance," Petula said softly to the others while they watched the other bowlers finish their game. "You have to knock down a certain combination of pins to get in."

"And you got all this from a dog?" Caitlin asked.

Petula huffed. "The dog led me to the bowling alley, and inside a guy in a pastel suit was bowling here on lane five. I stayed long enough to see two different Accelerati bowl the exact same pattern and then disappear."

"Disappear how?" asked Nick.

Just then, the bowlers ahead of them left. Petula put up her hand. "I've had it with these questions!" Instead of choosing a ball, she marched down the lane toward the pins.

"I don't think you're allowed to do that," called Mitch—but of course that had never stopped her before.

Petula bent over the pins and started knocking them down by hand, leaving a seven-ten split. Then she called back, "Hit reset!"

Nick hit the button. Petula scooted back as the pin-setter jaw came down, nearly chomping her. Once the new pins were set, she knocked down all but three and ordered another reset. Nick exchanged a glance with Caitlin, and pressed the button again.

Petula knocked down the second and third row of pins and, after the next reset, kicked them all over.

As soon as the last pin fell, to Nick's amazement, the far end of the lane began to sink, becoming a ramp into some dark, unknown place.

"Whoa," said Nick.

"Good going, Petula!" Mitch called.

"I don't believe it," said Caitlin. "No, seriously, I don't. How could she have known all this?"

"Because," said Mitch, standing up, "she's smarter than any of you give her credit for."

Nick raised his eyebrows. "I guess so."

None of the other bowlers seemed to notice the lane turning into an access ramp, or the kids walking down it. By now Nick knew the Accelerati well enough not to question it. It didn't surprise him that the secret society had a way of disappearing right before everyone's eyes.

*Smoke and mirrors,* he thought, *practically applied.* That was what Jorgenson had said to him on the day Danny caught the first meteorite.

Well, now it was time for Nick to apply some of his own sleight of hand and make the harp disappear. That is, if they could find it.

It was no secret that Caitlin and Petula did not like each other. For Caitlin it had nothing to do with the fact that Petula had a stalkerlike crush on Nick. It had to do with things like the voodoo doll Petula had made of Caitlin in third grade (which hadn't worked) and the stink-bomb shampoo she had given Caitlin in fourth grade (which had).

Caitlin had been nursing a what's-wrong-with-this-picture kind of feeling since the moment she arrived at Nick's house— but these days that was nothing new. Lately, the more appropriate question would be "What's *not* wrong with this picture?" Still, Caitlin had to admit that Petula had promised to get them into the Accelerati lair, and she did—so maybe Caitlin had misjudged her.

As for Mitch, he was proud that his girlfriend had, for once, done something helpful. And Nick? Well, his mind was already leaping ahead toward the harp.

The four of them went down the ramp to a dim hallway beneath the pin setter. About a dozen yards in, they came to an elaborately sculpted bronze double door.

"Rodin's *Gates of Hell*," said Caitlin, who knew her art. "But a different version. Interesting."

The bronze doors opened into what appeared to be a broom closet, but the room seemed to expand like an accordion with every step they took until they were in an absurdly grand, cathedral-like space, with windows that looked out over the snowcapped Himalayas—a nearly perfect three-dimensional projection.

Petula was right about something else, too: the place wasn't teaming with Accelerati. It was practically deserted.

But practically isn't completely. At the far end of the hall, two men in pastel suits were in the midst of a heated debate about time dilation. As soon as they saw the kids, they strode purposefully toward them.

"I got this," said Nick. He pulled the narc-in-the-box from his belt and started turning the crank. Mercifully, it did not play "Pop Goes the Weasel." But it did require several full turns for it to generate a sleep-inducing charge.

"Who let you in here?" asked one of the approaching men.

"Look away," Nick warned his friends. Then the clown's head on a spring popped out. The two agents gasped and collapsed to the ground, unconscious.

Nick pushed the puppet back down and latched the box again. "The harp is here. I can feel it."

"Can you feel us a map?" asked Caitlin. "And maybe some keys to get us through locked doors?"

Beyond the Great Hall there was a marble rotunda with corridors going off in all directions, like the spokes of a wheel. A stately bronze statue of a man holding a lightbulb stood in the center. Thomas Edison. The statue seemed to be pointing down one hallway. Nick could have taken that as a sign, but he doubted that a statue of Edison, Tesla's archrival, would give him any assistance whatsoever.

Then a short, plump man in a pale lavender suit entered the rotunda from one of the other corridors. He stopped short when he saw them. Nick recognized him as a member of the team that had tried to clear out his attic.

Nick held up the fan.

"The harp. Where is it?" Nick demanded.

The man hesitated.

"Don't make me use this!"

The man, who had seen what the fan could do, pointed down one of the hallways with a shaky finger.

Nick dispatched him with the narc-in-the-box, and they went down the hall until they got to a door labeled RESEARCH AND DEVELOPMENT.

The room was empty except for a crate in the middle already marked with a shipping label.

"New Jersey?" said Mitch, reading the label. "Why would they send the harp to New Jersey?"

"We don't know it's the harp yet." Nick unlatched a side of the crate and pulled it open. The harp was indeed inside, secured by some sort of magnetic restraint, which seemed extremely complicated, except for the switch labeled OFF. Nick turned it off, and the harp was free for the taking. It seemed so easy, Nick half expected an Indiana Jones kind of booby trap—like poison-tipped arrows shooting from the wall—but nothing happened.

"Don't pluck the strings!" Petula warned. "We don't know what they do."

"It has no strings," said Mitch.

Caitlin leaned toward it. "No—look closely."

Nick did so and still couldn't see any strings, but as soon as he started to shift his eyes away, he saw them. Not so much strings, but lines cutting vertically through space—invisible in a direct line of sight.

With Caitlin checking that the coast was clear, Nick and Mitch carried the harp out into the hallway and toward the statue of Edison—but there were six passageways converging on the rotunda, increasing the chances that they would be spotted. Sure enough, a group of men and women in pastel suits were coming down a hallway to the left.

Various shouts of "They've got the harp!" "Stop them!" and "Call security!" erupted.

"I got this one," Mitch said. He put down his end of the harp and planted his feet apart like a police officer about to take out a perp. He aimed the bellows and pumped the handles together, expelling a single blast of air down the corridor.

Within the confines of the hallway, it didn't create a mini-tornado; instead, it turned the passage into a wind tunnel. The multicolored gaggle were blown off their feet and so far back down the seemingly endless hall that they ceased to be a concern.

Nick considered the six entrances and couldn't remember the way to go. He couldn't even remember which way they had just come.

Caitlin read the look on his face and said, "It's this way, to the right of where Edison's pointing."

But the Accelerati were now alerted to their presence, and three more agents ran toward them from that hallway.

Petula took the initiative this time. "Fingers in your ears," she ordered. "Earwax-deep!"

Even with their ears plugged, they could still hear the horrific sound of the clarinet as Petula began to play. For Nick it was definitely the most unpleasant auditory experience of his life. Like steroid-infused nails on a chalkboard. Like microphone feedback injected directly into his brain. It made him weak in the knees—but with his fingers in his ears, and the bell of the instrument aimed down the hall and not at him, he and the others were able to withstand it. The approaching Accelerati were not so lucky. They were hit with the full force of Petula's soul-searing solo just as they entered the rotunda. They fell to the ground, clutching their heads in agony.

Nick grabbed the harp again, and Caitlin, who was closest, took the other end. They moved as quickly as they could. But as they reached the Great Hall, Nick realized they were one person short.

"Where's Mitch?"

Mitch hadn't come for the harp. He had a much more personal agenda. While Vince was powered by a long-life battery, and Nick was powered by his growing connection to Tesla's machine, Mitch was driven by something else entirely.

It had begun as a furious desire for vengeance when his father was wrongly imprisoned. Back then Mitch had no idea who to take vengeance on. When he learned it was the Accelerati who had used his father and tossed him away, his first wish was for all of them to suffer for the suffering they had caused his family. But Mitch's need for revenge had evolved. It was more important, he realized, to clear his father's name. And to make sure he received adequate compensation for the year of his life lost to prison. Seven hundred and fifty million dollars' worth of compensation, perhaps.

In the rotunda, while the other kids were focused on the harp, the clarinet-smacked Accelerati were scrambling away like the cowards they were. Mitch grabbed one of them before he could escape, and pushed him hard around a corner.

Mitch was not the biggest kid, but he did have the inertia of a few extra pounds. That, coupled with the keen focus of intense purpose, made him a force to be reckoned with.

Before the man could protest, Mitch shoved the tip of the bellows into his mouth, and the guy's eyes went wide.

"I'll bet you can guess what this does," he said. "Let's just say, a single pump and you'll blow up like a parade balloon. But since you're not made of rubber, you'll probably just go *pop*."

"Gwat goo oo gwant?" the man said, his words garbled by the large nozzle in his mouth.

"Where's the money?" Mitch asked. "The seven hundred and fifty million you guys framed my father for!"

The man shook his head "Gign't grame him . . ."

Mitch tightened his grip on the bellows handle. He wasn't bluffing, and the man knew it.

"Ro-kay, Ro-kay, I'll grell oo!" the man slurred.

"Then go ahead and tell me," Mitch said. "You've got three seconds."

"Brandon Gunther's alligator!" the terrified Accelerati member said. "Grinthon! Grinthon! Brandon Gunther's alligator." Then he knocked the bellows from his mouth and scrambled away, escaping down the hallway.

"Wait! What does that mean?" Mitch called after him.

What he'd said made no sense and that infuriated Mitch, so he pumped the bellows at him as he ran, but the wind just blew him farther down the hallway, aiding his escape.

Mitch would have gone after him, but Nick arrived and grabbed his arm.

"What are you doing? We've gotta get out of here!"

"Grinthon!" Mitch screamed. "Brandon Gunther's alligator!"

Nick looked at him like he was crazy, and now Mitch was wondering if maybe he was.

In the Great Hall, the few Accelerati who were present on a Sunday morning—and still had the nerve to face the enemy—made their stand. There were about ten of them. Nick didn't recognize a single face. *How many Accelerati are there, in how many cities?* he wondered; all living normal lives, like Petula had said, while secretly devoting their brainpower to the secret society. How could he ever hope to defeat a force so large and unseen? Well, if he could defeat the ones he could see in front of him right now, that would be enough for today.

A few of them raised weapons, and though Nick didn't know what those weapons did, he knew they would be "elegant," as Jorgenson was so fond of saying. The technology might artistically turn them inside out, or make them grow a third arm that would strangle them, or maybe convert them at a molecular level into a precious metal that the Accelerati could sell at a huge profit. In any case, the weapons would leave Nick and his friends elegantly dead.

"Force field!" Nick shouted.

Caitlin must have practiced at home, because she knew exactly what to do.

"Stay close!" she said, and she began cranking the handle on the flour sifter for all she was worth.

Nick suspected that if it were attached to a source of electricity it could create a truly impressive field. Hand-cranked, it created a barrier just large enough to protect the four of them. One of the men fired, and the bullet—or whatever came out—hit the force field and ricocheted, shattering one of holographic windows and ruining the illusion that they were in the Himalayas.

Nick's crew pushed forward together, toward the door, but as they did, Caitlin tripped over one of the coffee mugs dropped by the first two agents. It was just a slight stumble, but it was enough to jar her hand from the sifter crank, and the force field failed. With no time to think, Nick grabbed the fan and turned it on full blast.

The Accelerati reacted immediately, racing away before the cold front could hit them. Only one remained, and all he did was turn around—which seemed odd, until Nick saw that he wore the strangest thing on his back: a curved body-size shield that looked oddly like a tortoise shell. It was as if the Accelerati, in their underground lair, were turning themselves into mutant turtles of the ninja variety. Nick didn't want to even consider what that was all about.

He kept the fan aimed at the tortoise shell so the Accelerati on the other side wouldn't turn around.

"Go!" Nick shouted to the others, and they carried the harp through the doorway. As soon as they were in the clear, Nick hurried after them, slammed *The Gates of Hell*, and aimed the fan at the doors, icing the hinges so the doors couldn't open.

"Well, it's happened," Caitlin said, looking at Rodin's massive bronze doors. "Hell has finally frozen over."

The lack of a sizable force of Accelerati in their Colorado Springs facility had nothing to do with it being Sunday. In fact, Sunday was usually a day when their subterranean mecca thrived with activity. There were experiments, research, theoretical discussions, and, of course, Sunday brunch—which always featured a buffet of genetically modified species of unique flavor, which would eventually find their way into the global food supply.

One reason so few Accelerati were in their headquarters that day was due to the electromagnetic trouble that was growing beyond anyone's ability to ignore it. Even the world's most skilled deniers could no longer keep their heads in the sand.

The Accelerati were monitoring the exponential growth of static, magnetic anomalies, misdirected birds, and unplanned electrocutions. They had been secretly called upon by the Federal Aviation Administration to troubleshoot the navigational nightmare that had grounded the world's aircraft. This was more of a challenge than usual, because in other cases when the Accelerati were called in to solve a problem, they were the ones who had created the problem in the first place—and already knew the solution, making themselves appear more than just brilliant, but almost magical.

But, as Dr. Alan Jorgenson once pointed out to Nick Slate,

there was no magic involved, only scientific illusion. Smoke and mirrors, practically applied.

On that Sunday, some of the Accelerati were gathered in government think tanks, trying to puzzle their way out of the problem. Others were in the field, monitoring the levels of magnetic and electrical disturbances. Still others were negotiating for hiding spots in the deepest levels of NORAD, which was packing in high-level hiders trying to escape yet another end of the world.

This was the state of things when Harley Grabowski drove Petula, Nick, Mitch, and Caitlin back to Nick's house with the harp, no questions asked. Clearly the instrument was low on the list of contraband his vehicle had hauled.

In the open back of the pickup, it was hard to ignore the skies above, which were billowing with strange purple clouds that didn't have anything to do with rain. The clouds strobed with deep flashes, and occasionally lightning shot out—but the sound the bolts made was nothing like thunder. It was more like the hiss of a thousand snakes.

"I think we're in trouble," Caitlin said as the snapping and hissing from the sky grew louder.

But Nick was still too focused on the task at hand. "We have the harp—let's deal with one thing at a time."

"You can't ignore what's happening, Nick. Look at the sky!"

"Well, what do you want me to do about it?"

At that moment Mitch said something they had known for weeks but hadn't wanted to say out loud. It was a simple statement of fact. "This is because of us," he said. "All of it."

But Nick knew what he really meant. This was because of *him*. Nick was the one who had opened this world-changing Pandora's box. Well, how was he supposed to know? How could he possibly have foreseen what would come from a simple garage sale? "Just because it's worse than we thought, that doesn't mean the machine can't fix it. That's what it's for!" Nick said. "We have to complete the machine."

"What if we can't?" Caitlin asked.

He wanted to lash out at her. She had to *stop* making him *think*.

He looked up to the sky, if only to avoid Caitlin's gaze, which at the moment seemed all-seeing.

What he saw above was enough to shake him to his core.

There were still a few patches of blue sky through the building veil of smoky clouds, and now, through one of those patches, he caught sight of the orbiting asteroid. An object fifty miles wide might sound huge, but it wasn't by cosmic proportions. In daylight it could barely be seen from Earth—it was just a tiny gray dot in the sky. But now that dot was emitting menacing spiderlike sparks. That's when the truth finally hit home.

*He was too late.*

Yes, he had caused this; yes, he was also meant to fix it; and yes, the machine was the solution . . . but the machine wasn't finished.

He looked to the objects strung on their belts, but even with all of them, plus the harp, there were still too many missing parts. In spite of their victory against the Accelerati, in spite of all he had achieved, Nick felt useless—

—as much of a failure as when he had emerged from his burning house and realized that his mother was not behind him. He felt as helpless as when he'd seen the windows explode and the porch collapse and he knew there was no way to change what was happening. He had failed then.

And he had failed now.

∎ ∎ ∎

For Mitch, just a glimpse of the big picture was enough. He found it easier to deal with the more immediate problem of the Accelerati.

Freezing *The Gates of Hell* had barely even slowed them down. Three pearlescent SUVs were now in hot pursuit.

Everyone was in the pickup bed except for Petula, who was sitting comfortably in the cab with her cousin. Mitch pounded desperately on the rear window of the cab. "Can't he go any faster?" he yelled.

But Petula gave him the universal hand gesture for "I can't hear you," because the car radio was blasting death metal. As for her cousin, he was the definition of oblivious.

Nick was still staring at the sky; Caitlin was still watching Nick. Neither had even noticed that the Accelerati were gaining. And Mitch saw this as his opportunity to make up for all the times his actions had created more problems than they had solved.

He took the bellows, aimed it in the direction of the approaching vehicles, and began pumping the handles together, expelling wind at break-force velocity.

Wind—even at high speeds—behaves in very predictable ways. Hurricanes always turn in the same direction. Warm fronts meeting cold fronts form thunderstorms. And supercell storm clouds filled with violently shifting warm and cold air lead to tornadoes. One might not be able to predict how strong a force of nature will be, or on which path it will wreak its particular brand of havoc—but its basic behavior is as predictable as rain.

Not so for man-made wind. The bellows, which had not had millions of years of field-testing like the earth's standard weather patterns, was a loose air cannon, so to speak. There was no telling what it would do.

Its effect was cumulative, building with each pump of its

bladder. A single blast could create a stiff wind capable of blowing people down a hallway, as Mitch had already witnessed. Two blasts could create a gale that would capsize a sailboat. Not even Tesla himself knew what three blasts could do. But Mitch Murló was about to find out.

The first blast did little more than blow a Smart car off the road, clearing the way for the Accelerati. The second blast made a dust devil that the Accelerati handily circumnavigated.

The next blast was the charm. The closest SUV flipped into the second one, the third one was blown into the plate-glass window of a furniture shop—and now, in the middle of the street, there swirled an angry orphan tornado. Unlike a real tornado, it did not connect to the troubled clouds above; it was self-contained and self-sustaining, sucking in everything around it until its churning wind was dark with debris.

Pedestrians scattered, cars ran off the road to avoid it, and to his chagrin, Mitch realized that once again his actions had created more problems than they had solved.

Meanwhile, in a seemingly unrelated incident, a house filled with 437 miniaturized cats was struck by one of the many stray lightning bolts from the problematic sky. The energy from the strike did not electrocute anyone, but it was precisely the amount needed to destabilize the miniaturization process. Instantly, each cat expanded to its original size. The effect was not unlike a bag of microwave popcorn, if every single kernel popped at exactly the same instant. And if every single kernel was a cat.

Windows blew out, doors flew off their hinges, and cats exploded outward, filling the street like a plague.

As luck would have it, a freestanding tornado just happened to be sashaying down that particular street at that particular moment.

Of the 437 cats, 436 were drawn up into the tornado.

The last one remained in the crazy cat lady's arms. She watched the tornado pass, decided enough was enough, and promptly returned to the kitchen to open a single can of cat food for her only kitty.

Charles Fort, the man who, among other things, had coined the term "teleportation" in the early 1900s, kept a catalog of bizarre true events. Among the strange phenomena he recorded were reports of salmon and frogs raining from the skies in otherwise normal, peaceful towns. The theory was that these poor creatures were in the wrong place at the wrong time when a tornado or waterspout visited their particular body of water, sucked them up as if through a straw, and spit them out. Witnesses were torn as to whether this was a sign of judgment upon them, a gift from heaven, or simply one of God's many practical jokes.

As Charles Fort was a contemporary of Nikola Tesla, it wouldn't be farfetched to speculate that some of the odd events were caused by the inventor.

If Mitch had given a fourth blast, the tornado might have developed enough muscle to do major damage. In its current form, without a massive supercell to feed the funnel, it was more a curiosity than a disaster.

Had Charles Fort been alive today, he would have had plenty to write about.

Through no small coincidence, Theo Blankenship was out on the street at the time, trying to capture some freaky lightning pictures to share on Krapchat, when he witnessed and video-recorded the unexpected feline Rapture.

Now the disconnected tornado was a swirling, yowling mass of fur, throwing cats left and right at panicking citizens—which thrilled Theo, because this was bound to get him tons of likes and spice up his social media presence.

He recalled seeing a TV movie like this once, in which a tornado became infested with sharks. But that, of course, was ridiculous.

Also through no small coincidence, Ms. Planck was on the rooftop of her town house, sent there by the Accelerati when they realized that the kids who took the harp were heading in her direction.

In her hands was a significantly modified sniper rifle. She silently cursed Petula, for this was surely a betrayal, and she silently cursed Jorgenson for being absent when he was needed most.

Now she was the last line of defense, and as the pickup with the kids and the harp roared closer, she looked through her scope and leveled her aim.

Anyone else might have targeted the driver, but Ms. Planck knew that he was unimportant. It was the ringleader who needed to be taken out. And so she took aim at Nick, waited until she had a clear shot, and pulled the trigger.

At that very moment, however, a rogue tornado hurled a very disoriented calico at her. It dug its claws into her shoulder, forcing her arm to jerk just as she fired, which caused the bullet to miss Nick and strike an innocent bystander instead.

Theo was that bystander. Much like the aforementioned salmon and frogs, he had a particular talent for being in the wrong place at the wrong time. Fortunately for him, the projectile was of Accelerati design. It was not intended to kill, only to alter the target in a very specific way.

The shell was an antidimensional round, which effectively

removed the z-axis from any object or individual it struck. In other words, it rendered three-dimensional objects two-dimensional. To any observer, Theo now appeared to be little more than a projection on the concrete wall behind him.

Theo found this perplexing, but not entirely unpleasant. While others might have considered it a major inconvenience, Theo could adapt. Because, when it came right down to it, depth had never been one of his personal strengths anyway.

By now, Harley Grabowski had finally noticed the state of affairs outside of his limited worldview. He panicked, careening in and out of traffic to avoid the tornado, which was coughing up extremely miffed cats in all directions and showed no signs of stopping. Petula tried to keep him focused on getting to Nick's house, while in the truck bed, Nick and Caitlin clutched the harp tightly, attempting to keep it—and themselves—from being flung out of the pickup.

At the very back of the truck, Mitch kept his eyes locked on the twister. This was his fault. He had set the winds in motion—he had to be the one to stop them. So he climbed over the swerving tailgate just as Harley abandoned the road, jumping the curb, driving into Memorial Park, and mowing down Tesla's lonely memorial marker in the process.

"Mitch! What are you doing?" shouted Nick.

"Fixing my own mess!"

Bellows in hand, he leaped.

At that same moment, around the world, the effects of the building electromagnetic charge were reaching what could only be described as biblical proportions. In San Antonio, Texas, the bats of Braken Cave, which was supposedly the largest bat cave in the world, took to the air at noon, thinking it was twilight.

They were even more disoriented than birds, and so, instead of flying out of the cave in their normal swarm, they flitted around San Antonio in frustration and began biting the population.

In Sydney, Australia, a hailstorm began to pelt the streets. It might not have been so bad, except that the hailstones were coated in magnetically charged atmospheric particles, which discharged as they hit the ground. The effect could most accurately be described as "burning hail."

In Greenwich, England, where the world clock kept global time down to the millisecond, the official keepers of time were baffled, and more than a little bit frightened—for time had very literally stopped, or at least was on an extended vacation.

And in Colorado Springs, residents were trying to wrap their minds around a plague of cats.

The doomsayers who saw everything as a sign insisted that judgment was upon them—but if this was indeed Judgment Day, then Nick, Caitlin, Petula, and Mitch were the Four Horsemen of the Apocalypse. And a fifth was waiting at Nick's house.

# 31 THE GODS OF POWER

**V**ince had gone home to mull the state of his "life," but he soon returned to Nick's house and was waiting on the doorstep. He watched the skies with the same simmering dread as the rest of the world. Usually he loved electrical storms, but that kind of storm comes and goes. This one just came and promised to keep on coming.

He wondered if he should stand out in a field and attempt to be struck by the strange sizzling lightning. Maybe it would supercharge his battery. On the other hand, it could make it explode. He decided it was best not to try that particular experiment.

No one bothered him as he sat there. Nick's father, in spite of the weird weather, was out back, gardening, and Nick's little brother was nowhere to be seen. So Vince was where and how he liked to be: alone with his thoughts.

Today, though, his thoughts were poor company.

While he was not a team player, he could not deny that he had begun to feel like a part of Team Nick, which really ticked Vince off. It was hard to be a lone wolf when the pack kept drawing him in.

Vince rationalized that if Nick and the others didn't return, his presence wouldn't have made a difference anyway. But he had a hard time making himself believe that. Therefore, when he saw the rusty pickup truck turning into the driveway, he was so relieved he did something he rarely did. He actually smiled.

He didn't apologize when Nick saw him. Instead Vince just said, "C'mon, I'll help you with the harp."

There was an awkward moment when Vince actually thought Nick might refuse his offer. Then Nick said, "You were right, Vince. It's over. We risked our lives for this thing, and it doesn't even matter."

Under different circumstances, Vince might have offered a morose "I-told-ya-so," but the moment called for something else. Something equally depressing, but more helpful.

"So what?" Vince said.

Nick looked at him for a moment, not sure what to make of it. "Didn't you hear what I said? The sky is about to explode, and the only person who can do something about it went nuts and died, like, seventy-five years ago. Tesla isn't going to save us, and his machine will never be finished."

"Yeah, it's a lost cause," Vince said, "but everything in the world is a lost cause when you think about it, right? We all die, the sun eventually goes supernova, and the Milky Way collides with Andromeda. And don't forget that all of the stars in the billion billion galaxies will wink out of existence one day."

"Vince," said Caitlin, "you ever think about writing greeting cards?"

"I'm just saying that if we stopped fighting for lost causes, where would we be?"

Nick took a deep breath and nodded. "We'd be worse than lost," he said. "Let's get the harp up to the attic."

Petula, meanwhile, had concluded that making the future happen was a royal pain.

Precisely twenty-four hours earlier she had looked through

the time-bending periscope and had seen herself—along with Nick, Vince, and Caitlin—dragging the harp toward Nick's front door. The lens did not lie, so the harp's arrival here was inevitable.

Mitch was not present in the image, which meant that if he didn't leave of his own accord, Petula would have to find a way to *make* him leave to fulfill the future that she knew would happen. Or that she knows will have happened. Or that she had known was going to be happening.

*Grrrrr!* She hated seeing through that lens. The tenses alone were enough to make her want to kick out someone's spleen.

But when she exited the truck at Nick's house, she was delighted to see that, somewhere along the route, Mitch had apparently fallen out, solving the problem for her. It was nice that the universe had, for once, taken care of the future without making her do all the heavy lifting.

Meanwhile, in a sketchy part of town that was getting sketchier by the minute, Mitch stalked an irascible twister. It appeared to have a life of its own, getting neither stronger nor weaker. It was its own perpetual motion machine.

At one point, it began to double back and approach Mitch; then it seemed to stall, spinning in place, as if inviting a standoff. Mitch was ready. He raised the bellows.

A bellows, Mitch knew, didn't just expel air. It took in air as well, albeit much more slowly—and he guessed that if he pulled the handles of the bellows apart with the same force he had used to push them together, maybe, just maybe, he could reverse the process.

He stood in the middle of the road, amid panicking drivers and pedestrians who were barely able to comprehend the rain of cats and were probably expecting dogs to follow.

As he looked at the swirling wind, he was struck by a thought. In a sense he was looking at himself—not that he was filled with angry flying cats—but he knew what it was like to have all of his thoughts and feelings spinning out of control.

And that's when he realized this tornado wasn't just a random churning of wind. The bellows—like so many of Tesla's devices—tapped into something inside of the user. The bellows had reached into his soul and pulled out the cyclone that churned within him. Perhaps, he thought, if he could wrangle the one, he could wrangle the other.

As the tornado neared him, he took a deep breath, trying to calm himself. He put aside thoughts of the Accelerati and his father. He put aside thoughts of all the times he had fouled things up. Then he began pulling the handles of the bellows apart, filling the bladder with the tempestuous wind.

Once. Twice. Three times.

Like before, the third time was the charm. The tornado collapsed into a lazy eddy, and Mitch found himself buried beneath a veritable dog pile of cats.

As the wind stopped, the roiling turmoil inside him became still. The cats, dizzy and more than ready for a warm windowsill, staggered away. With all the other noise cleared from his mind, Mitch could hear the ring of truth. And it explained everything.

*There are things you don't understand,* his father had said of the Accelerati. Well, not anymore.

Nick, Vince, and Caitlin struggled to get the harp up the walk to Nick's front door, while Petula seemed more than happy to supervise without actually lifting a finger. To Nick the harp felt increasingly heavy as they maneuvered it. It was probably just because his arms were tired after having carried it out from the

Accelerati headquarters—but at this point he wouldn't put it past Tesla to imbue the thing with some sort of variable density that changed inversely to the exhaustion of the people schlepping it. It wobbled in their arms as they moved it toward the front door and began to tip. Caitlin reached up to balance it.

"Careful!" yelled Petula.

But Caitlin's hand accidentally brushed the strings, and Nick felt the vibration deep within himself. The feeling was both pleasant and unpleasant at once. Like a sudden chill up his spine, but warm. As it reverberated he could feel more than see a deeper perspective, a larger picture.

What happened today would be important. And it could go either way. There was no predetermination to Tesla's plan—just a series of probable outcomes. And today's probability was simple. It was no more complex than the flipping of a coin. Fifty-fifty. Reality, as they knew it, was going to change. Things could turn out very well, or horribly wrong. To see it in such simple terms was sobering—and heartening, because it meant he hadn't lost. Not yet!

"Never lose hope until the last pitch is thrown," his father often said, for with him, it was always about baseball.

His father!

Vince had told Nick that he was out in the backyard—and in that moment of clarity, Nick knew he needed to protect him, once more, from a reality he was not prepared to accept.

"Caitlin," Nick said, "can you go out back and check on my dad? Make sure he doesn't come into the house right now . . . and just make sure that he's okay."

He thought she might ask him what he meant, but she didn't. Instead she unclipped the flour sifter/force-field generator and handed it to him. "For lost causes," she said.

In spite of their dire circumstances, Nick found himself smiling. "Thanks, Caitlin. For everything."

Then he did something that not even he was expecting. He kissed her. It was just a quick peck on the cheek, but it carried with it a spark that was more than just static buildup.

"Ouch," she said reflexively, then she touched her cheek, laughing.

"Sorry," Nick said, although he wasn't sorry at all.

Caitlin strode off quickly, not wanting Nick or the others to see her blush. Mercifully, Petula had been looking the other way, almost as if she had known the kiss was coming, but Vince stared with a creepy, detached amusement that had nothing to do with being undead.

She found Mr. Slate in the backyard, digging—but he wasn't exactly gardening. He was in the process of unearthing a huge steel slab.

At least it looked like steel. Stainless, perhaps, because although it had been buried in the ground, it showed no signs of rust. Mr. Slate had exposed about eight feet of it—enough for Caitlin to see that it was more than a slab, it was the top edge of a band of metal, over a foot wide and slightly curved. The thing was so big that he hadn't found the bottom yet.

"Hi, Caitlin," said Mr. Slate, not looking up from his work. "I keep thinking just one more foot and I'll get to the end of it, but it keeps on going."

Following the curve with her eyes, Caitlin suspected that the band formed a perfect circle around the house.

"Now it's a mission," Mr. Slate said cheerfully.

Caitlin looked at him curiously. There was something about him that troubled her—and when he finally glanced at her, she saw something in his eyes that troubled her even more. She'd seen that vague gaze before. Meanwhile, up above, lightning arced between two clouds, oscillating like a jump rope.

"Mr. Slate," she said, "you shouldn't be digging around something metallic. I mean, look at the sky."

"Yes." He looked up, noted the massive sparks that volleyed between the clouds, then adjusted his baseball cap. "Beautiful, isn't it?"

"But . . ." Caitlin couldn't understand how the man could be so blasé, as if there was nothing unusual at all. . . .

She gasped when she realized the reason, and she turned back toward the house. "Nick!" she yelled, running. "Nick! Don't go in the attic!"

But Nick was already there, pulling the harp through the trapdoor.

Vince pushed from below as he climbed the spring-loaded attic ladder, lifting his end of the harp through the opening. "So where does it go?"

Nick knew with a single glance. "Move the weight machine to the side."

Vince took a deep breath. "Okay." He rolled up his sleeves, put his hands on the weight machine, and pushed with all his strength. The machine didn't budge.

"Oh, right," said Nick. He reached over and turned the weight machine on. "Now try."

Vince easily slid the machine out of the way then, and Nick put the harp into place. It actually clicked into position, fitting perfectly up against the tall stage lamp.

Nick dragged the weight machine back so that its handles gently grazed the invisible strings of the harp. He could feel the resonance within him as those strings began to vibrate. But the vibration felt off somehow. He could sense a gaping absence at the center of the machine, the void left by the items still missing. He could reconnect the fan, bellows, and other items they had used in their assault on the Accelerati, but that wouldn't change the fact that the core of the machine was mostly hollow. The completion of Tesla's great design was so close, and yet was only as close as the farthest object. Wherever that was.

It was painful to be this near to completion. So painful that his head hurt. But it hurt a whole lot more when he was hit from behind and knocked out.

The clarinet was a heavy thing. Much heavier than an actual instrument. Perhaps that's because it was made of a cobalt-molybdenum alloy. Not a conductor's choice for an orchestra, but superb as a conductor of electricity.

The Accelerati had wanted to weaponize it, but at the moment it was good enough as is. Good enough for clobbering Nick over the head, anyway.

Petula hoped she hadn't cracked his skull. She had practiced on some melons at home, and found the perfect combination of vector and force that would dent the melon without cracking it. She had to trust that Nick's melon offered a similar level of resistance.

"Hey," said Vince, a bit slow to react, "what are you—"

Petula ripped the sunglasses from his face, disconnecting him from the battery in his backpack. She wondered with an unpleasant shiver whether ending the life of someone who had already died multiple times could still be considered murder. Well, it wasn't something she could stop to think about now.

She lifted the backpack from his shoulders as he dropped. She hadn't expected Vince to fall down the attic ladder, but he did—picking off Caitlin, who had been on her way up.

"A twofer!" said Petula.

"Petula! Help!" Caitlin screamed from below, clearly not yet grasping the full extent of the situation.

"The Lord helps those who help themselves," Petula said. Then she yanked up the spring-loaded attic stairs, slammed the trapdoor shut, and wedged the broken baseball bat through the spring so the stairs could not be pulled open from below. Now Caitlin and the re-dead Vince were locked out, and no longer her problem.

When she turned, Jorgenson crawled out from under Nick's bed, like the proverbial monster.

"Well done," he said as he stood up, towering over her. "Very well done."

While Jorgenson examined the machine, Petula checked Nick's pulse. He was out cold, but still alive. His head wasn't even bleeding. Score.

Jorgenson regarded the invention with awe. "It was right under our noses all along. I was up here, but I didn't see it for what it was." He looked at Petula with very nearly the same regard. "I'm sorry I ever doubted you."

Twenty-four hours and five minutes earlier, when Petula had looked through the time-bending periscope and had seen them dragging the harp toward Nick's front door, she knew there were only two possible scenarios:

Either she would betray the Accelerati, as it had appeared she was doing . . .

. . . or she could play the situation to her personal advantage.

Then the periscope had revealed Nick giving Caitlin that awful little kiss, and she knew there was really only one choice.

"What do you see?" Jorgenson had asked her.

"See for yourself." She stepped back and allowed Jorgenson to watch the scene through the periscope. After a quiet moment, he glanced over at her coldly, ready, she assumed, to call security and have her removed. But before he could say a word, she took the wind out of his sails.

"Don't bother locking me up," she had told him. "If you're seeing it, then it's going to happen, no matter what you do." Then she added, "But we can make sure that it happens on *our* terms."

And so—without even letting the other Accelerati know what he was up to—Jorgenson left the harp unattended in a shipping crate, with only a skeleton crew at headquarters to defend it. Then he went to Nick's house, subdued Mr. Slate with a new and improved mind-numbing fob, and waited for the boy to return—which, of course, Jorgenson knew would happen, because he had already seen it.

Had he kept watching through the periscope, however, he also would have seen what came next—and things might have been very different. . . .

"Do you know where the items go?" Jorgenson asked as he studied the machine in Nick's attic.

"I think . . ." Petula began. She put the clarinet where she had seen Nick place it before. Then she took the jack-in-the-box, sifter, and fan from Nick's belt and added them as well. Once she was done, Jorgenson reached into his pocket and pulled out the time-bending lens. He secured it to the frame of the box camera—which was now aimed right into the bell of the clarinet.

Up above, through the pyramid of glass at the apex of the attic, Petula could see the spidery-sparking asteroid thousands of miles above their heads.

"The battery!" Jorgenson said. "Its leads must connect to

these posts on the washboard!" With each passing moment he began to sound less like the reserved professor and more like the mad scientist. His gray hair, teased by static, made the image complete. "It's a primer engine!" he announced. "Don't you see? It's like the ignition of a car. And I can hot-wire it! I can turn it on!"

"But it's not finished!" Petula reminded him.

Jorgenson dismissed the thought with a wave of his good hand as he examined the machine, his eyes rapidly darting from piece to piece, his mind trying to take it all in. "It's incomplete, but I believe there are enough components here for us to be able to see what it does."

Petula hesitated. She looked to the harp, remembering the feeling it had given her when she first plucked it. "But . . . but *I* must complete the circuit," she told him.

He turned his gaze to her with predatory smoothness. An owl eyeing a mouse. "I've been waiting my entire life for this moment," he said. "Don't even think of taking it away from me."

Petula pulled the battery from Vince's backpack. "It can't be you," she told him, "You don't understand—it has to be me! *I complete the circuit!*"

She tried to hold the battery out of his reach, but he grabbed it from her, pushing her backward. She stumbled over Nick, who was beginning to stir, moaning his way back to consciousness.

"Now we will know what Tesla knew!" Jorgenson took the battery's leads in his hands. "Now *we* shall be the deity electric! The gods of power!"

But Petula kicked him behind the knee, causing his leg to buckle, and he dropped the battery.

"I complete the circuit!" Petula insisted. "The harp told me!"

Jorgenson turned to Petula, ready to tear her apart for her

insolence, but she was more than ready for the fight. After all, she had taken an online course; she was a black belt in theoretical jujitsu.

Nick's head pounded. His ears rang. He was dazed, but he understood the gist of what was going on. Somehow Jorgenson was here. He had knocked Nick out and Petula was valiantly trying to fend him off.

Before him was the battery. Vince's battery. And beyond that, the machine.

The hissing, snapping sizzling sounds from the heavens had grown deafening—and that's when Nick knew what he had to do. The machine was not finished, but even so, he had to turn it on. Even if it failed, even if it blew up, he had to do it. Because if he didn't, everyone would be toast. Literally.

While Petula battled Jorgenson, getting in some theoretically accurate martial-arts moves, Nick crawled to the machine. Through the pyramidal skylight, he could see the asteroid, its orbit having brought it directly overhead.

Nick grabbed the negative and positive wires of the battery. Jorgenson, on his back, saw what he was about to do.

"No!" Jorgenson yelled like a spoiled child. "Mine!"

But the machine was not his. It would never be.

Nick held his breath and hooked the electrified wires on the posts of the shimmering washboard.

# 32 MYSTERIOUS ERRAND

There are some who believe that the great Tunguska "comet" blast that leveled two thousand square kilometers of Siberia in 1908 was actually caused by one of Tesla's experiments gone awry. According to this theory, he was attempting to transmit energy wirelessly via a massive Tesla coil—very much like the device that now filled Nick's attic.

While the inventor's connection to the Tunguska incident remains speculative, it is verifiably true that he constructed a giant Tesla coil atop a tower 190 feet high in Shoreham, New York. He believed that Wardenclyffe Tower, as it was called, would create a resonant electrical pulse through the earth, thus providing free electricity to everyone on the planet. None of the rich businessmen who funded Tesla, however, were interested in anything that was free, so they killed the project before the world could see its potential.

Tesla went broke, and what was arguably the greatest invention in the history of the human race was torn down and sold for scrap to pay off his debts.

Legend has it, however, that in 1903, before the wrecking ball came a-calling, Tesla fired it up once, and only once. The glow from the great coil could be seen hundreds of miles away in Connecticut, across Long Island Sound, and some say they could feel the electrical charge as far as Paris. The *New York Sun* reported that bolts of electricity shot out in all directions, as if on some "mysterious errand."

The day Nick Slate turned on the unfinished machine, a new mysterious errand began.

Danny, who had spent the day out with his teammate Seth, was riding home with Beverly Webb at the same moment Nick fired up the machine in the attic.

The car had just turned on to Danny's street, and he immediately knew something was wrong at home, perhaps because his house seemed taller than it was when he left it that morning.

The attic was, in fact, rising.

The levitating triangular shape looked something like the image on the back of a dollar bill: the pyramid with the glowing eye at its top. The attic didn't have an eye, but it sure was glowing.

Beverly saw it a moment later. "What on earth?"

The sight must have absorbed all of her attention, because she began to veer into an oncoming car. She jerked the steering wheel and successfully avoided a collision, but she jumped the curb and killed a poor defenseless mailbox.

Danny climbed out of the car, ignoring Beverly's colorful language, and hurried toward his family's supremely weird home. People who had already been outside to eye the troublesome sky were converging on his house to gawk.

Now that he was closer, he could see that the attic wasn't levitating at all. It was being lifted skyward by a series of gears, cranks, and support struts . . . ?

"That's cool," said Seth, coming up behind him. "I wish my house could do that."

■ ■ ■

Mr. Slate saw the attic rising, too. And he saw the steel band that he had unearthed in his yard begin to shimmer with static flashes.

But, with the logic centers of his brain currently blocked by Accelerati technology, he found nothing unusual about this. An attic rising 190 feet above the rest of the house? Such things happened every day. Didn't they?

He wanted to return to his digging, but deep inside him, in a place he couldn't quite reach, he had a nagging suspicion that he was missing something important.

Then, when a massive and continuous bolt of lightning shot down from the distant asteroid and right through the glass skylight of his attic, it occurred to him what was wrong.

He had been so busy digging, he had forgotten to eat lunch.

Petula Grabowski-Jones was a great believer in self-preservation. Sacrificing herself—either for the benefit of others or the benefit of science—was not part of her psychological makeup. She firmly believed that others didn't deserve it, and as for science—well, Jorgenson would be a far better sacrifice, him being a professor and all.

And so, the moment Nick connected the battery and everything in the room began to shake, Petula decided it was time to make a quick exit. She unwedged the broken baseball bat and pushed open the attic stairs.

To her surprise, she found that the attic stairs no longer reached the second-floor landing. The attic had begun to rise, and if she didn't get out soon, it would be too far to jump.

"Where's Nick?" Caitlin yelled at her from below. "Petula! Where's Nick?"

Petula turned to see Nick standing by the machine. She might have grabbed him then and pulled him out with her, but the weight machine made gravity shift just enough for her to lose her balance.

She fell down the ladderlike steps, until they ejected her like a playground slide ten feet above the rest of the house. Caitlin moved out of the way as she fell. Vince, still dead as a doornail, would have broken Petula's fall, but she missed him and hit bare wooden floor, breaking her arm in three places.

Jorgenson knew that turning on Tesla's machine was a calculated risk—but it was his risk to take. Then Petula had attacked him, and now the Slate boy had wrested control. As the machine began to grind into action, Jorgenson pushed his way to his feet.

This was, and had always been, his destiny. His life had been spent searching for the machine before him. He would not let the boy steal his glory. The Jorgenson Power Transducer, as he would name it, would secure his place in history.

As Jorgenson stumbled across the shaking attic, he didn't notice the room rising. Or Petula falling. All he could see was the boy at the controls. As he gripped the boy's shoulders, the electrical charge that had built up in the trillion-ton copper asteroid suddenly found a place to go, and it blew Jorgenson across the room.

Down below, the gawkers took off in all directions when the powerful blast of lightning struck and the attic walls exploded. Beverly dragged Seth away, but Danny took off toward the house.

He ran to his father in the backyard, who was now staring at the attic, slightly bemused, as bits and pieces of smoking lumber settled all around them.

"Oh, hi, Danny," he said.

"Dad, what's going on?"

"Our attic just exploded," Mr. Slate said cheerfully. "Hey, how about we go to Hometown Buffet? I feel like I could eat a horse."

Danny couldn't quite believe what he'd heard, so he pretended he didn't.

"Where's Nick? He's not up there, is he?" Danny turned to see Petula running out of the house, grimacing as she gripped her weirdly dangling right arm—but Nick didn't come out with her. "Dad!" Danny said, shaking his father. "Where's Nick?"

And at that moment, high above them, a key chain was blasted out of Alan Jorgenson's pocket. It fell nearly two hundred feet into Danny's now-roofless room and into his fish tank, where it immediately shorted out.

Mr. Slate snapped out of his haze in an instant. His eyes filled with the dark dread of understanding as he looked at the scene before him.

"Oh my God!" Then he raced into the house to save his son.

Nick had no idea what had happened. All he knew was that a steady stream of electricity was shooting down from the sky into Tesla's machine—and the machine was alive!

The curlers pumped like pistons and the hair dryer glowed like a reactor while the toaster produced blue spiral pulses that the camera lens focused into a stream of pure power down the bell of the clarinet. The weight machine was pumping, directing its antigravity field downward and causing the entire attic to rise.

Nick could feel his own mass decrease to what he might weigh on the moon. Or on the asteroid.

The walls of his attic were gone. They had been blown away completely, leaving only the floor, and the machine.

Nick could sense that the machine wasn't working properly. It was missing too many parts. It was taking in the electricity, but it didn't have any way to disperse it.

Then he heard someone yelling. He followed the sound to the jagged edge of what had once been his bedroom. There, hanging by one hand, was Alan Jorgenson. He was just outside the machine's gravity field—far enough that it wouldn't save him from falling to his death if he lost his grip. The man's Madagascan spider-silk suit no longer shimmered with pearlescence. It was shredded and singed. Nick saw no regret or pleading in his eyes, just coldness, as if his soul had been frozen by his own remote control. Maybe it was the persistent vibrations from the cosmic string harp, but Nick felt like he could almost read the man's mind.

*I am now going to die,* Jorgenson's expression said. *This miserable boy who has ruined everything will now ruin me.*

Nick could have just stood there and watched Jorgenson fall. The man certainly deserved it. No one would blame Nick.

But as awful as Jorgenson was, Nick simply couldn't do it. Letting a man fall to his death was not the kind of victory he wanted. So he reached out his hand.

Nick read Jorgenson again. *I don't trust him! He'll take my hand and cast it off, sending me to my death.*

Nick didn't say a word. It didn't matter what Jorgenson believed about him. Nick just kept his hand extended. Jorgenson would either take it, or he wouldn't. That would have to be his choice.

In the end Jorgenson reached up with his free hand—the hand with the painfully chipped-off pinkie—and grabbed Nick's.

Nick leaned back and, using a buckled floorboard to brace

himself, pulled Jorgenson up and out of danger. And in that moment Nick realized something.

He had just shaken hands with Dr. Jorgenson.

From the second floor of Nick's house, Caitlin had watched the attic rise toward the heavens.

She felt the jolt as the asteroid discharged, and took cover as the attic exploded. At first she figured there was no way Nick could have survived. Then, when she saw Jorgenson hanging from the edge of the attic, she nurtured a sliver of hope that Nick was still alive.

The only way up there was to scale the accordion-like scaffolding that still connected the attic to the house. So she began to climb.

Nick knew that the machine was overloading and the next explosion wouldn't take out just his attic. It would leave a crater miles wide.

"It's no use!" Jorgenson said. "We have to get out of here!"

"And how are we going to do that, Einstein?"

Jorgenson, genius that he was, had no answer.

The machine shook violently. The spatial distortion coming from the cosmic strings of the harp seemed about to shred the very fabric of space, and still power shot down from the supercharged asteroid.

That's when Caitlin arrived, out of breath, but looking ready to rip out one or more of Jorgenson's internal organs.

"You!" she growled. "I should have known you were behind this!"

"Forget him!" said Nick, realizing how truly unimportant Jorgenson was, in spite of all of his superior airs. "We've got to shut this thing down!"

"There's some sort of metal ring around your house," Caitlin told him. "Maybe it's a part of the solution."

As soon as she said it, Nick instinctively knew it wasn't the solution, but part of the problem. The machine was designed to discharge somehow. The ring his father had found must have been some sort of power storage cell—but since the device wasn't complete, it couldn't connect with the ring.

Just as he had turned the machine on, he had to be the one to turn it off. The question was, when? When would enough energy have been discharged? If he did it too soon, the world would be back in the same state it was just a few minutes ago. If he waited too long, the machine would blow up, killing him, Caitlin, Jorgenson, and everyone else within the blast radius.

Caitlin surmised the situation, and ripped the wires of the wet-cell battery from the washboard posts—but it made no difference. The machine didn't stop.

"The battery was just to start it," Nick told her. "To give it 'life.' The asteroid's supplying all of the power now."

Nick knew that to shut down the machine, he would have to dismantle it from the inside out. He would have to be the monkey wrench jammed into the works. So he stepped toward the machine, and took a deep breath, preparing to get elbow-deep in the overloading mechanism.

"Don't!" Jorgenson shouted over the electrical wail. "You don't know what will happen!"

He tried to move toward Nick, but Caitlin held him back. "Nick knows what he's doing. Even if you don't."

Nick would have laughed if their lives weren't hanging in the balance. *I have no clue what I'm doing. But I've got to do it anyway.*

The electrical whine around them was degrading into a failing warble. There was no time to second-guess himself; not an instant to lose. Gritting his teeth, Nick thrust both hands into the heart of the machine.

The pain was immediate and intense. It jolted his body and mind, enveloping him as if he had shoved his hands into a—

*—fire!*
*His house was on fire!*
*On hands and knees*
*A glance back*
*His mother behind him*
*Telling him it will be okay*
*He can barely see her in the swirling smoke, and—*
*—is someone else there?*
*Is that someone behind her?*
*His imagination?*
*What else could it be?*
*And then he's out on the lawn*
*Coughing, gagging*
*And she's not there*
*She's not behind him.*
*And the windows explode*
*And the porch collapses*
*And the world Nick knew is gone gone gone.*

Screaming in pain, Nick forced away the memory. He grabbed the clarinet and ripped it out of the machine. He knocked the electrified hair curlers to the ground, and he kicked the weight machine away from the harp.

At last the circuit was broken. The machine finally stopped, and its electrified components began to disgorge energy, shooting spidery bolts in all directions. The toaster began to angrily shoot out what looked like miniature spiral galaxies, then it blew off of the F.R.E.E. and hit Nick in the head.

· · ·

Electricity does not like to be disrupted. Like a storm-swollen river, it doesn't just have direction, it has intention—and when its intentions are foiled, its wrath is unleashed down new and unexpected paths.

The moment the circuit was cut, an electromagnetic pulse blew out from the heart of the device—an EMP more powerful than any ever recorded.

For a strange and glorious moment, every electrically powered object within a three-mile radius turned on whether it was plugged in or not. Vacuum cleaners and hair dryers and WeedWackers roared to life as if possessed. Every radio blared unrequested music, and every lightbulb—even the ones still boxed at hardware stores—began to glow.

It was, for that one instant, a twisted fulfillment of Tesla's dream—free wireless energy for all.

And in the next instant, everything died. Appliance motors burned out, cell phones burst into flames in people's pockets, and computers fried, their hard drives irretrievably erased.

The pulse had only slightly dissipated by the time it reached NORAD, deep in the heart of Cheyenne Mountain. As the EMP blasted past, NORAD's data and defense grid was protected by the tons of granite above, and many paranoiac layers of lead shielding, for it was NORAD's job to plan for things as unlikely as a technology-killing pulse from a quaint, hundred-year-old home.

Farther away, the pulse weakened; its effect was less intense, but still noticeable. A neighborhood in Salt Lake City experienced a mass garage-door opening, and in Las Vegas, three thousand slot machines paid off simultaneous jackpots.

One would expect that anything at the heart of the pulse would have been incinerated, or at least boiled from the inside out like meat in a microwave—but Nikola Tesla was not so cavalier as to think his inventions could never go wrong. For this reason he had built in some rudimentary protections, such as a force-field generator disguised as a flour sifter, which not only deflected attack from the outside, but also protected things within the field as well.

Of course, if someone was foolish enough to shove his hand into the middle of the Far Range Energy Emitter . . . well, there's not much the sifter could do about that.

Nick fell to the attic floor, reeling from the pain of the electrical burns, and the strike of the ballistic toaster—and then realized that he was still falling. With the weight machine turned off, the spindly struts that had elevated the attic could no longer bear the weight of the machine. Joints buckled, gears flew, the struts collapsed, and what was left of the attic began to crash back down upon the house.

Caitlin had shielded her eyes when the machine failed, and although the force field protected her from the explosion, it could not protect her from the half-eaten peanut butter and jelly sandwich Nick had left on a plate on his bedroom floor. She slipped on it, the plate went shooting off into oblivion like a discus, and Caitlin fell through the attic trapdoor, much like Petula had. Unlike Petula, however, Caitlin managed to catch herself on the struts supporting the elevated attic—but when the pyrotechnics ended and the attic started to fall, the struts began to collapse. With the framework crumbling around her, she knew there were only three possible outcomes: she would be crushed to death; she would fall to her death; or she would be impaled by jagged steel and bleed to death. As she tried to decide which was the least awful way to die, a fourth possibility presented itself. Without a second to lose, she jumped toward

Danny's room, which, like all the other rooms on the second floor, had no roof.

Her aim was true. She landed on Danny's bed with enough force to shatter the wooden frame.

An instant later, the attic met the second floor. Wood and steel and plaster came raining down, leaving the fish in Danny's aquarium to ponder the madness of the nonliquid world.

When Wayne Slate reached the second-floor landing, his heart nearly stopped, until he realized the body lying there wasn't Nick, it was someone else. When he realized it was the twin brother of the kid who had died in his house a month earlier, his heart nearly stopped again.

But all of that was blown out of his mind as the elevated attic began to collapse.

He dove for cover as the attic came down, buckling the walls of the second floor, destroying what little structural integrity the house still had. And then, like a gift from heaven, the spring-loaded attic stairs popped open, and Nick was ejected into his arms, bloody and bruised, but still very much alive.

"It's okay, it's okay, it's okay," his father said, holding Nick in his strong embrace. Though clearly nothing was okay, his son was alive, which meant that everything was okay.

The first thing people noticed in the aftermath of the discharge was the silence. Every power station and transformer within a three-mile radius of Nick's house had exploded, and every electrical device was beyond repair.

But the silence was more than just the quiet of stilled machinery. The sky was peaceful, too, all around the world. The strange sizzling lightning had ceased everywhere, and the skies between the Arctic and Antarctic Circles no longer flared with the aurora. The asteroid was once more just a reddish-gray spot in the sky, a fraction the size of the moon.

By the time Mitch arrived at Nick's house, followed by seven cats convinced he was their savior, the first responders were already there.

The house looked like it had been sat upon by a giant. Fire trucks and ambulances sprayed red light through the smoke and dust, and Mitch knew beyond doubt that Nick had turned on the half-built machine.

Petula was being attended by paramedics and basked in the attention like a dying diva.

In the driveway, Nick was being loaded into an ambulance on a stretcher, with Caitlin on one side and his father on the other. Mitch could see that he was alive by the way he gripped his father's hand, but the ambulance left before he could ask about Nick's condition.

And then, out of the ruins of the house, strode Jorgenson. Mitch's one consolation was that he looked as ruined as the rest of them.

As soon as Jorgenson emerged, medics rushed to help him, but he waved them off with such an imperious air that they let him stride on.

Mitch confronted him. There were a million things that he wanted to say to the man, but one in particular bubbled its way to the surface.

"My father's one of you, isn't he? You didn't frame him—he's one of you."

Jorgenson gave him a disgusted look, like Mitch was something nasty he had spotted on the sidewalk. "He *was* one of us. We disavowed him. Accelerati don't get caught." And then he added: "It took you long enough to figure it out."

"I'm going to figure out 'Grinthon,' too. And 'Brandon Gunther's alligator.'"

Jorgenson's disgusted glare took a turn toward bafflement. "I haven't the foggiest notion what you're talking about," he said. "But if I did, I would say the same."

On the street behind them, a couple of Accelerati SUVs arrived, along with more police and emergency vehicles. Mitch didn't care.

"I will take you down. Every last one of you," he said.

"I sincerely doubt it," said Jorgenson, nice and smug. "I think it's clear that—"

"—*things won't end well for you,*" Mitch blurted. And he smiled, because he knew it would come true.

Jorgenson, only mildly disconcerted, brushed him aside. "If you will excuse me, I have a disaster area to contain."

Mitch thought about using the bellows, to give him a nice sharp blast and send him off to Oz, but he was distracted by the sight of two paramedics carrying a body bag out of the house.

"It's weird," he heard one of them say, "but this looks like the same kid we took out of this same house a few weeks ago."

So, when no one was watching, Mitch snuck back into the house and made his way up the shattered stairs to the remains of the attic. He left the bellows like a flower on a grave, and then picked up the battery.

A few minutes later, when the dead kid disappeared from the body bag, the paramedic decided it was the perfect cherry to top off this day.

# 33 QUID PRO QUO

**N**ick awoke in a comfortable hospital room, if anything about a hospital room can be called comfortable.

"Hey," said a familiar voice.

He turned to see Caitlin by the door. "They said I couldn't visit without an adult," she told him as she walked over to his bed, "but it's amazing how little they seem to care when you pretend you don't hear them." She glanced at his bandages and the swollen fingers protruding from the white layers of cotton gauze. "It looks like you really did a number on your arms."

"It couldn't be helped," Nick told her. "How's everyone else?"

"We all survived," she said. "Except for Vince, of course."

Nick sighed. "Are we going to have to go resurrect him again?"

"Mitch already did."

"Good," Nick said, leaning back and closing his eyes.

"I know, right? After the first time, I'll never look at jelly beans and spandex the same way again."

Caitlin explained that Mitch was making a special trip to Colorado State Penitentiary to talk to his father, and that the newly re-re-reanimated Vince and his mother were leaving town, because they couldn't risk the Accelerati finding him and taking away the battery.

"He told me they were going to Scotland," Caitlin said. "I couldn't tell whether or not he was joking."

As for Petula, she had vanished entirely. "And if she ever shows her face around me again, she won't have a face left to show," Caitlin vowed.

Nick turned to look out the window. "Clear blue sky today," he said. He reached up to her as best he could, and touched Caitlin's arm with a fingertip. "There's no shock."

Caitlin smiled. "I don't know about that," she said. "I mean, I felt something."

Nick could feel himself starting to blush, but before the moment got too awkward, he said, "Hey, did you see my dad and Danny around?"

"I know they were here—maybe they're in the cafeteria getting lunch," Caitlin suggested. "Hey, there's a vending machine down the hallway. Why don't I get us something to drink. We can make a toast to you for saving the world again."

She left, and Nick looked out the window once more. A moment later, he heard someone enter the room.

"Your ability to foul the waters of everything you touch is truly remarkable."

Nick turned his head to face a gaunt figure in a brand-new vanilla suit.

"You're the only foul thing in here, Dr. Jorgenson."

Jorgenson took a step forward and glanced at the machine that was monitoring Nick's vital signs.

Nick got worried. "Are you going to kill me?" he asked.

"I have plenty of justification for ending your life and the lives of your friends. It would solve a myriad of problems, too. For that I would feel no remorse. Except for one thing. Quid pro quo."

"English please," Nick said.

"You saved my life when you didn't have to," Jorgenson told him, "and decency dictates that I spare yours."

"So you're letting me go?"

"Let's just say I'm leaving your destiny in the hands of a higher power."

It took several attempts before the vending machine accepted Caitlin's money.

When she finally returned with two cans of sparkling Dr Pepper, Nick was not in his room. In fact, the bed had been stripped and the room was clean, as if no one had been there for quite some time. Her stomach began a long, bottomless fall.

"Excuse me," she said to a passing nurse, her voice shaky. "The boy who was in this room—where did he go?"

"You must be mistaken," the nurse said. "No one has been in this room all day."

And when Caitlin demanded that they check the hospital records, there was no evidence that Nick had ever been there. Nor did she find Mr. Slate or Danny in the cafeteria or anywhere else.

Caitlin knew, without question, that the Accelerati had pulled yet another magic trick. Smoke and mirrors, practically applied.

# 34 SOMEWHERE IN NEW JERSEY

First by private jet and then by limousine, Nick was taken to an old house secluded in deep woods. He had no idea where he was, but the flight took several hours, and by the speed of the sunset, he knew they had traveled east.

Nick was accompanied by two Accelerati who, he assumed, were there to make sure he behaved, and to subdue him if necessary. Nick was not a cooperative passenger for obvious reasons, not the least of which were his burned arms. They were still swollen, and the blisters were still raw beneath the bandages. And now, on top of the pain, there was a constant itch in both arms that he couldn't scratch. The doctors had said itching was good. It meant his arms were healing. Never mind that it was driving him crazy.

The two Accelerati had been tight-lipped on the flight. He had tried to talk to them, to ask questions, to find out where they were going, but their response was always a terse "We've been instructed not to converse with you."

When they arrived at their destination, Nick was practically carried to the front door in the grip of his escorts, lest he try to run for it. Like his ruined home in Colorado Springs, this house was Victorian in style, but it was larger, and much better maintained. He was greeted by a kindly housekeeper who had an odd air about her.

"There 'e is!" she said cheerily. "Why, we've been waiting for you, we 'ave!"

Nick's two travel companions left them alone. He fleetingly thought about trying to escape, until he noticed that the door had triple-bolted itself behind him.

"Would you like some tea?" the housekeeper asked. "Or some nice chilled water? Our quantum cooling gizmo is working just fine now."

"No, thank you." She was so upbeat that Nick had no choice but to be polite, even though he felt like being anything but.

She led Nick into a parlor that at first appeared to contain only furniture—antiques in mint condition. Then he noticed an old man in the shadows.

The man was seated in a high-backed leather chair that had been converted into a wheelchair. He wore a wool suit that, like nearly everything else in the house, seemed old-fashioned, yet not old. The man, however, *was* old. Very old.

"When is a house not a home?" the man asked, his voice raspy and rough, like a flag flapping in a strong wind. "When tourists are traipsing through it seven days a week!" He rolled a few inches forward, but not far enough to be directly in the light. "This house is not the original. It's just a replica. An accurate one, however. The original is several miles away in West Orange, owned and operated by the National Park Service."

He reached out a withered hand, and beckoned Nick. "Come closer," he said, then added "please" as an afterthought.

Nick did not move. "Who are you?"

"Me?" The old man chuckled. "I am the one who sets things in motion. I am the one who can turn your lowly lump of coal into a diamond, if you let me. I am the éminence grise behind the éminence grise."

This man loved to hear himself talk. Just like Jorgenson.

"English, please," Nick said. He was getting tired of saying it.

"Behind every man who appears to wield power is someone else wielding *him*, because"—he pointed at Nick's bandaged arms—"as you've no doubt learned, power is best not handled directly."

Nick said nothing. He found the only power he had in the situation came from his conspicuous silence.

The old man took a long drag on his cigar, as if he had all the time in the world, and blew the smoke in Nick's direction. Nick did his best not to cough.

"My Grand Acceleratus certainly made a mess of things, didn't he? Don't get me wrong—Jorgenson is a fine scientist. But hubris can spoil the best of them. Bloated pride—the bane of success. Rest assured he will be severely disciplined for his actions." He waved his hand and smoke rose in a lazy spiral. "Luckily, you managed to discharge the Bonk Object. The charge won't build up to lethal levels again for a month, at least. That gives us some time to devise a more permanent solution."

The man rolled himself out of the shadows. He looked familiar, though Nick couldn't place him. He was more than just old. He was decrepit in a way that was hard to fathom. His skin seemed like crinkled papier-mâché, gray and tissue-thin. His eyes were yellowed, and the skin around them sagged.

Then, all at once, it occurred to Nick who this must be—but he banished the thought as preposterous. It was impossible. Unless . . .

Nick stepped forward. Behind the chair was a large cylindrical object covered by a red satin sheet. Nick reached up and pulled it off. The old man didn't stop him.

Beneath the blanket was a wet cell—just like Vince's, but larger. It stood six feet high. Its liquid was clouded, its terminals corroded, and attached to those metal studs were heavily insulated wires that snaked over the back of the leather chair and disappeared beneath the man's collar.

The old man offered him a Halloween grin. "Ah," he said, "you've discovered my little secret." And he laughed.

"You . . . you're . . . Thomas Edison!"

"Thomas *Alva* Edison," the old man said. "My friends call me Al. And I'd very much like to be your friend."

Nick backed away until he stumbled against a lamp, knocking it off the table. He barely registered the sound of breaking glass.

He could feel himself hyperventilating. Edison would have to be about 170 years old—but what did age mean when you were connected to an eternal life battery?

The crash of the lamp alerted the housekeeper. "Oh dear, oh dear. This won't do." She picked up the broken lamp and left, returning moments later with an identical replacement.

Nick had to slow his breathing to keep from passing out.

"Let me out of here!" he demanded.

"The wet cell, as I'm sure you surmised, is a technology I borrowed from our mutual friend, Mr. Tesla, many, many years ago."

"*Stole it*, you mean! Tesla hated you. And I hate you, too!"

Edison heaved a sigh for the ages. "You hate me because I succeeded where Tesla failed. I was not Nikola's enemy—he was his own enemy, insisting on doing things his way, when his way led to one financial failure after another."

"Maybe he wasn't interested in money." Nick crossed his arms in defiance, even though it hurt to do so.

"Genius without money is like a bulb without a filament," Edison said. "Your hero never learned that. It was his fatal flaw."

"You destroyed him!"

Edison raised his voice only slightly, betraying his anger.

"Tesla destroyed himself! He was a genius, but a remarkably bad businessman. We could have worked together, but he didn't want to share in mutual success. He wanted to 'beat Edison.' So I became richer and even more famous, and he died broke and forgotten—through no fault of mine! Let the historical record show that my only crime was leaving him alone!"

Then Edison softened. It was hard to read expressions on his sallow, sagging face, but this one seemed like genuine sorrow. "Do you think I enjoyed seeing that pompous, loudmouth Marconi take credit for the radio, when it was clearly Tesla's invention? Do you think I rejoiced when Wardenclyffe Tower was torn down and the coil sold for scrap? Far from it! I was saddened beyond measure."

"You could have saved Wardenclyffe! You could have paid Tesla's debts."

Edison sat stiffer, clearly insulted. "I never pay another man's debts!" he said. Then he heaved his frail shoulders in a labored shrug. "But even if I had offered, he would have refused the slightest bit of charity. I suppose I would have done the same in his position. Proud men soar solo, or fall alone."

"And the Accelerati?"

Now Edison looked away. "I knew Tesla had hidden his greatest inventions, and I suspected that after his failure at Wardenclyffe he went on to perfect his Far Range Energy Emitter in secret. Because he would rather leave the world in darkness than let me share an ounce of his genius."

"He gave the world light!"

"Yes, well, so did Prometheus. So did Lucifer, for that matter, and you see where it got them."

They stared each other down for a few moments longer. Finally, Edison pulled out a lace handkerchief and wiped a trace of spittle from his lips. "I have a proposition for you, Nick," he said. "An offer that I believe you will like a little bit more than you will hate."

"I'm listening," Nick said firmly.

"I'm not sure if you know this, but your father is in jail. He's charged with treason."

*"What?!"* Nick took a few steps forward.

"The government believes your father used classified technology that he stole from NORAD to create the device in your attic."

"That's not true! He had nothing to do with it!"

"You and I know that, but the government sees it differently."

Nick's heart pounded—he could feel the pulse painfully in his injured arm. "Where's my brother?"

"In the custody of Child Protective Services, until he's placed in a foster home."

The thought of Danny ripped from their father and placed in some stranger's house made Nick want to rip the wires out of Edison's back—but he knew that would only make things worse.

Then the old man clapped. The sound was like the slamming of an ancient book. "Here's my proposition. The Accelerati are well rooted in the criminal justice system, and they also maintain a presence in various other government agencies. It will take substantial effort, but I can make all the charges against your father go away. I can reunite him with your brother. I can let them get on with their lives in peace."

"In exchange for what?"

"You," Edison said simply. "Jorgenson despises you so intensely because deep down he knows you are a worthy rival. You're smart. You have powerful scientific instincts."

"I'm not that smart."

"No? The records from your school in Tampa say otherwise."

"Those records disappeared when I moved to Colorado."

"Not at all. We had them here all the time. You tested at the genius level in math and science in third grade."

"That was then. Now I just get B's."

"There's a reason for that, isn't there?"

Nick shrugged.

"Your mother knew how smart you are."

Nick glared at him. "Don't talk about my mother."

But Edison ignored him. "She wanted you to go to a special school for exceptional children. Which, I suspect, is why you kept your grades low. You didn't want to go. After a while, it became a habit. You've hidden it from everyone. Even from your closest friends." Edison leaned forward. "Even from yourself."

"An IQ test isn't the real world."

"No. But it is a measure of potential." Edison leaned back in his chair, smug in his assessment of Nick. The fact that he might be right irritated Nick even more. "We have recovered all the items from your attic, except for the battery," Edison said, "and there are several more we managed to get our hands on, thanks to the list you provided to Evangeline Planck."

"No!" said Nick, not wanting to believe it.

"Yes, she's one of us. Has been from the beginning." Then the old man sighed. "But we're still missing three other objects, as best we can determine. And we don't know exactly how everything fits together. That's where you come in," he said, his eyes twinkling. "Join the Accelerati, Nick. Join us, and I will see to it that your father goes free."

"And if I don't?"

Edison's face drooped. "In that case, justice must take its course." Then he held out something to Nick. Something shiny. "Finish Tesla's machine for me."

Nick looked closer. It was a gold pin in the shape of an *A*, with an infinity crossbar.

"You were born to be one of us, Nick. We are meant to be on the same side. In time you'll realize this."

Nick knew the Accelerati were about power. They were about control. And greed. They were about everything Tesla was against.

As if reading his mind, Edison said, "Don't make the same mistake poor Nikola did, son. Your story does not need to end tragically. It can be glorious and bright."

Nick reached out and took the pin, turning it over in his sore fingers while Edison, ancient Edison, waited to see what Nick would do.

His soul in exchange for the lives of his brother and father. Edison had said it was his choice, but what choice did he have, really? Perhaps that's what made Edison such a successful businessman. He left his rivals only two options: bad or worse. Nick thought of Caitlin. He thought of Mitch and Vince. His one consolation was that they were not a part of this equation. This was between him and Edison.

"Choose your path, Nick. I promise I will honor whatever choice you make."

Indecision would indicate weakness, and that was the last thing he wanted to show the man. Without any further hesitation, enduring the pain of his blistered fingers, and aching heart, he affixed the gold pin to his shirt.

Edison smiled and put his crinkled papier-mâché hand on Nick's shoulder.

"Welcome," he said, "to the Loyal Order of the Accelerati."